C / K M

6.00

D1396593

ᒧ

The Scoop

FERN MICHAELS

The Scoop

**Doubleday Large Print
Home Library Edition**

KENSINGTON BOOKS

KENSINGTON BOOKS are published by

Kensington Publishing Corp.
119 West 40th Street
New York, NY 10018

ISBN-13: 978-1-61523-392-2

Printed in the United States of America

The Scoop

Chapter 1

Charleston, South Carolina

It was an event, there was no doubt about it. Not that funerals were, as a rule, events, but when someone of Leland St. John's stature bit the dust, it became one. The seven-piece string band playing in the downpour, per one of Leland's last wishes, had turned it into an event regardless of what else was going on in the world.

Then there was the tail end of Hurricane Blanche, which was unleashing torrents of rain upon the mourners huddled under the dark blue tent and only added to the circuslike atmosphere.

"Will you just get on with it," Toots Loudenberry mumbled under her breath. She continued to mutter and mumble as the minister droned on and on. "No one is as good as you're making Leland sound. All you know is what I told you, and I sure as hell didn't tell you all that crap you're spouting. He was a selfish, rich, old man. End of story."

Toots's daughter leaned closer to her mother and tried to whisper through the thick veil covering her mother's head and ears. "Can't you hurry it along? It's not like this is the first time you've done this. Isn't this the seventh or eighth husband you've buried? I'm damn glad that preacher said his name, or I wouldn't even know who it is that's being planted. I gotta say, Mom, you outdid yourself with all these flowers."

Toots rose to the occasion and stepped forward, cutting the minister off in midsentence. "Thank you, Reverend." She wanted to say his check was in the mail, but she bit her tongue as she took a step forward and laid her wilted rose on top of the bronze coffin. She stepped aside so the other mourners could follow her out from under the temporary tent, which was open on all four sides. She stepped in water up to her ankles, cursed ripely, and sloshed her way to the waiting limousine, which would take her back home. "That's just like you, Leland. Why couldn't you have waited one more week, and the rainy season would have been over? Now my shoes are ruined. So is my hat, as well as my suit. Too bad you don't know how much this outfit cost. If you did, you would have waited another week to die. You always were selfish. See what all that selfishness got you. You're dead."

"What are you mumbling about, Mom?"

Toots slid into the limousine and kicked off her sodden shoes. Her black mourning hat followed. She looked over at her daughter, Abby, who looked like a drowned rat, and said, "Of all my husbands, I liked Leland the least. I resent having to attend his funeral under these conditions. He was my only mistake. But one out of eight, I suppose, isn't too bad."

Abby reached for a wad of paper napkins next to the champagne bottle that seemed to come with all limousines. "Why didn't you just crisp him up?"

Toots sighed. "I wanted to, but Leland

said in his will that he wanted to be buried with that damn string band playing music. One has to honor a person's last wishes. What kind of person would I be if I didn't honor his, even if he was a jerk?"

"Don't you mean if you didn't honor those last wishes, what's-his-name's money would have gone to the polar bears in the Arctic?"

"That, too." Toots sighed.

The woman born Teresa Amelia Loudenberry, Toots to her friends, stared at her daughter. "How long are you staying, dear?"

"I have a four o'clock flight. I left Chester with a sitter, and Chester does not like sitters. There's just enough time for me to grab something to eat at your post feast, change into dry clothes, and get outta here. Can't you hear California calling my name? Don't look at me like that, Mom. I didn't even know that guy you married. I met him at your wedding, and that's the sum total of our relationship. If I remember correctly, you said he was a charmer. I expected a charmer. I did not get a charmer. I'm just saying."

"Maybe I should have said snake

charmer," Toots said vaguely. "Leland was like this gorgeously wrapped present that when opened was quite . . . tacky. I was stunned, but I did marry the man, so I had to make the best of it. He's gone now, so perhaps we shouldn't speak ill of him. I'll mourn for ten days for the sake of appearance, then get on with my life. I'm going to find a hobby to keep myself busy. I'm sick and tired of doing good deeds. Anyone can do good deeds. Anyone can garden and grow one-of-a-kind roses. I need to do something that will make a difference, something challenging. Something I can really sink my teeth into. That's another thing. Leland wore dentures. He kept them in a cup in the bathroom at night. I could never get used to that. He wasn't very good in bed, either."

"That's probably more than I need to know, Mom."

"I'm just saying, Abby. I don't want you to think your old mom is callous. You have to admit I did have seven happy marriages. I should have hung up my garter belt when Dolph died. Did I do that? No, I did not. I let Leland sweep me off my feet, dentures and all. Sometimes life is so unfair.

"That's enough of a pity party for me. Tell me how it's going out there in sunny California. How's the job going? What's the latest hot gossip, and who is doing what to whom in Hollywood?"

Abby Simpson, Toots's daughter by her first husband, John Simpson, the absolute love of Toots's life, was a reporter for a second-rate tabloid, *The Informer,* based in Los Angeles. She was a second-string runner, which meant she had to hit the pavement and find her own stories, then elaborate on them for the public's insatiable appetite for Hollywood gossip.

"Rodwell Archibald Godfrey, otherwise known as Rag to us underlings, called me into his office and told me he wants more product. I can't make it happen if it isn't out there. All the A-list papers seem to get the stories first. I think this is just another way of saying he is not happy with my work. I applied to the other tabloids, but they're full up and not taking on anyone new. I'm doing my best. I just manage to make my mortgage payment every month and have enough left over to buy dog food. No, you cannot help me, Mom. I'm going to make it on my own, so let's not go down that road. My break is coming, I can feel it. By the way, I brought a stack of future issues for you to read. I have stuff in all of them."

"I can't get used to the idea that you people make all that stuff up, then it happens. And you print weeks in advance of what's happening," Toots said.

Abby laughed. "It's not quite that way, but you're close. Well, we're home, and you have guests. You really know how to throw a funeral, Mom."

"Event, dear. *Funeral* is such a dreary word. It conjures up all kinds of dismal thinking."

Abby laughed as she climbed out of the limo and marched up the steps to the wide veranda of her mother's house.

Both women raced upstairs to change into dry clothing before they had to meet with the guests who would be coming by to pay their last respects.

Toots looked at herself in the long mirror in her room. Yes, she did look bedraggled, but wasn't a widow supposed to look a little bedraggled? "Black is not my best color," she muttered to herself as she tossed her mourning outfit into a heap on the floor in the bathroom. She donned another black dress, added a string of pearls, brushed out her hair, sprayed on some perfume, and felt refreshed enough to go downstairs and socialize for an hour or so.

Burying the dead was so time-consuming. Even the aftermath took an eternity. All she wanted to do was retire to her sitting room to read the pile of tabloids Abby had brought with her. Not for the world would Toots ever admit that she was addicted to tabloid gossip. But for now, she had a duty to perform, and perform it she would. She had all evening to read her treasured tabloids and guzzle a little wine while doing so. She'd drink to Leland, and that would be the end of this chapter in her life.

Time to move on. Something she was very good at.

Chapter 2

The minute the last guest walked out the door with a go-bag of food, the bereaved Toots galloped up the stairs and headed for her three-hundred-square-foot bathroom, where she ran a bath. She made two trips to the huge Jacuzzi with the pile of tabloids, four scented candles, a fresh bottle of wine, and her favorite Baccarat wineglass. She paused a minute to decide which bath salts she wanted to use, finally settling on Confederate jasmine since the scent was more or less true to the flower. She was, when you got right down to it, a transplanted Southern belle.

Toots stripped down, and the clothes she was wearing went on top of the sodden outfit she'd discarded earlier. She'd never wear them again. Then again, since she was a stickler for protocol, maybe she'd tell her housekeeper, Bernice, to leave them until her ten days of mourning were up. That way she wouldn't be cheating. And to think she had to wear black, which really made her look washed out, for another ten days. Nine more if you counted today. Well, she was definitely counting today.

Toots sniffed at the delicious aroma emanating from the Jacuzzi. Wonderful! She lowered herself into the silky water and sighed happily. Toots leaned back and savored the first few moments of the exquisite bath before leaning forward to pour herself a glass of the bubbly that Leland had bought by the truckload for his wine cellar.

"To you, Leland," Toots said as she held her wineglass aloft. She turned up the glass and swallowed the contents in one long gulp. Now she could move on. She'd done her duty.

Toots refilled her glass, leaned back, and fired up a cigarette. Smoking was a truly horrible habit, but she didn't care. She was way too old to worry about what was good or bad for her. She was all about living and didn't give a thought to the fact that cigarettes would interfere with that. Besides, she had every vice there was. She loved vices because they made for such good conversations. She liked to drink, smoke, was a sugar addict and a closet tabloid reader. She'd long ago convinced herself that being a vegan made up for all her bad habits. That shit, Leland, was forever giving her grief for her, as he put it, unsavory habits. "Screw you, Leland!"

Toots was on her third glass of wine and on page four of the issue she was reading before she realized she couldn't remember what she'd just read. What was wrong with her? Nothing ever interfered with reading her beloved tabloids. Until now. She closed her eyes and tried to figure out what it was that was interfering with her universe.

Something was lurking somewhere inside her. She'd already scratched Leland. Abby was okay, at least for the moment. Did she feel rudderless? Did she need a man in residence? Hell no, she didn't.

Then what was bothering her? The nine days of mourning she allowed herself? She snorted. Any woman worth her salt could get through nine days of mourning by going out to breakfast, lunch, and dinner every day. Fit in a little shopping, and she'd be good to go.

By the fourth glass of wine, Toots decided she needed . . . no, she didn't need, she *wanted* to stir up some trouble. She needed some excitement in her life. Her thoughts carried her back in time to when she was young and full of piss and vinegar with her friends. Friends she hadn't seen near enough throughout the past twenty years. They e-mailed, called, and sent Christmas cards, but life got in the way sometimes. Maybe it was time to call all of them and invite them for a visit. They were, after all, Abby's godmothers. Everyone thought it strange that her daughter had three godmothers. Especially that shithead, Leland. She didn't find it strange at all. Neither did her friends.

Toots peered into the wine bottle. Empty! She climbed out of the tub, dried off with a towel the size of a tent, powdered herself, slipped into a black nightgown—

because she was in mourning—and tottered out to the minioffice in her bedroom. It wasn't really an office, just a little table where she sat to write notes to people she didn't give two shits about, pay a few bills that she didn't want her business manager to know about, and use her laptop to check out TMZ and Page Six several times a day.

Toots fired up her laptop and proceeded to type an e-mail to her friend Mavis, who lived in Maine in a little clapboard house near the ocean.

"I want you to come for a visit, Mavis. You were always the one with the ideas. How soon can you get here? By the way, I just buried Leland today, and I'm in a funk."

Five minutes later, the laptop pinged receipt of a return e-mail.

"Sorry, Toots, I can't afford a trip like that. I can't leave Coco, my dog. She's really my only friend these days. I'm sorry your dog Leland died. I didn't even know you had a dog. It's terrible when your beloved pet dies. Sorry, Toots, I'd love to see you, but my pension just won't cover a trip at this time."

Toots blinked. How weird that Mavis

thought Leland was a dog. She wondered why she thought that, then it dawned on her what her old friend meant.

She hit the REPLY button.

"I'll send a first-class ticket for you and Coco. Leland was my husband."

The next response from Mavis was: *"LOL, I forgot you married again. Too bad, too sad. You'll get over it, Toots, you always do. I'll be happy to accept your tickets and look forward to seeing you. It's been way too long. Are the others coming, too?"*

Toots fired back, *"I'm working on it now. More tomorrow."*

Toots's next e-mail was to Sophie, who'd married a philanderer, now with one foot in the grave and the other on a banana peel, according to Sophie's latest e-mail. It was a known fact among the foursome that Sophie hated her husband and was only sort of/more or less taking care of him because of the five-million-dollar insurance policy she'd taken out on him some years ago. "I'm sticking around long enough to collect, then I'm outta here," she'd said.

"Sophie, I'm e-mailing you to invite you for a visit. I'm willing to send you a

ticket if you can clear your calendar. It's been way too long since we've seen each other. I have something in mind that I think you and the others will find interesting. It will be like old times."

Sophie's response came through so quickly that Toots was surprised. *"I can't leave him here alone. This old bird is taking way too long to die. I didn't pay that mountain of premiums all these years to get aced out of the payoff. Besides, I want him to sweat every day and wonder if I'm going to give him his meds and feed him. Which, of course, I do. What kind of person would I be not to do that?"*

Well, Toots decided, she could certainly relate to that. *"Not to worry, Sophie. I'll get you a nurse 24/7 for your husband. So you'll come, then? By the way, I buried Leland today."*

Sophie shot back. *"Okay, I'll clear my schedule that's not really a schedule. Just let me know when my departure date is. Who is Leland?"*

Toots responded to her e-mail. *"I'll get back to you on the date. Leland was my husband. I have to do that ten-day mourning thing. Nine days if you count today. I am definitely counting today. You can watch me and know what it's like, so you'll know how to behave when that dud you married bites the dust. Mourning is tricky. You have to do it just right, or people will talk about you."*

"What number is Leland?" Sophie queried. *"I think you've been married more times than Elizabeth Taylor."*

Toots quickly replied, *"Leland was number 8, and I am never getting married again. More tomorrow. I have to e-mail Ida now. She's going to be tough. Remember how we hated each other and pretended we didn't? I think she's still ticked off that I married the guy she wanted. She'd be a widow now if I hadn't. I tried to tell her he was a big nothing, but he did have all that money."*

Toots didn't bother waiting for a response before she e-mailed Ida. She got right to the point. *"Ida, it's Toots. I'm e-mailing you to invite you for a visit. Mavis and Sophie have agreed to come, and it will be like old times. I have this plan, Ida, and I want to involve all of us in it. I hope you aren't still holding a grudge against me. It's time for us to forget about all that old silly stuff. Believe it or not, I did you a favor by stealing whatever his name was. Even his money didn't make up for how boring he was. But he was gentle and considerate. So, what do you think? By the way, I buried Leland today. I'm in mourning, have nine days to go."*

Ida's response was short and curt. *"Count me in. Tell me when you want me to arrive. Oh, boo hoo about Leland."*

Toots rubbed her hands together and closed her laptop. She was on a roll, she could feel it. Though what this big plan was, she hadn't a clue just yet. She'd think of something. She always did.

Chapter 3

Toots had wakened at five A.M. every day of the week for as long as she could remember, but today, on her tenth and final day of mourning, she woke up at three, more excited than she'd been in ages. Sophie, Mavis, and Ida would be arriving first thing in the morning. Today was her "get my ass in gear" day.

Out of habit she quickly made her bed. She'd let Bernice, her friend and housekeeper, worry about dusting and vacuuming later. This day was to be a new beginning for her. She wanted to live like a woman half her age, not like some old fuddy-duddy who buried husbands like ancient treasures, then spent the rest of her life memorializing them. No, no, no, that was not for her.

Thrilled she could finally toss her black mourning clothes, Toots chose a bright hot-pink blouse to wear with a cherry red skirt. Just a bit over five-seven, and thankfully she hadn't acquired a hump on her back like many women her age, her reddish-brown hair still glistened. Of course she colored her hair, but that was her own secret. She tied her hair in a loose topknot. *Not bad for sixty-five,* she thought as she gazed in the full-length mirror. Three of her husbands had told her she looked like Katharine Hepburn, though for the life of her she couldn't recall which ones. It didn't matter anyway. She smiled at her reflection. The colors were loud, but after ten days of black, she planned to dress like a rainbow from here on. No more husbands, so there would be no need for black. With that thought in mind, Toots yanked everything black out of her closet, tossing all of it into a laundry basket. She'd donate the clothes to charity. That accomplished, Toots headed downstairs to the kitchen, her favorite room in her house.

The old pine floors shone like molten gold. With the sunrise, Toots knew the freshly washed windows would sparkle like diamonds. She and Bernice had spent yesterday scrubbing and shining them with white vinegar and newspapers. Red and emerald green throw rugs were scattered around the floor like Christmas gumdrops. Custom-made red cabinets, which Leland had called gaudy and tacky, lined three walls. On the fourth wall was a fireplace made from large rocks she had gathered herself in the mountains of North Carolina. Leland had thought that was cheap. She'd reminded him this was *her* house, and he was free to live in the guesthouse anytime he chose. He chose to stay put, the old shit. But he'd kept his mouth shut after that. Well, Leland was dead and gone. She could paint the walls purple if she wanted to.

Obliterating all thoughts of her deceased spouse, Toots prepared a pot of coffee, found her cigarettes in the kitchen drawer where she hid her secret supply of Pay-Day candy bars. When the coffee finished brewing, she filled her favorite Maxine cup with the hot brew. Cigarettes and coffee in hand, she went outside to sit on the back veranda.

She loved this time of day. The birds were starting to awaken, the potpourri of their chirping music to her ears. The flowers and shrubbery were still glazed with early-morning dew. Freshly plowed dirt from her neighbor's garden seasoned the morning air, reminding her that summer was just around the corner. The bouquet of night-blooming jasmine she'd gathered last night sat in a vase on a wicker side table, filling her senses with its pungent odor. God, she loved this place. She couldn't imagine living anywhere else in the whole world.

Taking a big swallow of coffee, Toots went over her mental "get my ass in gear" list. She and Bernice had worked like troupers yesterday cleaning most of the house inside and out. Pete, her longtime friend and gardener, weeded the flower beds, spruced up the shrubs, cut the grass, then trimmed the dead leaves from her two angel oaks. The hummingbird feeders were replenished, dried corn sprinkled around for the squirrels in hopes they would stay away from her bird feeders, but that was a lost cause. She did this every year and saw no reason to stop anytime soon. She had a routine, liked sticking to it most days, but there was a yearning in her now, something she hadn't been able to silence since Leland's death. The best she could come up with was that a sort of restlessness was flowing through her veins. Was this what getting old felt like? Lost, with no sense of purpose? No! No! No! She would not allow herself a pity party by believing in that crap.

Her best friends in the whole world were on their way for a visit. A dark mood was not on her agenda. She liked to count her blessings and reminded herself of all she had to be thankful for. At sixty-five she was healthy as a horse, according to her physical three months ago. She had a beautiful daughter who seemed to be thriving in Los Angeles. Her dearest friends were still alive. She had more money than JPMorgan Chase, at least today she did, and she didn't see that changing anytime in the near future. Life was lookin' good.

She took a slurp of the now-cold coffee, lit another cigarette, and inhaled the toxins before releasing the acrid smoke into the fresh air. Ida would be on her ass like white on rice when she found out that Toots still smoked. Ida thought everything in life that felt good was actually bad for you. Breathing was bad for you, according to her. Mavis said Ida had something the professionals called OCD, obsessive compulsive disorder, whatever the hell that was. Didn't anyone just get constipated anymore? Why did every disease have to be reduced to initials?

New beginnings, Toots thought as she went inside to refill her cup. *Brand-spanking-new beginnings*. No husbands to fret over, not that she ever had, but for the first time in a very, very long time, Toots was on her own. She wasn't sure if she liked the idea or not. She'd always had some distant family close by or, God help her, a husband to contend with. With Abby on the West Coast and her friends scattered across the country, Toots realized that the feelings she'd been experiencing were feelings of loss, of not being needed. Shit. Someone always needed something. She would simply find a new need, fill it, and live heartily.

Never one to wallow in self-pity, Toots drank two more cups of coffee and smoked three more cigarettes before fixing herself a bowl of Froot Loops cereal doused liberally with extra sugar and whole milk. She laughed loudly at what she thought of as her wicked ways.

"What on earth are you doing up at this hour laughing like a loon in *my* kitchen?" Bernice asked from the front door, where she'd been watching her crazy employer, whom she loved more than she had ever loved her own deceased husband.

Toots almost jumped out of her skin. "Damn, Bernice, you scared the snot out of me! I didn't hear the front door open. I might ask you the same thing. Why are you here so early?"

"We have a long list of things to do today. You said so yourself last night. All those hoity-toity friends of yours will be here soon. I wouldn't want them to think you lived like anything but a queen. I'm here at your command. Remember how you taught me to say that after your third husband died?"

Toots grimaced. She couldn't remember any such thing, but she nodded anyway.

Bernice was more friend than employee. When Toots had told her about her friends' upcoming visit, Bernice wasn't the least bit thrilled. Not wanting her to feel left out of the swing of things, she'd asked her to help with a few extra chores, hoping it would make her feel included, part of the gang, but instead Bernice acted like she'd been stung by a nasty bunch of bees, then mumbled something about being the hired help.

"Oh, stop it already! You're acting like a baby. You don't have to stick around while the girls are here. I'm sure you have plenty of other activities to occupy your time." Toots and Bernice both knew this was bullshit. Bernice's family consisted of a son she hadn't seen or heard from in four years and was supposedly traveling the world in search of his roots.

"If you weren't my employer, I'd tell you to just kiss my wrinkled old ass," Bernice said with a trace of her old humor.

"Yeah? And if you weren't my favorite employee, I'd tell you you're fired. So there," Toots shot right back.

"Did you drink the entire pot of coffee?" Bernice asked.

"Yep, what's it to ya?" Toots singsonged. "You the coffee police this morning?"

"You know I like at least three cups before I start working. Make another pot while I fix myself some toast."

"Yes, sir—ma'am!" Toots said, smiling. This was their normal morning routine. Bernice was a bit on the possessive side, though in a good way, when it came to her friendship with Toots. The truth was, Toots knew she'd just lie down and die if Bernice deserted her. She consoled herself that once Bernice got to know the girls on this visit, since they would all be here at once, she'd come around. They'd have plenty of time for gabbing and getting to know each other all over again. Bernice included.

The phone rang, alarming Toots. She'd learned through eight marriages that early-morning and late-night phone calls never brought good news. She hesitated before answering, then remembered there weren't any more husbands to bury.

"Hello?" she said in a brisk voice.

"Mom, are you really awake at this

god-awful hour or just pretending to be?" Abby asked.

"I could ask you the same question. Knowing you're on the West Coast probably means you are winding down your night's work. So what gives? Why are you calling me at this ungodly hour? You're okay, aren't you?" Toots asked anxiously.

"It depends on what you mean by okay. Am I healthy? Yes. Is my mortgage paid? Yes. Is Chester okay? Yes to that, too." Abby sighed. Chester was the German shepherd that Abby had adopted three years ago on Christmas Day. Abby called her Sweet Baby Love for short. Chester never responded to that endearment.

Toots knew her daughter, and she knew that she wouldn't call her at this time of day, or early morning as was the case, unless there was truly something bothering her. "So what's the problem? Is it a man? If you've met another jerk, and he needs to be taken care of, I'll be on the next flight out."

Abby ignored the gibe. "Mom, I just heard some disturbing news. It seems dear old Rag is in trouble. The entire staff knew he had a gambling problem. We just didn't know to what extent. We had a staff meeting yesterday afternoon. He told us he was putting *The Informer* up for sale. Said he was tired of working, but we all know it's to pay off his gambling debts. He spends most weekends in Vegas. I don't know what I'm going to do for a job. In one of his usual small spiteful moods, he told us one of the conditions to selling the paper would probably be that all former employees have to go. I'm just venting here, Mom."

"Oh, honey, that's terrible. From everything you've told me about him, he might just do himself in. You also said he threatens to sell from time to time and never does. Hold tight until you have something a little more definite to go on. Just out of curiosity, do you have any idea how much he's asking for the paper?" Toots asked, as an idea hit her like a lightning bolt.

"I don't know, Mom. I'm sure *The Globe* or *The Enquirer* will pick it up for a song if it really does go up for sale. If they do, they've got plenty of people to staff or pick up the slack. It just pisses me off that someone else's bad habit is putting me and a handful of others out of a job. I just hate the thought of possibly having to collect unemployment."

"You could come home, Abby. *The Post and Courier* would hire you in a heartbeat. You know that." Amanda Lawford, the owner and publisher of *The Post and Courier,* had worked with Toots on at least a dozen mutual committees and had told her time and again if Abby ever decided to move back to Charleston, she'd give her a job on the crime beat. Abby hadn't been interested. Maybe this time things would be different.

"Thanks, Mom, but no, thanks. I'm twenty-eight years old. The last thing I want to do is come crawling home with my tail between my legs. Besides, Amanda Lawford just wants me around to date that nerd son of hers."

Toots laughed. "You're right about that. He always asks about you when I see him."

"Tell him I said hello next time you see him. He's not a bad guy, just not my type. Besides, I could never date a guy named Herman. Reminds me of that show I used to watch as a kid."

"*The Munsters!*" Toots laughed as she

recalled how Abby sat glued to reruns of the old television show and, to her knowledge, never missed an episode.

"Yep, that was it. So when do all my godmothers arrive? I can't believe you actually orchestrated a visit for them at the same time. It's been like forever since I've seen them."

"Come home, and you can see them, Abby. They'd love to see you," Toots encouraged. "I'll buy you a ticket."

"The timing is off. With the dark stuff about to hit the fan at the paper, I don't think it would be in my best interest to take a vacation. Besides, I was just there."

"Your room is waiting if you change your mind. Bernice takes great pleasure in freshening your room every day in case you decide to make a spur-of-the-moment visit."

"Thanks, Mom. You're the best, but right now I just needed to cry on your shoulder. I'll figure something out. I can always work for the *Los Angeles Times*. I get e-mails from my former editor at least once a month trying to lure me back."

"You wouldn't be happy writing about

stuffy politicians and government," Toots said.

Toots could hear Abby's deep sigh over the phone. "If it comes down to that, I'll consider it. I have bills to pay, and no, I'm not going to allow you to cover my ass, so let's not even go there, okay?"

Toots smiled in spite of herself. Abby was just like her father. Fiercely independent. "Whatever you say, dear. Just know that help is out there if things get too rough."

"How did I ever get so lucky to wind up with a mother like you?" Abby asked.

"The luck of the draw, kiddo," Toots said. She hoped Abby would remember those words in six months.

Chapter 4

Toots raced around the kitchen, opening and closing drawers. "Where is my address book? I know it's in here somewhere."

"It's on your desk in your room. Remember, you always leave it there," Bernice said between bites of toast.

"Of course! You're right. What was I thinking?" Toots snapped.

"You weren't," Bernice quipped.

"Would you stop it already?" Toots tossed over her shoulder as she raced upstairs. She heard Bernice mutter something just as she found her address book on her desk. Toots laughed and shook her head. Bernice had been with her since Abby was a baby. At the time, she'd been recently widowed herself, with a young son, when she'd answered an ad for a housekeeper Toots had placed in the paper back in New Jersey all those years ago. When John Simpson, her one true love and Abby's father, died in a car accident, they'd left New Jersey behind with no regrets. Bernice hadn't hesitated for a skinny minute when Toots asked her to come to Charleston. Abby had been five at the time. Where had all the years gone?

Bernice knew her better than had all eight of her husbands put together. She'd been with her through the good times and the bad. While a dear friend, Bernice was forever mindful of her position as an employee. Toots trusted her to the ends of the earth.

Toots flipped through the pages until she found the number for her stepson, Christopher Clay. She looked at the clock and realized it was probably too early to call. Shit! If Christopher was anything like his father, he got up with the chickens. Toots dialed the number despite the three-hour time difference. This was important. Screw propriety. As she waited for the call to go through, she tried to remember where Garland, Christopher's father, ranked on the husband scale. Maybe the fourth. Christopher had been in boarding school when they married.

Toots remembered fearing Chris would view her as his evil stepmother, but that hadn't been the case at all. Garland's first wife, Chris's mother, had died when Chris was a baby. He'd been thrilled at the prospect of having a "real mom," and they'd hit it off from the beginning. To this day, Toots still thought of him as her son. When Garland died and left her everything, she'd immediately turned the millions over to Chris, who'd just started law school. She'd kept the home they'd shared simply because Chris hadn't been ready for the responsibility of home ownership at the time. When the time was right, she'd give him the house as well. Toots had fond memories of their life together. She hoped Chris's memories were just as pleasant.

"This better be good," a throaty voice came over the wire.

"Christopher, good morning! It's Toots,

how goes it, baby?" she said cheerfully. Everyone in Hollywood called each other baby.

The voice on the other end of the line chuckled. "I should have known it was you. Typhoon Toots, you're the only one crazy enough to call me this time of night ... morning." Typhoon Toots was a name Chris had bestowed on her the week he'd graduated from college and she'd arranged the party of all parties for two hundred of his friends in a matter of just a few hours.

Toots smiled. She'd always admired and respected her stepson and was glad they'd remained close through the years. She knew she could count on him no matter what. When Abby had decided to move to Los Angeles, knowing Chris was there in the wings to watch over her was a tremendous weight off Toots's shoulders. He was as responsible as his father had been.

"Look, I'm sorry for this early-morning call, but it's important; otherwise, I wouldn't be calling. I need some legal advice, Chris, and you were the first person who came to mind. Plus you're in Los Angeles, which stacked the deck."

"Thanks for the vote of confidence, Toots. What's going down in LA?"

"It's Abby," she said. "She's in trouble."

"Damn! Why didn't you say something?"

"I'm saying it now. And, Christopher, it's not life-threatening. At least not at this point." Toots did have thoughts of choking Rodwell Archibald Godfrey, but she kept them to herself. "Clearly, Abby is alive and well, or I wouldn't be talking to you. She's having trouble at work."

"She still writing for that rag?"

Abby replied in a firm yet kind tone. "Yes, Christopher, she is still writing for that rag. She loves her work regardless of who approves or disapproves."

"No need to defend her, Toots. I'm an entertainment attorney. We don't rate so high in the legal world, either. So what kind of trouble has Abby gotten herself into?"

That was more like it. It reminded her of why she'd married Garland. He'd had a quick wit and all of his own teeth. Like father like son.

"The paper's owner needs to pay off his gambling debts. He told the staff he's selling the paper."

Christopher laughed. "What does this

have to do with Abby? Doesn't she want to work for someone else? She's good, Toots. She could have her pick of beats at any of the large newspapers."

"As her mother, I already know that! Abby absolutely loves working for a tabloid," Toots said, her voice crisp and clipped. "Sorry, Chris, I'm just so ticked off right now. I didn't mean to go all snarly on you. Apparently one of the conditions in selling the paper is that the current employees, including Abby, have to go their own way. Abby says it's the owner's way of being petty and spiteful, and I tend to agree, but then again, I know nothing about how newspapers work."

"Toots, I know where this is heading, and as an attorney, I am going to advise you to stay out of it. Financially, *The Informer* is a flop. It's low on the tabloid totem pole. Very low, as I'm sure Abby's told you. I haven't a clue what the circulation is, but—"

"Find out as soon as possible. Offer them double their asking price. No questions, Chris. It is what it is."

"It's not a good investment, Toots. I strongly caution you against going down this road. You just said you don't know anything about newspapers. If your mind is made up, I won't stop you, but I am going on record that it is a poor move. I'm not keen on acting as your broker, either. Have you really thought this through, Toots? What does Abby think about this?"

Damn, how did she know he would ask her about Abby? "I have thought it through, Chris." Toots took a deep breath and let it out in a loud swoosh. "Currently, Abby is unaware of my intentions."

"I assume you don't plan to share them with her, either," Chris said sourly. He was not liking this conversation one little bit.

Was she that obvious? Hell yes. She was a mother. She had to do what she had to do for her daughter. Any woman/ mother in her right mind would do whatever she could to help her daughter's career. So what if it was just the type of unscrupulous excitement she'd been looking for anyway? She couldn't wait to tell Sophie, Mavis, and Ida.

"Your assumption would be correct, darling boy."

"Okay, Toots. Give me a day or so to get the ball rolling."

"You're a good man, Chris, just like your father. I knew I could count on you."

Ten minutes later, Toots was downstairs pouring her umpteenth cup of coffee. There was a twinkle in her eye that hadn't been there since . . . forever.

"Bernice, I have a good bottle of scotch hidden around here somewhere. I say let's find it and make a toast." Toots ran around the kitchen, rifling through the cupboards, searching for the bottle. She found it next to the Comet cleanser beneath the sink. Bernice held out her empty mug. "Mind telling me what we're toasting?"

Suddenly, Toots was afraid she'd jinx the possible deal if she spoke about it before it was a fait accompli. She'd always been superstitious. "Yes. No. I'm not exactly sure. Never mind." Toots held her Maxine cup high. "Here's to new beginnings and happy endings."

The women clinked their mugs together, spilling coffee and liquor on the newly polished floor. Bernice dropped a kitchen towel onto the floor and used her foot to mop up the spill.

"I do like the way you clean, Bernice dear, but the Ladies' Society would frown on that particular method. Personally, I don't care; I'm just saying. I'm thinking they would call us both tacky," Toots said, before pouring each of them another bounteous spot of scotch.

"You didn't think that way yesterday while you were working me like a mule."

"Oh, for crying out loud, Bernice, stop whining. I did not work you like a mule yesterday. You have the cushiest job in Charleston," Toots said, before tipping her mug back.

"Don't get carried away, Toots."

They both laughed at the absurdity of their state of affairs. Each had it made, and they both knew life couldn't be better. They just liked to devil one another to, as Bernice put it, get the other's goat.

"So now that we're half snockered, do you want to tell me why we're drinking scotch at five o'clock in the morning?" Bernice asked.

"Nope, but let's just say this. I might be taking a trip to the West Coast. Soon. As in day-after-tomorrow soon."

"What about your friends? You can't

just leave me here to entertain them! I don't even know them." Bernice started to flutter around like a lost hen.

"They'll come with me, of course. You can come with us, too, if you want, you know that, Bernice. I'm not leaving you out."

"Not me! No, ma'am, I will *not* get on an airplane. That's not in my job description. I'll stay here and make sure Pete keeps the bird feeders full, thank you very much."

"Oh, Bernice, you need to live a little. Life's too short to allow fear to bog you down."

"Toots, I'm seventy years old. If God wanted me to fly, he would have given me wings. I've made it this far in life without flying, and I plan on keeping it that way. I've never been on an airplane in my life. I don't think it's going to matter one way or another at this point in time if I'm fearful of flying or not. I just can't see how it would improve my life," Bernice said, in defense of her lifelong fear of flying.

Toots thought about what her housekeeper had just said. She supposed it made sense from Bernice's point of view.

"You're probably right, but still, you could give it some thought."

"Still nothing. It's unnatural. If people were meant to fly, we would've been born with wings." Bernice made her usual argument when the topic of air travel came up, and she never cared how repetitive she was.

"I suppose you're right about that, too, but you don't know what you're missing. There are still so many places I want to visit. Actually, I plan to become bicoastal. It's the new 'in thing' with seniors, at least healthy, well-to-do seniors." If she succeeded in purchasing *The Informer,* she would *have* to live bicoastal.

"You're certainly well qualified for that lifestyle," Bernice said tartly.

"Yes, I am, I won't disagree. Now let's get my 'ass in gear' list and zip through what's left. I still have some shopping to do. I think I'll have Pete drive me since I've . . . imbibed a little."

"Well, I, for one, need to rest a minute. That booze doesn't sit well in my stomach this early. We should have eaten some cornflakes first. Go on to the store. I'll put the fresh sheets on the guest beds while you're gone."

"Good idea. Thank heavens Walmart never closes. If you think of anything we didn't put on the list, call my cell," Toots called over her shoulder. Grabbing her purse and the keys to her Town Car, she walked out the back door without another word as she went in search of her gardener.

Two hours later, the early-morning sun flashed through the kitchen window as Toots dumped fourteen bags on the countertop. She skimmed through her list, checking off each item as she removed it from a bag. "Damn, something *is* up with Ida," she said out loud.

Bernice skirted through the kitchen like a summer breeze. "You back already?"

"Yes. Six in the morning is the perfect time to shop. There are no lines. Look at all this stuff." Toots indicated three bags of disinfectant and germ-killing products.

Bernice foraged through the bags. "What's all this for? We've got plenty of cleaning supplies."

A bit bewildered, Toots shook her head. "Ida said she'd need a few things for her visit. This must be what Mavis was telling me about. Something about Ida's fear of germs. She called it OCD, obsessive compulsive disorder."

Bernice removed a box with a picture on the front label that resembled a cell phone. "What kind of dumb-bunny gadget is this?"

"It's called a germ-zapping light. Apparently you wave it around a germy area, and it's supposed to kill off any germs in ten seconds. E. coli, staphylococcus, salmonella, cold and flu germs, stuff like that. Mavis said Ida wouldn't come if I didn't buy one."

"Think she'll wave it over the toilet seat? Lord, I'll have to douse it with Clorox every two minutes."

Toots laughed. "Probably, but I don't think you need to concern yourself with Ida's germ disorder. I've bought everything under the sun and then some. Besides, this house is as clean as it's going to get. So what if there's a little germ here and there? Ida will just have to get over it."

"I suppose," Bernice said as she began transferring the canned goods and staples Toots had purchased to the pantry shelves. "I don't see why the need for all this food. You said yourself you gals were going to the West Coast. Who's going to eat all this?" she asked, waving her arm around to indicate the already overstocked shelves.

"Actually, Bernice, I'm stockpiling just in case I'm in California longer than planned, you know, more than, say, ten days. I don't have a clue at this juncture just how long I'll be staying, so I want to go with a free mind, knowing you and Pete will be covered until I get back. The freezer is chockfull." Toots wondered if she was putting the cart before the horse. Yes, she probably was, but she had a feeling this "project" might turn into something more than a simple bicoastal quickie business venture.

Maybe what she should do was cover all her bases and have Christopher check into purchasing a jet and hiring a full-time pilot so she wouldn't have to give up her Charleston digs. She beamed at the thought. *Yes*, she thought, it was all doable.

"Did you get any of those raspberry jelly rolls I like?"

"Don't I always? I don't see how you eat the silly things and not gain an ounce."

"The same way you do, Typhoon Toots. I smoke, drink, and thrive on the adrenaline rush I get when I see the stock market climbing. It keeps my metabolism high. Don't tell anyone I said that, because they won't believe you, but it's the honest-to-God truth." Bernice cackled.

"I'm sure it is." *When pigs fly.*

Chapter 5

Fortunately, Toots's travel agent had been able to book Sophie's, Mavis's, and Ida's flights within an hour of one another. She'd discussed it with Sophie and Mavis the previous night on the phone, explaining everything in detail. All three agreed they were fine with hanging out in the airport lounge until Ida's flight arrived.

Before she left for the airport, Bernice made Toots promise she would not touch a drop of anything alcoholic until she returned safely with the girls. As if she needed to be told, but it was Bernice's way of watching over her employer, and Toots was careful not to say anything to upset her since she'd been running around like a chicken with its head cut off all morning in preparation for the arrival of the guests.

Forty minutes later, Toots maneuvered her Range Rover through the entrance at Charleston International Airport with ease. Soon she'd have a jet of her own and wouldn't need to use commercial airlines. At least that was her plan. Spying valet parking, she pulled to the curb, gave the attendant—a slim, dark-haired boy who looked to be at least six feet tall, still growing, and not a day over eighteen—her keys. She made him swear he wouldn't smoke any of the cigarettes she'd left lying on the passenger seat, telling him they would stunt his growth. He swore he wouldn't. Toots counted the three packs of Marlboro Lights just in case.

Inside the airport, she spotted the arrival gates and hurried toward them. Mavis's flight was first to arrive. She wanted to be visible so Mavis would see her the minute she passed the security line. She wondered if Mavis was as happy as she was over this little reunion.

Knowing Mavis was traveling with Coco,

her Chihuahua, she'd called ahead to make sure they would be allowed to keep the dog with them while they waited for Sophie and Ida. Toots was assured it would be fine as long as the dog was kept in its carrier.

Had it not been for the pet carrier, Toots wouldn't have recognized Mavis. Though they talked on the phone once a week, e-mailed every day, and sent birthday and Christmas cards to each other, it had been almost six years since they'd seen each other. What she saw waddling toward her was not the dear friend she remembered. Mavis was at least a hundred pounds heavier, possibly more, since the last visit.

Mavis spotted Toots waiting behind the velvet ropes. She waved, her plump arms flapping like sheets in the wind. "Toots! Over here!" she called out, pausing mid-way to catch her breath.

Toots plastered a big grin on her face, then waved back in acknowledgment. "Hurry it up, woman! I can't wait to give you a big hug."

When Mavis finally made it past the ropes where friends and family were allowed to wait, she was huffing and puffing.

Perspiration dotted her upper lip and fore-head. She reached into her pocket for a tissue to mop her face. "Lord, it's hot here. I don't see how you stand it."

Toots hugged her friend and planted a kiss on her cheek. Another plan was forming in her brain, which was already on overload. She smiled. Mavis needed her, and that made her extremely happy. Toots loved it when people needed her. "You get used to it after a while. I'm so glad you could make it, Mavis. I've got a big surprise for you, but I can't tell you what it is until Sophie and Ida arrive."

"Yip, yip!"

"This must be Coco," Toots said, peer-ing inside the pet carrier.

Mavis struggled to speak normally, but she was still winded. "It is, and she's thirsty. A surprise, huh? I can only imag-ine. Let's find a ladies' room, then I'll see if I can pick your brain while we wait for Sophie and Ida."

"Right around the corner." Toots pointed to the restroom. "What about your lug-gage?" Toots glanced at the small brown canvas bag slung over Mavis's shoulder. Surely she'd packed more than that.

"This is it. I like to travel light. I only have three outfits anyway. My pension doesn't allow for a lot of extras. Property taxes are killing me. I hope you have a washer and dryer," Mavis huffed.

"Of course I do." Toots took the pet carrier from her, then anchored Mavis's tote around her own shoulder. "Go on. I'll hold this while you do your thing."

Mavis nodded and trundled off toward the ladies' room.

Travelers with every color, size, and shape of luggage dotted the terminal. Toots heard bits of conversation here and there, an occasional cry from a baby as she waited outside the restroom. Coco barked at a young man whizzing through the airport in what amounted to a golf cart with a flashing yellow light on top. The *beep beep beep* sound must've scared the little dog. Cooked onions and old grease from a nearby fast-food restaurant filled the air, the scent so overwhelming it made her stomach roil. How people could eat that fast-food junk was beyond her. A bowl of Froot Loops with a cup of sugar and some light cream was all she needed to qualify her as a happy camper.

While she waited for Mavis, Toots's mind raced. First she'd contact a friend who owned Liz's Stout Shop and purchase some clothing. Mavis would need it once they were in California, that is, if she agreed to make the trip. Then she'd hire the best weight-loss guru money could buy to get her friend down to size. Of course she'd have to make sure Mavis was physically able to withstand any vigorous activity before she was put on an exercise routine. All she had to do was call Joe Pauley, her own personal physician, and ask him to make a house call tonight. Friends forever, she knew Joe would do as she asked.

Mavis emerged from the restroom looking fresh as a daisy. Or maybe a sunflower. Toots reasoned she was a *large* woman. And sunflowers were the largest flower she could come up with.

More yipping from the carrier.

"Let's take a quick scoot out to the pet area and then we can come back in and wait for Sophie," Toots suggested.

Toots removed the little Chihuahua from the carrier, allowed the small pooch to give her a few wet doggie kisses, then handed her to Mavis. "This way," she said, motioning to an outside area where several other dogs and a few cats roamed about with their owners.

Ten minutes later, they were back in the lounge. "Let's have something to drink," Toots suggested.

"Sounds good to me. I sure could use a thick chocolate shake right now. All they offered on the plane was soda and pretzels. I was so sure they would at least serve a sandwich or something," Mavis grumbled.

Toots knew in her gut if she wanted to help Mavis she had to start now. "Mavis darling, I don't know how to tell you this, but you know me, I've never been one to beat around the bush. The last thing you need right now is a chocolate milk shake. You're heavier than you've ever been and I'm worried."

There! She'd said it.

Mavis took a deep breath and nodded. "I know. I almost backed out because I thought I wouldn't be able to fit in the seat on the plane. They had to give me a seatbelt extender. I was so embarrassed. I just can't seem to get a grip on my eating habits. First it's one ice cream, then a

couple of donuts, and from there it esca-
lated to two and three bags of chips a
day." Mavis looked down. "And you see
where it's got me."

Toots's eyes filled with tears over her
friend's dilemma, if you could call being a
hundred pounds overweight a dilemma. It
was more like a heart attack waiting to
happen. "If you want to lose weight, you
know I'll help out any way I can." Toots
wasn't about to tell her she already had a
plan in mind. She'd need Sophie's and
Ida's help to keep Mavis out of the refrigerator and on the treadmill.

"Then I'll accept whatever help you're
offering. It's just me and Coco. As you can
see, she's tiny, doesn't require a lot of exercise or food. Most days I sit in my
Barcalounger with her at my side. I watch
the soaps, and Coco scrambles after my
crumbs. I haven't had the money to buy
her decent dog food in ages. I figured
what went in my gut was good enough for
her, too, but then I see the way I look, and
I just want to curl up and die. Then I'll think
of Coco and Abby and you girls, I'll eat
salads for a week, then little by little I slide
back into my old routine."

"Mavis, I should kick your butt! Why didn't you tell me things were that rough? You know I've got millions. No, make that *billions.* I'll never live long enough to spend all that money."

"You do enough, Toots. Thanks to you, I have a live Christmas tree delivered every year and beautifully decorated packages to place beneath it. Plus all the other stuff you do, like that laptop computer you sent me. I know you paid off my mortgage, too, so don't insult me by lying."

True, Toots thought, but she hadn't seen any reason to shout it to the world. Mavis knew, and that's all that mattered. She knew there was a pride issue, too. Mavis didn't like accepting charity, so she'd simply done what she felt Mavis would allow without kicking up her heels. Had she known things were as bad as they were, though, she would have done more, *much* more. That was about to change. She'd call Henry Whitmore, her old friend and president at the Bank of Charleston, and set up an account for Mavis. And if Mavis didn't like it, too bad. Eventually she'd get over it.

Things are about to change, Mavis

Hanover, and if you don't like it, well, to quote Bernice, "you can just kiss my wrinkled old ass."

Toots spied a sports lounge close to the exit gates. Flat-screen television sets were suspended from the ceiling, each tuned to a different sports network. Loud guffaws from a group of men filled the small lounge as the women found a three-seater booth close to the exit.

The two women slid into the soft leather booth, placing Coco's carrier next to Toots since Mavis's bulk took up most of her seat. A waitress wearing a hot-pink shirt, black shorts, and a name tag that read TAMMY came to take their order. "We'll each have a bottle of sparkling water with a twist of lime."

"Nothin' to eat?" the waitress asked in a distinct Charleston drawl. Toots wondered if she was old enough to drink legally, let alone serve alcohol. Several bangle bracelets clinked against one another as she wrote their order on a pad. The girl had at least five earrings in each ear, along with other piercings.

Toots looked at Mavis, who was practically salivating. "Yes, we'll have two tossed salads, no dressing, with extra lemon on the side."

"I guess this means I'm on a diet now?"

"Yep, but it won't be that hard really. I'm a vegan, and I'm rarely hungry." Toots wasn't about to mention her sugar addiction.

"If you say so," Mavis acquiesced.

They spent the next half hour catching up and reminiscing.

"Remember when Ida's 'tits' fell out of her prom dress?" Mavis said. "I thought she'd never come out of hiding after that episode."

Toots smiled at the memory. "I think I would've done the same thing. Her being prom queen and all. Having the pair of rolled-up socks stuffed in your bra fall to the floor during the coronation isn't the most pleasant memory. It was funny, though. Sophie peed in her pants, she laughed so hard. We never shared that with Ida. We were full of fire, weren't we?"

"That we were," Mavis agreed.

"I wouldn't trade those memories for anything in the world." Maybe a few, but she'd keep those to herself.

"It's amazing after all these years that

we're still friends. I can't imagine my life without you girls. Abby, too. Lord, if it weren't for her, I don't know if we would've remained as close. Since the rest of us never had children."

"We all went our own way, that's true. Isn't e-mail great? I can just imagine what our phone bills would be without it. It's just so darn instant," Toots exclaimed in amazement.

"I get e-mails from some of my former students. Actually, one of them is running for state senator. I can't wait to see if she's elected."

"For your sake, I hope she is. And I hope she'll acknowledge what a fantastic English teacher you were."

Mavis laughed. "I don't know about that, but it would certainly do my old heart good to see someone I had a bit of a hand in molding making it to the state senate. Lord knows what's in there now isn't doing me much good. I keep fearing my Medicare will get cut, and then where would I be?"

Toots reached across the table, placing her hand on top of Mavis's. "You'll never have to worry about anything if it comes to that, so don't concern yourself over it."

Bracelets jingling against the background noise coming from the televisions and the group of rowdy drinkers at the bar, Tammy returned with the check.

Toots removed a twenty-dollar bill from her wallet and placed it inside the leather check holder. She smiled at the young waitress before glancing at the diamond watch on her wrist. "Sophie's flight is due to arrive any minute. I think I'll run and check the boards just to make sure. I wouldn't want her roaming around thinking I've forgotten her. Why don't you order coffee or tea and wait here. There's no need for you to lug Coco and her carrier through the airport." Toots thought that was a rather nice way of saying her friend was just too heavy to walk through the airport without a hassle.

"Sounds good, even though I'd rather have that milk shake."

"Don't you dare! Now sit here and enjoy the scenery. I'll be right back."

"If you insist," Mavis replied with a smile. "Don't worry, I promise not to sneak."

"Good." Toots pulled another twenty out of her wallet. "For the coffee."

In reality, Toots wanted to prepare

Sophie for Mavis's bulk so she wouldn't be as shocked as she herself had been when she'd seen her struggling to walk the short distance from the gate to the arrival area.

As Toots raced to greet Sophie, she couldn't recall being this happy. Her friends were there, and they needed her, or at least Mavis did.

At this precise moment, all was right with the world.

Until she saw Sophie emerging from the masses exiting the plane.

Lord! She had her work cut out for her. And to think she was going to be managing a newspaper on top of everything else. Maybe.

"Tootsie!" Sophie hollered, using the pet name that only she was allowed to use.

Once again Toots plastered a big smile on her face. "Sophie Manchester, if you aren't a sight for sore eyes!" Toots wrapped her arms around Sophie's bony frame. She couldn't weigh a hair over ninety pounds, if that. Mavis was obese, and poor Sophie looked and felt like a skeleton with a layer of skin stretched around it.

"You look stunning," Sophie said. "Of course you always do. So where's Mavis?

You said she was arriving before the rest of us."

Without mentioning Sophie's weight, or lack thereof, Toots was momentarily at a loss for words. How could she tell one friend that the other looked like Two-Ton Tessie while Sophie looked like a Starving Scrawny Sue?

"She's waiting in the lounge," was the best she could come up with.

"I can't wait to see her; it's been ages. Thank God for the Internet; otherwise, I'd be completely out of the loop. With Walter on the brink of death, it's the only link I have to the real world. You would think that old fossil would've kicked the bucket by now. But no, he's too damned ornery to die. Every day I wake up—and I hope *he* doesn't."

Toots wanted to tell her that was a terrible thing to say, but she alone knew what Walter had put Sophie through. As far as Toots was concerned, the old fossil had lingered on way too long, but she wasn't going to voice her opinion at the moment.

"Maybe he'll perish while you're gone," Toots said.

"Perish?" Sophie laughed. "I want the

old poop to *die.* D-I-E," she spelled the letters out. "*Perish* sounds too good for him."

"How did Walter react when you told him you were leaving?" Toots had kept her promise and arranged for a nurse to stay with Sophie's husband twenty-four/seven. Sophie had yet to tell her of Walter's reaction.

"You really want to know? I didn't even tell him I was leaving. I figured if he was nervous or scared—if Walter even knows what that feels like—I thought maybe once he discovered I flew the coop, it would speed things up. Like massive heart failure or something."

Toots couldn't help but laugh. Walter *was* a mean old man.

"Speaking of heart failure. Mavis is heavier than she's ever been, so don't be shocked when you see her. Act normal. I told her she was going on a diet while she's here. She agreed, but something tells me it isn't going to be easy for her. I've got more things in the works for her, like a good checkup, so don't say anything about her weight unless she brings it up first.

She's got this adorable yacker of a dog. Focus on the dog."

Briefly, Toots wondered if she could feed Sophie Mavis's leftovers. Kill two birds with one stone type of thing. She'd think of something to help Sophie put on a few pounds. Sophie had always been the prettiest of the four. Thick, shiny black hair with almond brown eyes. She'd had a figure to die for, too. Now all she had to do was figure out a tasteful way to get Mavis to *stop* stuffing and a way to get Sophie to *start* stuffing. She smiled at the thought.

They retrieved Sophie's four suitcases from the luggage carousel. Toots was glad she'd driven the Range Rover instead of the Town Car.

Toots pulled the largest of the two bags behind her while Sophie wrestled with two smaller pieces.

"Here." Toots directed her gaze to the lounge. "Now, remember, not a word about her weight."

Toots skillfully maneuvered their way through the throngs of travelers, hearing scattered bits of varied conversations in dozens of languages as they made their way to the lounge. The group of loud men at the bar had been replaced by a group of women who were just as loud, if not more so. Amidst the chatter, Toots led Sophie to the booth where Mavis and Coco waited.

Sophie hid her surprise at Mavis's appearance, but Mavis didn't bother to restrain herself.

"Girl, you look like a stick! Do you ever eat?"

They hugged and air-kissed before Sophie answered, "Yes, I do but not enough. I'm so busy taking care of that old goat, I don't have time to eat." Sophie raked her gaze over Mavis's bulk. "From the looks of you, I can see food or lack of is not an issue with you."

"Sophie!" Toots admonished.

"It's okay, Toots, I know I'm fat and need to lose all this blubber. Maybe Sophie can teach me a thing or two."

"I never thought our roles would be reversed. Remember when I went through my fat phase our junior year? I didn't think I'd ever lose those extra thirty pounds. It's not easy to lose, especially at our age," Sophie said as she pulled a chair up to the end of the booth.

"Don't discourage me, Sophie. I just promised Toots I'd go on a diet. I don't know if I'm up for this or not, but I sure as hell am going to go for the gusto." Mavis eyed the next table in front of her as the waitress delivered a heaping plate of french fries with crumbled bacon and melted cheese piled on top. "If it doesn't work, I'll just die fat and happy!"

"Like hell you will! Tell me you don't remember all those nightly jogs we took through the park? If memory serves me correctly, Mavis dear, *you* were the skinny little shit that ran alongside me encouraging me, reminding me that Billy Bledsoe wasn't worth all those late-night binges," Sophie recalled.

"I do remember that. I was skinny, too. Well, I don't know if I'll ever get as thin as I was back in high school, but I wouldn't mind losing some of this fat. It's so uncomfortable at times, I want to take a knife and slice it off!"

"Lose the weight, and I'll check into reconstructive surgery if you're healthy enough, that is, if you want it," Toots volunteered.

Mavis shook her head. "Don't know

that I'd go that far, but it's something to consider. Just promise me one thing? The both of you." Mavis looked at Toots, then Sophie.

"Anything," Toots said.

"Whatever you want," Sophie added.

"Whatever you do, keep the ice cream, potato chips, cakes, and pies out of the house. I don't know if I could resist if I saw a pint of Cherry Garcia. Those four things are what got me in this mess."

"I'll make sure there's nothing in the fridge to tempt you. Now"—Toots glanced at her watch again—"I'd better go see if Ida's flight arrived. She'll be pissed to the teeth if I'm not there to greet her and roll out the red carpet." She rummaged through her purse, thrust another twenty on the table, then gave her car keys to Sophie.

"Take these to the valet and wait for us there. Ida and I might need a few minutes alone."

"I can't believe she's still ticked at you for stealing away what's-his-name after all these years. You two go through this routine every time you meet," Sophie said.

"Ida expects it. I can't start disappointing her now," Toots replied.

"True," Mavis said.

"Yip, yip!" from the carrier.

"Apparently, Coco agrees. Now just follow the signs to the exit. I'll meet you both at the car. By the way, it's a Range Rover in case the valet attendant asks."

Toots left the women in the lounge, knowing Mavis would tell Sophie she had a surprise for all of them. They'd spend their time waiting trying to figure out exactly what the surprise was. She smiled at the image.

Ten minutes later, when she saw Ida emerge from the plane, Toots almost fainted. Mavis and Sophie had weight issues for sure. Ida on the other hand . . . what the hell *was* her problem?

Toots observed her friend as Ida carefully made her way through the group of debarking passengers, careful to stay as far away from human contact as possible. Ida was neither fat nor skinny. She was just right. Hair graying nicely though plainly styled. Toots thought her old friend was gorgeous, with her perfectly even features, nothing too large or too small. Every feature was where it was supposed to be. Toots always thought she herself was too tall and her lips too thick, but now wasn't the time to start tallying up her issues against that of her former rival. More immediate issues were at hand. Like why did Ida have on latex gloves and one of those masks surgeons wear?

Her voice muffled by the mask, Ida asked, "Teresa, is that you?"

"Of course it's me. Who did you think it was, King Kong? I haven't changed that much, have I?" *Here I go*, Toots thought, *all those damned insecurities slapping me in the face like a cheating lover caught in the act.*

"I'm not sure. Let me take a look at you."

Toots leaned in to give Ida a hug and allow her a close-up look. Ida almost fell over backward. "Do not touch me!"

"What?" Toots asked, sure she hadn't heard Ida correctly.

"Let's get out of here. Did you bring all the supplies Mavis told you I'd need? Don't tell me she didn't tell you what's wrong with me, because she called me right after she hung up talking to you last night."

Yep, other than the germ factor, Ida was still a snippy bitch. Toots planned on curing her, like real quick.

Toots grabbed Ida by the hand. "Follow me, and don't you dare tell me not to touch you!"

Chapter 6

"Bernice," Toots announced, "you've out-
done yourself again. I don't know when
I've enjoyed a meal as much." With Toots
a vegan, Mavis on her new diet, Sophie
needing to pile on the pounds, and Ida
fearing anything she put in her mouth was
laced with germs, Toots had called ahead
to warn Bernice about the weird eating re-
quirements of her friends. She'd success-
fully put together a menu that would satisfy
each of their needs. Poached salmon and
a watercress salad for Mavis, a thick New
York strip steak and mashed potatoes for

Sophie, and a plate of boiled vegetables for Ida.

Acting the role of maid, chef, and pot scrubber, Bernice merely nodded, then began clearing their plates from the table. With a smirk on her face, Bernice asked, "Would the Missus care for coffee and dessert now?"

"Of course. We'll have it outside on the terrace." Toots saw Bernice roll her eyes. If she wanted to play the roll of indentured servant, Toots was game. "Make sure the coffee is hot, too. And I'll want Half & Half, no skim milk for me, though I'm sure Mavis will want hers black, and she'll pass on dessert. Ida? Sophie?"

Mavis was the first to speak up. "I don't want any coffee, but I would like to take a sniff at whatever you're offering for dessert. I can't do this cold turkey."

"Of course you can't," Toots confirmed. "Bernice, slice a plate of fresh fruit for Mavis. In bite-size pieces."

Toots couldn't help but smile because she knew under ordinary circumstances Bernice would have told her to "kiss her wrinkled old ass" or flipped her the single-digit salute. For the moment, she was on her best behavior.

Meekly, with her eyes lowered, Bernice replied, "Yes, Missus Toots."

"Sophie? Ida? Dessert and coffee?" Toots asked the pair seated across from her.

"Hell yes, I want dessert! All I've heard since I arrived is how skinny I am," Sophie said with a grin.

Thank goodness her eating disorder wasn't self-inflicted, Toots thought. She'd just been too occupied with Walter's care the last year to take proper care of herself. That was about to change.

"Ida?" Toots inquired.

"Nothing, thank you."

The minute Ida had stepped foot in the house, she'd asked to go to her room, where she took the germ-zapping light Toots had purchased and proceeded to scan it across every inch of the room. Apparently it had been to her satisfaction, for she hadn't complained. At least not yet. A small bathroom that Toots herself had scrubbed with Clorox and then with ammonia—even Toots knew better than to mix the two if she wanted to be alive when her friends got there—met her standards as well. Ida needed psychiatric help. Big-time and soon. Toots made a mental note to ask Dr. Pauley for a referral.

While the others familiarized them-selves with their rooms, she'd called and arranged for the doctor to stop by later that evening. She'd also spoken with Henry Whitmore. He would fax her the re-quired papers so she could set up an ac-count for Mavis. With those tasks out of the way, all she needed was to hear from Christopher to see if the sale had gone through. She said a prayer that it would. Abby would never have to know she'd purchased *The Informer,* because she'd told Christopher she must remain a "silent owner." Big businesses did that all the time, she reasoned. Abby would never know her new boss. Toots had big plans for her daughter's future as a tabloid reporter.

Ten minutes later, they scattered around the long expanse of what Toots always referred to as the terrace even though it was a front porch that stretched around the entire perimeter of her home. Old houses in Charleston were like that. They had sunporches, sunrooms, verandas. Toots simply referred to the area as a terrace, and the name had stuck.

When Toots bought the old plantation house years ago, she hadn't hired a decorator the way most of her friends had. She'd simply bought pieces she liked, and in doing so created a welcoming, homey atmosphere inside and out. Old wicker chairs and tables were arranged so that one person or a group of twenty could converse comfortably without too much effort. Colorful handcrafted pots purchased from many of Charleston's local artists held a variety of green plants, ferns, and brightly colored flowers. Discreetly placed outdoor lighting created a soft, warm glow all the way around the long porch. Toots loved the varied scents that permeated the outdoors this time of the day, when the world was settling in for an evening of rest, or should be. She always thought of evenings as a time to reflect on the events of the day, both good and bad. Though today she must focus on her guests and what tomorrow would bring.

Bernice served dessert and coffee with as much aplomb as she had earlier. A chocolate mousse with whipped topping and chocolate shavings and a large array of fruit for Mavis and anyone else who cared to forgo a trip down sugar alley.

"How long has it been since we were all together like this?" Mavis asked, between bites of pineapple.

"Six years ago, when Abby graduated from college. Then, when she up and decided to move to California, you girls came to my rescue, remember?" Toots said. "It was the worst day of my life," she added, recalling how sad and empty she'd felt after Abby flew the coop. That's when that damned Leland had stepped into her life, trying to charm the pants off her. Stupid her, she'd let him, then felt guilty and married him. Shit! What *had* she been thinking?

"Toots!" Sophie said none too quietly. "Earth to Toots!"

"I bet she's planning her next wedding," Ida offered, more like the old Ida they all knew and loved. Not the germaphobe who wouldn't hug or kiss them in return.

"Oh, shut up! I was thinking about Abby," Toots said, explaining her temporary private mental mission.

"You should have asked her to come for a visit. I don't know about the rest of you, but I haven't seen my goddaughter nearly enough," Mavis stated.

"I invited her, but she's too busy with work. Actually, that's something I want to talk to you all about. Abby's boss at *The Informer* has a gambling problem. I'm not clear about all the details, but apparently he's selling the paper to settle his gambling debts. Abby said a condition of the sale may be that all current employees must go."

"That's not fair," Sophie said, sipping her coffee. "Can't she sue him? Discrimination, something like that?"

Toots shook her head. "I didn't ask." She took a deep breath. "That's what I wanted to talk to you all about. I know each of us has something going on in her life right now, but I don't think any one of us has something so important that she can't put it off for a few weeks or . . . months." Toots let the statement hang in the air, allowing the girls a chance to absorb her words, hoping they'd know she was leading them to something bigger and better than what they currently had. Not so much a monetary thing, except for Mavis, of course, but a chance for some real excitement. Toots wanted to add some much-needed excitement to her life and her friends' lives. With her owning and operating a tabloid, the opportunity for some exhilarating thrills was theirs for the taking. *If* they saw it that way. *If* they would welcome a new challenge in their lives. *If* they were willing to relocate temporarily to California. There were a lot of *if*s.

"I know you too well, Teresa. You've got something up your sleeve. You've always been such a sneak," Ida said. "I should know," she added, referring to the past.

"Oh, get over it, Ida! You only wanted Jerry when you thought Toots wanted him. Face the facts, she got him, you didn't. From what I gather, you're the lucky one. So what if he left all his millions to Toots? She deserved it after all those years of his cheapness and lack of sex drive. If you want my opinion"—Sophie held up a slim hand—"and I know you don't, but I'm going to give it to you anyway. Toots did you a favor by snatching him away. So get over it. And you need to get over this germ thing you've got going on. Do you realize there are medications for people like you?"

Toots could barely contain her laughter. Leave it to Sophie to call an ace an ace and a spade a spade.

"Is that what you think?" Ida asked indignantly.

"No, it's what I *know.* You two have been going at it for years, and I, for one, am damned sick of it. It isn't like you never married. How many times was it?" Sophie looked to Mavis for an answer.

"I can't remember. Between her and Toots, I lost count. I think it's a competition thing between the two of them," Mavis said.

"Three, if you must know," Ida shot back.

"Bullshit. More like five. I'm not that old that I don't remember those two idiots you married from Georgia. The ones you claimed were related to Jimmy Carter. The ones you never wanted to talk about. Weren't they cousins or something?" Toots said to her former rival with a huge grin plastered on her face. She knew it ticked Ida off when someone reminded her of her not-so-perfect past.

"I'll have you know I had both marriages annulled. And no, they were not cousins.

They were very . . . *distant* cousins, not close at all. They didn't even know one another until I came along," Ida said with an air of haughtiness that was *so Ida.*

Snickering, Sophie said, "I wonder if they ever compared notes."

Ida stood up. "I don't know why I even bother with you three. All you do is crack jokes about one another and talk about sex."

"Sit down, Ida. We're teasing, and you know it. Stop acting like some lily-white puritan. We're your friends, or have you forgotten that?" Toots asked.

Gingerly, Ida sat back down on the edge of a stool. "You won't let me. I know we're friends, but truly when you took Jerry away, well, let's just say my life hasn't been the same. I've been trying to find a . . . substitute to replace him if you must know. He really broke my heart. And so did you," Ida added, tears streaming down her face like two silvery rivers.

Toots thought Ida had missed her calling. She should've been an actress. This repeat performance was getting old. Ida needed a new script. If she'd stop caterwauling long enough, Toots was about to offer her, *all of them,* the opportunity of a lifetime.

Toots passed Ida a tissue while Sophie lit a cigarette and Mavis snarfed down the last piece of fruit on the platter.

"I have a proposition I'd like to offer for your consideration. It's not set in stone yet, but something tells me that's just a formality." When Toots saw she had her three best friends' undivided attention, she continued. "It's about Abby." Now she really had their attention. Faultless they were not. Godmothers, they were the best.

"Is she sick?" Ida asked.

"I bet she's getting married!" Sophie shouted exuberantly.

"Is she a lesbian?" Mavis asked timidly.

"No, no, and no." Toots looked at Mavis questioningly. "Why would you even ask such a question?"

"I don't know. Abby's not getting any younger. I never hear anything about her dating anyone special. I just thought I'd ask. It's not that big a deal anymore. Not like when we were young. Remember Sheila Finkelstein? She's a lesbian. I saw her with her partner years ago at the theater in New York when I took my English class there for their senior trip. I always suspected it when we were in high school. There was just something about her, you know, the way she would watch you undress in gym class. I never felt comfortable around her."

"That's more than I needed to know," Toots said. "I do remember her, though. Never thought too much about her sexual preference then, either."

The four women laughed deep, bellyhurting laughs. Just like old times. Yes, they all had their quirks, but they had the ties of almost fifty years of friendship to bind them.

It would take another fifty to unravel them.

Chapter 7

"*California?* What am I supposed to do about Walter?" Sophie squealed. "He's on the brink of death! At least I think he's on the brink of death. Maybe it's more wishful thinking on my part. California!"

"Yes, California. Stop fretting, Sophie. Dear old Walter can die just as easily with a nurse in attendance as with you. You can go back for the funeral if it happens. Like Abby says, crisp him up, and it's a done deal. You collect your insurance check, and it's all just a memory."

"Yes, but I thought this was just a quick trip, a minivacation. I needed a break," Sophie argued. She fired up a cigarette. "What if he dies while I'm in California?"

"Then you'll have your wish and five million bucks to boot. It's your call. Either you're in or out."

Toots stared at the group gathered around the dining room table. After dessert and coffee, they'd gone inside, where Toots found the half-empty bottle of scotch. Half-empty cups littered the table. Sophie used hers for an ashtray. Ida perched on the edge of her chair, ready to spring at any second, while Mavis eyed the bowl of apples and oranges in the center.

"Sorry. When Walter's name is mentioned, it brings back all those years of bad memories, not to mention bringing out my bad side."

The women nodded. They understood perfectly.

"Here's my plan. I'm thinking at the very least we'll need to hang out west for at least six months if we're to accomplish our goal, which is to make *The Informer* a source to be reckoned with. The other tabloids have ruled the market for years. It's time they had some healthy competition." Toots took a sip of scotch. She shuddered as it made its fiery descent into the pit of her stomach.

"Sounds good, but exactly what do you plan to do? News is news no matter if it's Hollywood news or national news. You just can't make it happen. It could take years to develop sources in the business. You need someone on the inside, you need reliable snitches, friends who hate their best-friends-forever and sell them out for money," Sophie said.

"Remember, we're talking about Hollywood. News that may not be considered real news is news out there. For instance, remember when Helen Heart disappeared? The tabloids reported that she'd taken a trip to Europe for plastic surgery when in reality she'd been in rehab right in their very own Malibu Hills. While this isn't important to the world in general, it's *very* important to those in the business. Would you want to hire an aging drunk for your next blockbuster? I don't think so. So, to answer your question, the type of news we'll be working on isn't important in the sense that it will affect the world, but it will affect Helen Heart's career and others just like her. The big guns in the business read this stuff even though they'll never admit it. Abby told me this. *She knows*."

"I don't understand," Ida said. "What can you do that the former owner didn't do?"

"That's where Abby will come in. She has contacts. She's told me on more than one occasion that she had *breaking news* before the other reporters, but old Rag didn't believe her, then the next day, it would be splashed on the front page of *The Enquirer* or *The Globe.* Abby said it happened a lot. Enough that it made her wonder if her boss was on the take. I have no clue what she meant by that. The stories Abby writes are newsy but not front-page news, according to her, even though I tend to disagree. I enjoy reading whatever she writes."

"Same here," Sophie said.

"I am very proud of my goddaughter, no matter what she writes. She's a very skilled writer, too," Mavis added. "I bet she could write a novel if she set her mind to it. It would probably be a best seller, too. Nothing like that tacky Jackie Collins stuff, either. I have never liked her books."

"Then why do you read them?" Ida questioned.

"Supposedly her characters are loosely based on real people. I always try and figure out who the 'real' people are. Not that I know them, but it's interesting. I don't believe all those wild sex scenes, either. What kind of woman has sex with five different men a night?" Mavis said.

"Tramps," Toots offered.

"Sluts," Sophie said, "or at least those who want to get a jump start in the business. Happens all the time."

"And how do you know this?" Ida demanded fretfully.

"I don't know it for a fact, but it's been happening since the beginning of time. People use sex as a trade-off." Sophie looked at Ida, then at Toots. "Right?"

"If you're insinuating that I've done something similar in the past, you would be wrong. Though there were times when I was rather happy that my poor mate couldn't, well, let's just say rise to the occasion." Toots laughed. "And in that sense I was grateful for the payoff. Which was no sex with a man who'd passed his prime."

"Why do we always end up discussing sex?" Ida asked.

"Because none of us are getting any," Sophie said with a huge grin. "At least none that I know of." She glanced at her three friends seated at the table, wondering if one of them was lucky enough to dispute her statement.

Zip.

"Says something about us, doesn't it?" Toots challenged. "We're not *that* old. We're going to Los Angeles. I think it's time we changed our status. What about the rest of you? Are you game for a change?"

Toots eyed her friends seated around the table as she waited for an answer. Her hands in her lap, she crossed her fingers.

"As long as I can bring Coco, I'm in. I can get Phyllis, my neighbor, to close up my house for the summer. Better yet, she can use it when all of her grandkids come to visit after school gets out. She's always complaining about how cramped she is when they visit. This will work out just perfect!" Mavis clapped her pudgy hands together, smiling from ear to ear.

"Ida?" Toots asked. "What about it?"

"I don't know. There's this condition . . ."—Ida looked down at her hands covered in latex—". . . ah . . . problem. I know you all think it's irrational, but I can't seem to help myself. I wouldn't be an asset to the paper or to the three of you, so I should probably head on home when you all leave."

Sophie chimed in. "So that's a no? You won't even give this a try? You want to spend the rest of your years wearing latex, struggling to breathe behind a mask, and smelling like bleach?"

Good old Sophie, always going straight to the heart of the matter. Toots smiled. This is what Ida needed, a good dose of reality, and there was no one better than Sophie to serve it up with a large dollop of her smart-ass humor.

Ida turned to face Toots, tears pooling in her eyes. "What should I do, Teresa? I don't want to be like this. I've tried to fight it, but it's a losing battle. And before you ask, I've been to three different shrinks." She held out her gloved hands.

The three old friends had convinced Ida to get rid of the surgeon's mask when

Sophie threatened to shoot out her kneecaps. Toots figured it was more or less a start of sorts on Ida's rehabilitation. After a little too much scotch, Ida confessed her obsession with germs started when Thomas, her last husband, died from the E. coli he'd consumed by eating tainted meat. The friends' ready solution was unanimous: *Stop eating meat*.

"I can't make the decision for any of you. Either you want to come along or not. I can't say it doesn't matter one way or the other because it does matter. I would like nothing more than to have Abby's godmothers, my oldest and dearest friends, accompany me on this adventure. And I guarantee it will be an adventure, but if you can't or won't, I understand," Toots said coolly. She'd be damned if she'd reduce herself to begging.

"What the hell! If Walter dies, I'll rush back to New York, fry his ass, and collect my money. Count me in," Sophie said, a little too gleefully.

Toots grinned. She could always count on Sophie.

"I'm in." Mavis giggled, evidence of too much scotch.

Toots suddenly remembered her promise to take Mavis to Liz's Stout Shop for a new wardrobe. Maybe she could coax Bernice into doing it.

"Oh, phooey, if you girls can put up with my disorder, I suppose I could give California a try," Ida offered hesitantly.

Toots thought her old friend looked like a deer caught in the headlights. She clapped her hands in approval. "Then it's settled. We'll spend tomorrow making whatever arrangements we need to make to put our current lives on hold, then it's off to California. Deal?" She caught the eye of each woman and held out her hand, palm up. This was the secret handshake they'd had since high school.

Mavis placed her hand palm-down on top of Toots's. Sophie laid her hand on top of theirs, then Ida, latex glove and all, placed hers gingerly on top of the others.

On the count of three, the women fanned their arms up in the air, then in unison shouted, "Deal!" Toots and Sophie each fired up a cigarette. Mavis reached for an apple from the bowl on the table, and Ida took a sip of scotch, sealing the deal.

Toots announced in a grave, solemn voice that they were about to become secret *Informers.* All she needed now was confirmation from Christopher that her offer to purchase *The Informer* had been accepted, at which point they would be bona fide *Informers.* She couldn't wait to tell Abby her godmothers were coming to visit.

"Now that we've all agreed on temporarily relocating to Los Angeles, one of us needs to come up with a feasible excuse as to why we're there. I've got the first week covered. I'm going to tell Abby I convinced you all to come for a visit since she wasn't able to come east to see all of you. The second week I think we all could use a spa vacation. I'll invite Abby along though I know she won't go. This is as far as I've planned. And I'm not one hundred percent sure any of this will fly. Abby's a smart girl. She'll know soon enough we're up to something," Toots said.

"Why don't you just tell her the truth?" Sophie suggested.

"I should, but I can't. At least not yet. Heck, I'm not even sure that derelict she calls her boss accepted my offer. I thought for sure I'd hear something by now." Toots was a bit worried that she was jumping the gun, but if push came to shove, they'd all have a nice visit with Abby, a trip to a fancy spa, and they'd call it a day. She could always fall back and regroup until she figured out some other way to help advance Abby's career.

The phone rang, focusing their attention on Bernice, who answered on the second ring, then passed the phone to Toots. "It's for you."

"Hello? Yes? *Really?* Why, of course I will. That much? Well, I did say double the offer. Fine. And, Christopher, remember, Abby is not to get wind of this. I'll see you day after tomorrow." Toots hung up the phone, then waved her fist high in the air.

"Bernice, listen up! I am now the official owner/publisher of *The Informer*! Well, I will be as soon as we get to California to sign the papers and turn over the money. What do you think of that?" she asked dramatically.

Muttering and mumbling under her breath about crazy people not knowing what they were doing, Bernice returned the phone to its stand. "Lord help us all."

"And we're your new second-string cub reporters, right?" Sophie added.

"Not yet, but be careful of what you say. I have a sneaky feeling all of us are about to launch a new career," Toots observed. She couldn't help but visualize Leland gyrating six feet under at the price she'd just agreed to pay for a tabloid rag. Ten million bucks. Double what it was worth. Toots wasn't one to give up easily. She'd make that damn paper profitable, come hell or high water. Caution warned her to keep the financial end of things to herself. She'd pay the girls a whopping salary for whatever she needed them for. Whatever came after, she'd play by ear. She'd always been pretty good at doing things on the fly.

Who would've thought Toots, *Teresa Amelia Loudenberry,* would be the proud owner of an honest-to-God, at least sometimes, newspaper? She could see the headlines now: RICH WIDOW RAISES A RAG!

"I can take care of the grammatical stuff. What's proper and what isn't," Mavis offered. "I *am* a retired English teacher."

"Of course you can. I never thought of that, but I assume there has to be someone who checks that sort of thing," Toots said. "Remember, though, this is all on the QT, at least for now."

"What about a fact-checker?" Sophie asked. "I could do that when the time is right."

"Sophie, don't be such an idiot. Tabloids don't check facts. They make things up and print them. Pure and simple. Isn't this right, Teresa?" Ida stated matter-of-factly.

"I think there's a little more to it than that, but in a nutshell I'd say you pretty much have the gist of it. I do believe little granules of the truth are simply embellished to make it more exciting and stir up the public's interest. At least that's what Abby said when I asked her where she comes up with all of her stories," Toots said.

"You know, I did work for a photographer when I first moved to New York," Ida said, looking at the others. "I'm sure you'll need pictures to go with your stories."

"Ida, times have changed since you were snapping that Kodak Brownie or whatever it was back in the day. Have you ever heard of digital photography? Photoshop? How else do you think the tabloids get pictures of humans mating with aliens? They fix the photos. Can you do that?" Sophie asked her.

"I can learn. I'm not stupid, Sophie." Ida grimaced.

"I didn't say you were. You want to take pictures, you're going to have to get your hands dirty. You can't wander around Los Angeles with latex gloves on and expect all the Hollywood starlets to pose for you. They'll look at you like you're the nut that needs to be photographed."

"Sophie has a point," Toots said as she looked pointedly at Ida's gloves.

"You're both right. Until I get this disorder under control, I can't run around in a dirty city filled with God knows what kind of germs and expect to act as your photographer. I'll work in the office. That is, if you want me to."

"Look, let's get this cleared up now before it goes one step further. We're all going to be in this together. We'll pitch in where and when needed, but something you all need to know up front, no matter what the circumstances are, Abby must never associate us with *The Informer.* We'll all be working behind the scenes, so to speak. I don't have all the details figured out just now, but I will. I promise.

"We have a lot to get done between now and tomorrow. Mavis, you need a new wardrobe. I've arranged for Liz, a friend of mine who happens to own a clothing store in Charleston, to open the doors for you later this evening after they're closed for the night."

"Toots! You don't have to do this. As long as I have a washer and dryer handy, I'm good to go. Really, all I need is water and a place to let my clothes drip dry. Besides, I doubt your friend carries my size," Mavis said, her words garbled in embarrassment.

"Stop being so negative. Washers and dryers aren't like cell phones. Hotels don't have them for guests. Liz's is a shop exclusively for large-size women. Liz has everything you'll need right down to your undies. And since you're starting over in a sense, with your new diet and all, don't you dare buy any of those old granny panties. I want to see something sleek, sexy, and in color. Black and red. You're a beautiful woman, Mavis, and it's high time you acknowledged the fact." Toots knew for a fact that when you look better, you feel better. The minute she'd shed her mourning clothes, she felt like a breath of fresh air had washed over her. She knew that once Mavis got used to the idea of caring for herself, both inside and out, she wouldn't need any additional encouragement. Her own would be enough.

Toots turned to Ida without giving Mavis a chance to respond. "We can live with the latex gloves for a while. We can say you have some weird skin disorder like psoriasis or eczema. You have to promise me you'll take the help I'm offering. Dr. Pauley will be here around midnight to give Mavis a checkup." Toots watched Mavis to make sure she was okay with this. She nodded, and Toots gave her a thumbs-up.

"He knows a doctor in Los Angeles who specializes in OCD. He'll contact him first thing tomorrow and schedule an appointment. Are you okay with this, Ida?" Toots asked.

Ida nodded. "Yes, it's about time I got over this. I won't make any promises. All I can do is try."

"That's all I'm asking," Toots replied.

"And what about me?" Sophie asked.

Toots shook her head. "You, my friend, are as full of shit as a Sunday outhouse. You need to gain back some of the weight you've lost. You also need to prepare yourself for Walter's funeral. I've plenty of experience in that department, so when the time comes, I'll make sure you're ready to act as though you're in mourning. I did donate all of my mourning attire to charity, so you'll have to buy black clothes for your own mourning debut. It's not as easy as it sounds."

"Black? Mourning clothes? Surely you jest. The second they throw the last shovel of dirt in Walter's grave, I'm celebrating. Mourning is not for me. I don't give a good rat's ass what society expects. I will be celebrating the old coot's demise. I'll be five million dollars richer, too."

"Well said, my friend." Toots clapped her hands. "We've got our work cut out for us. Quoting my dear friend Bernice, I say let's get our wrinkled old asses in gear and get this show on the road. There's lots to do between now and midnight."

The four women looked at one another. They knew their lives were about to change. Majorly.

Chapter 8

Money talks.

On the spur of the moment, Toots hired a private jet for their trip to California since she knew it would be impossible to get reservations on such short notice. Flying alone would give them a chance to make sure they had their stories straight. The clincher, though, was that the pilot promised they could smoke on the five-hour flight.

Toots held up her hand, reminding the others that Abby was no fool. "One slipup, and we're toast. She'll never forgive any of us, so keep that in mind, ladies."

A small part of Toots's being felt disloyal for going behind her daughter's back to purchase *The Informer.* Another part of her, the motherly part, felt it was her God-given duty to do what she could to assure her daughter's happiness and well-being. Spending ten million dollars on a failing tabloid was beyond extreme, but sometimes the only things that worked were extreme measures. Toots might be old, but she wasn't an *old fool.* With the help of her friends, she was certain she could make this work for her and Abby, and at the same time give her friends a new lease on life. It was just the details she needed to figure out—all ten million of them.

Sophie stood and stretched. "I don't know about the rest of you, but I'm going to call it a night. All this talk of working and sex has worn me out. I'm going to dream about Brad Pitt."

"He's happily married to Angelina something and has six kids. You ought to be ashamed of yourself," Ida said.

"Nah, it'll just make the dream more exciting." Sophie gave Toots a hug, leaned down to kiss Mavis on the cheek, and then, before Ida could stop her, she gave

Ida a wet kiss squarely on the lips. "Think about those germs in your dreams. Night, girls."

Ida yanked a packet of antibacterial Wet Ones from her pants pocket and proceeded to wipe her lips with such force Toots was sure she'd peeled a layer of skin from her mouth.

"I have to go to the bathroom." Ida raced out of the room so fast Toots thought for sure she'd been beamed up to the *Enterprise* by Scotty.

"She is a quick one," Mavis said. "I'm glad I'm not her. I'll take fat over germs any day. I need to shower before my exam. I am slightly intoxicated, in case you haven't noticed." Mavis struggled to get out of her chair. Once she was able to stand, she moved unsteadily toward the hallway that led to her room.

"I noticed, Mavis," Toots called out. "Are you sure you don't need any help?"

"I'll be fine once I take a cold shower. I haven't had an alcoholic beverage in years. I have to admit, Toots, I liked it."

"Yeah, me, too. Call if you need me. I'm going to put on a pot of coffee before Joe gets here." The last thing she needed was

Joe thinking she and her childhood friends were a bunch of lushes.

With the girls respectively sleeping, disinfecting, and showering, Toots made a fresh pot of coffee, drank two cups, and smoked three cigarettes. She found a bottle of air freshener beneath the sink and sprayed the kitchen and dining room before lighting a scented Yankee candle. Like she was going to fool Joe.

Now all she had to do was wait for him.

A light tapping on the back door jarred Toots into action. Dr. Pauley. Dr. Joseph Pauley. *Joe to* her. She hurried to the door. The night air held a slight chill, which was unusual for this time of year. Toots hoped they weren't in for a cold summer, then remembered if all went according to plan, she would be in sunny California for the summer and into the fall.

"Toots, I wouldn't do this for any of my other patients, I hope you know that."

Toots stood aside as her old friend made his way through the kitchen. "Bullshit. I know of at least a dozen people that you make house calls to, so don't try and feed me a line of garbage."

Dr. Pauley had been Toots's physician

since her move to Charleston more than twenty years ago. He was at least seventy-five but could pass for sixty. A full head of snow-white hair, sharp blue eyes that didn't miss a beat, at least six feet tall without an ounce of fat on him. Toots thought him handsome and debonair. She'd had her eye on him when they first met. Once they became friends, and Toots knew there was no hope of anything more than friendship, she'd treated him like the older brother she'd never had. She liked to think of Joe as "good people."

"I can at least try, can't I?" He grinned. Placing his brown leather bag on the kitchen counter, he glanced around. "So where is my new patient?"

"She'll be down in a minute. Her name is Mavis. We've been friends since high school. Anything she needs, just do it. She only has Medicare and lives off a small pension. Make sure you send me the bills. I don't want her worrying about the cost of this house call, any lab work that is needed, or meds."

"I can do that. Now, just so you know, there isn't much I can do without taking her down to the office. I'll draw her blood for a

complete blood count, check her choles-
terol. I'll run a lipids test, check her blood
pressure and heart rate. That's about all I
can do. If I think she's a health risk, I won't
lie to you. I'm not just some old quack, you
know."

"I know a lot of things, Joe. Quack you
are not. How long will it take you to run the
lab work? I want her to start exercising as
soon as possible."

"I'll have it first thing in the morning.
But she has to have a stress test before
she can exercise. I'll set it up for tomorrow morning. I'll call you if there's anything that means she can't have the test
right then. A regular test won't work for
her; she'll have to have what's called a
chemical stress test. It's for people who
can't walk very far, and I assume that's
the case."

Mavis entered the kitchen, smelling like
White Diamonds. "Are you talking about
me?" she asked.

"Yes, we are. Mavis, this is Joe. He's
my friend and doctor. Are you sure you're
okay with this? If you feel pressured or
uncomfortable, now is the time to speak
up." Toots raised her eyebrows.

"I need this, Toots; it couldn't have happened at a better time. If I get any fatter, I'll die, and who's going to look after Coco?" Mavis held her hand out to greet the doctor. "Nice to meet you, Joe."

They shook hands. "Likewise. Now, young lady." He searched her face, saw the twinkle in her eyes. "I hope you're not afraid of needles."

Half an hour later, after Mavis had been poked and prodded, Dr. Joe Pauley left, promising to call as soon as he had Mavis's test results and the time for the stress test.

"Now it's time to go shopping," Toots said, grabbing her purse from the counter. "I do love to shop." Bernice had put her foot down and said she wouldn't be caught dead in a fat-ladies' store, and she could just take her friend herself, to which Toots had replied, "Up yours, Bernice."

"You don't have to do this, Toots. When I lose all this blubber"—Mavis grabbed a large hunk of flab around her waist— "I'll just need more new clothes anyway."

"Then we'll go shopping again. Besides, once we're in LA, you won't have time to wash and dry those three outfits every day. We'll be too busy. Liz loves dogs, so get Coco's leash. I just love to shop, did I mention that?" Toots exclaimed excitedly.

"I'm glad you do, because I hate it," Mavis remarked. "When you're as big as I am, it's downright embarrassing."

"Oh, stop it! Get Coco, and let's get out of here. We've tons to do before morning."

The ride to Liz's was made in silence, both women lost in their own thoughts. Fifteen minutes later, Toots tucked the Town Car into a narrow alley behind a cluster of small shops, the spot reserved for special customers. "This is it. Come on, I can't wait to get started."

Toots hurried around to the passenger door to assist Mavis. "Remember, this is only the beginning. A year from now, you'll love shopping as much as I do."

"I doubt that, but I'm open for new experiences, especially when my three best friends and goddaughter are involved. Lord knows I need some excitement in my life. Liz must be a special friend to open her shop this late at night just for us."

Coco squeaked from her carrier in the backseat.

"Liz is a very special lady. I'll get Coco," Toots said.

Toots removed the little Chihuahua from the carrier, snapped her leash to her jeweled collar, placed her on the ground, then took Mavis's hand. "Let the fun begin!"

Mavis laughed loud and hearty. "I have never been shopping this late. I still can't believe your friend opened up just for me."

"That's what friends do. You'd best get used to it. The life you've lived in Maine is a thing of the past."

Mavis stopped. "I don't want my life to change that way, Toots. I love Maine. It's been my home since Herbert died. I couldn't imagine living anywhere else."

Toots stopped in her tracks. Was this their first glitch? "Then why did you agree to go to California?"

"It's not like I'm going to be there forever, right?"

"True, but I'm not sure how long we're going to be there. Like I said, Mavis, think bicoastal. You have to be okay with this from the get-go."

"I am, I am. Change is a bit frightening, that's all. Like I said, I've lived in Maine since Herbert died, and that's been, what, fifteen years? Time passes quickly the older you get."

"And we're wasting our time talking about it. Come on, let's see what Liz has in the way of sexy lingerie."

Mavis shook her head. Coco scampered alongside her as they entered the dimly lit dress shop.

Chapter 9

Liz's shop was designed with privacy in mind. There were no price tags on the clothes, no sale tables offering unheard-of discounts, no coupons to receive 50 percent off. Everywhere she looked, Mavis could tell Liz's customers knew they were in an upscale clothier for overweight women. There were no tiny mannequins wearing clothes that would fit a three-year-old, no racks with sizes 0–2, no pictures with Barbie-size models wearing designer labels. Mavis thought the store resembled some of the celebrity closets she'd seen on the Style Network, only Liz's was ten times larger.

A small woman barely five feet tall, who didn't weigh more than a hundred pounds, greeted them. "You must be Mavis. I'm Liz." The little lady wore a slim black pencil skirt with a crisp white blouse tucked in neatly and a black-and-white-checkered jacket. Her tiny feet were encased in red leather boots that added at least three inches in height.

Mavis glanced at Toots questioningly.

Toots laughed. "I know what you're thinking."

Mavis remembered her manners. "It's very kind of you to do this for me. I just hate that it's so late. I hope I'm not keeping you from your family," Mavis said in one long breath.

"It's my pleasure, and no, you're not keeping me from anything. When Toots told me you were a friend of hers in need of a clothing makeover, I jumped at the chance," Liz said. Her voice was light, almost musical, and easy on the ear.

"Liz likes to dress people. She used to work as a dress designer for some of

Hollywood's hottest stars. A few years ago," Toots added. It had been more than a few years but, at their age, Toots figured twenty was "a few."

"Oh, you did! Whom, if you don't mind my asking, did you dress?" Mavis loved anything connected to Hollywood. Almost as much as Toots loved her tabloids.

"Doris Day was one of my favorites. She let me have free rein when it came to her personal wardrobe. She was a dream to work for."

"I am impressed. Whatever you think I can fit into, I'll try. I'm so fat, I'm ashamed of how I've let myself go."

Toots left Mavis's makeover in Liz's very capable hands. She took a seat on a blue velvet bench outside the dressing room door while the two women bustled in and out of the dressing room.

Three hours later, with a trunkful of bags and boxes, Toots and Mavis returned to the house, exhilarated from shopping. They carried their purchases inside, dropping them in the entryway.

Her voice ringing with tired excitement, Mavis said, "I've never had so many clothes in my life." She plopped down on a comfortable chair, with Coco resting on her ample lap. "I don't even want to know how much this cost. I'd probably die of a heart attack."

"I figured that's why you hurried to the car once Liz started tallying up the clothes. Trust me, it will be worth every penny when you see how much better you look and feel. Once you start dropping the weight, we'll do this all over again."

Thrilled to see the effect their midnight excursion had on Mavis, Toots made a silent promise to herself to do this with all the girls, no matter if they could afford it or not. Seeing the huge grin on Mavis's face as she tried on dozens of outfits was worth every penny Toots had spent that night, and more.

"I don't know about that. I'm pretty handy with a needle and thread. I'll just take in whatever I need to as I lose weight."

"Bullshit! Stop that right now. You'll do no such thing. I'm rich, Mavis. Hell, I'm dis-gustingly rich. I won't live long enough to spend the interest I earn, so forget about 'taking in' your clothes. You're just going to have to get used to the finer things in life. If you don't like it—"

"Then I can kiss your wrinkled old ass?" Mavis shot back with a smile.

"Exactly!"

"That wouldn't be my first choice of things to do, so—for now—you can refer to me as your 'poor relation,' and I'll accept your kindness."

"Good, because the visual I have of you kissing my ass isn't pretty."

Both women boomed with laughter at the mental image.

"It's late, Mavis. Why don't you go on to bed? You have a stress test this morning, and I've got a few loose ends to tie up, then I'm going to call it a night myself."

"I don't know when I've enjoyed myself as much as today, Toots. Thank you for making me want to live again. I feel like Cinderella at the ball minus the handsome prince." Mavis wobbled over to give Toots a hug.

"The prince was way overrated as far as I'm concerned." Toots smiled, surprised at how good she felt.

"He was, wasn't he? Well, I—for one— am beat. Shopping is much more physical than I thought. Night, Toots."

"Night, Mavis."

During the next hour, Toots made three phone calls and ate a huge bowl of Froot Loops with a cup of sugar and half a cup of milk. The first call was to the Beverly Hills Hotel. They would need a place to stay while she decided exactly how she was going to operate her new third-rate rag. She reserved four of the hotel's famous bungalows, specifically requesting one of the bungalows where Elizabeth Taylor had honeymooned with six of her eight husbands. They would all have their privacy in the lap of luxury. When the time was right, she would purchase a house. If things worked according to plan.

Maybe she'd buy Aaron Spelling's old digs. When the time came, she'd check the listings on Mansions for Sale online. She loved pretend house hunting there, often imagining how she'd redecorate something she "bought" online.

Oh, she was going to sleep so well tonight.

Chapter 10

Abby Simpson was as beautiful as the stars she wrote about, maybe even more so if she believed her coworkers' gossip when they thought she wasn't listening. She hated the lunchtime scuttlebutt and thought the comparison preposterous. If anything, Abby took extra measures to downplay her good looks because of their gossip. She'd learned very fast that beauty and smarts weren't the best mix in her chosen profession. At least not in LA. Inheriting her father's naturally curly blond hair and clear blue eyes was almost a curse. Factor in a petite frame with curves in all the right places, and she was often mistaken for one of the starlets she wrote about when she hit LA's hot spots searching for her next story.

A starlet she was *not.* Just the thought gave her a stomachache. And Toots would have been horrified at the comparison.

Abby had been offered a few small acting jobs when she'd first moved to LA but declined them all. All she wanted to do was cover the stories that made for such scandalous entertainment, not *star* in one. She hesitated calling it "news" because it wasn't news in the true sense of the word. She wrote to entertain, but the core of all of her stories contained the truth. She simply made her articles more exciting to read. No one wanted to read about the perfect lives of the admired and cherished. That would get too old too fast. However, when the admired and cherished went to rehab, gained weight, divorced, or engaged in behavior that showed their humanity, the public loved reading that their idols also experienced life's tragedies—as everyone else did. She just spiced up her stories a bit.

Now with *The Informer* up for sale, Abby

wasn't sure how long she would even have a job. Had her financial situation been more secure, she would have considered making an offer on the paper, but it was too much of a strain on her already tight budget. She'd invested most of her available cash in purchasing her first home, a 1950s ranch-style house located in Brentwood, an exclusive area west of Los Angeles.

Her mother would have given her the money in a heartbeat if she'd asked, but that wasn't her way. And there was no way she was going to touch her trust fund. As soon as she'd been legally able to work, at sixteen, she found a part-time job taking in classified ads over the phone for a small family-owned paper, *The Daily Gazette,* in Charleston, working there until she finished high school. She worked as an editorial assistant at a small publishing house while attending the University of South Carolina, where she majored in journalism, and at twenty-eight she hadn't slowed down and had no intention of doing so until she achieved her dream: owning the biggest and best tabloid possible, one with worldwide distribution.

To some, her goal might have seemed foolish because tabloids were *tabloids.* Abby reasoned that, like anything else, they had their purpose. She smiled when she thought of her mother's secret addiction to them. Since elementary school, Abby had also had an affinity for them, hence her present employment. So what if they weren't *The New York Times* or *The Wall Street Journal*? Abby was unashamed of her profession. If anyone gave her grief about it, she dished it right back at full throttle.

Like her mother, Abby rarely slept. When the phone rang around one A.M. LA time, she answered on the first ring. "Abby Simpson."

"Are you awake?" her mother asked.

"Of course I'm awake. I wouldn't be answering the phone if I weren't, now, would I? You know full well that I never sleep." Abby was a noted insomniac. Some of her best work had been achieved during the wee hours of the morning.

"No, you don't. Your father never slept much, either. At least when he was in bed with me." Toots giggled.

"Again, more than I need or want to

know." Abby laughed. Her mother was quite the character, but she wouldn't have her any other way. "Is everything all right? You don't usually call this late."

"It *is* almost four in the morning here. But it is earlier in LA, unless I have it backwards—again. Tell me I'm not getting senile."

"You, senile? Never!" Abby said.

"Thank you for the vote of confidence. I called because I have a surprise for you."

Oh no, Abby thought. "Okaaayyy."

"You don't sound very happy. Do you have company? Is there something you're not telling me?" Toots asked.

"I'm fine, and no to both questions. I wish I had company," Abby added wistfully. "Chester is great company, but he doesn't always understand what I say." Poor Chester. She'd spent many a night with him lying beside her, ears perked, head tilted in question, tail wagging patiently as though he were really trying to interpret his mistress's words. Most of the time, she liked her life as it was and didn't want it any other way. She enjoyed her freedom and didn't have time for a serious relationship. Well, there *was* one man she'd been attracted to forever and a day, but she didn't pursue him because she knew he wasn't interested in her in the way she wanted him to be. Her dear older *former* stepbrother, Christopher Clay, her protector and biggest ally in Los Angeles. And he just happened to be one of her best friends.

She'd had her eye on him since the first time she met him, and he'd been lingering in her thoughts as a potential lover ever since. She smiled. Lord, he was a hunk of hot maleness!

"Abby, are you listening to me?" her mother queried.

"Uh, yes, sorry I got distracted. Now, you were saying you had a surprise for me. I'm all ears."

"You know your godmothers are here. They're sleeping, as far as I know, but I wanted to be the first one to tell you. Sophie can't keep anything to herself, you know that," Toots said affectionately.

"Mom!" Abby loved her mother, but her flair for the dramatic got old at times. "Tell me, or I'm going to start singing. And you know I can't sing."

"I do, so let me save both our ears.

Here's the surprise: I've convinced the girls to fly out to LA for a visit. We're leaving later today if all goes according to plan. I even hired a private jet."

"Mom, that's fantastic news! I haven't seen my godmothers in forever. I won't ask how you managed to talk them into this. What about Ida? I thought she had some disease or something? Sophie sent me an e-mail saying she wore gloves all the time."

Abby heard her mother's deep sigh across the wires.

"Yes, and it's not pretty, either. I feel terrible for her. Joe has arranged for her to see a doctor in LA who specializes in obsessive compulsive disorder, OCD, they prefer to call it."

"I'm familiar with it. Seems to be on all the talk shows. I think Oprah did a piece on the subject a while back. Knowing what I know, I don't see how you managed this, but I know you and your powers of persuasion. I'll borrow a rollaway bed for Mavis. You and Sophie can sleep in my room, and we'll put Ida on the sofa. It's not much, but it's all I have to offer at the moment. Renovating's finished, but I haven't started to decorate the spare bedrooms yet." Abby had inherited her mother's love of decorating. When she'd purchased her fifties house, she'd sunk what cash she had left into remodeling, doing most of the repair work herself. She'd pulled out the old carpets and, much to her delight, had discovered solid cherry flooring. When she wasn't out chasing a story, she'd sanded the floors by hand. It'd taken a couple of months, but her hard work had paid off. The flooring throughout her house was as smooth and shiny as glass. She'd saved the original windows and the French doors that led to an enclosed courtyard, another area she'd admired when she purchased the place. Though it was overrun with elderberry vines, honeysuckle, and morning glory, Abby refrained from cutting them back because their fragrance was so intoxicating. Maybe if she were forced to look for another position, she would use her spare time to work on restoring her garden to its original splendor.

"Thanks, Abby, but I've already made arrangements for us to stay at the Beverly Hills Hotel. I rented four of the bungalows. I'm staying where Elizabeth Taylor honeymooned with several of her husbands. I can't wait. It'll be like old times, the four of us living side by side."

Hearing the excitement in her mother's voice, Abby grinned. She had heard many stories about the years her mother and godmothers had lived within walking distance of one another as teenagers. Some of the stories were so outrageous, it was hard to imagine her four greatest role models actually acting as they had.

"Perfect. Call me as soon as you're sure of your arrival time, and I'll arrange for a car to take you to your hotel." Abby drove a bright yellow MINI Cooper. With Chester always riding in the front, and the backseat packed with her gear, there was no room for passengers.

"Thanks, Abby. That was my next phone call."

"Then you'd better hit the sack and try to get some sleep if you're leaving soon. When I see you, I want you bright-eyed and bushy-tailed."

"On that note, I'll say good night. I'll see you in a few hours. Love you, dear."

"Same here," Abby said, then replaced the phone in its stand. With only a few hours before their arrival, Abby went on a cleaning binge, something she'd been wanting to do since last weekend but hadn't had time.

In her bedroom, she stripped the pink floral sheets off the bed, tossing them in a laundry basket for later. Since her washing machine and dryer were located in the attached garage, doing laundry would be last on her list because she had to go outside. She looked down at the Wonder Woman nightshirt she wore.

Abby dusted her bedroom furniture with lemon Pledge, ran a Swiffer across the wood floors throughout the house, then followed that with a quick damp mop. Times like this, she was glad she'd finished the floors with polyurethane rather than a "real" traditional finish. She scrubbed the bathtub and the tile in the shower, cleaned the sink, and returned her makeup to the drawer where it belonged.

In the kitchen, she scoured the counters with a nonscratch cleanser. They were the original Formica counters with metal edging and a light blue-and-gray swirly pattern typical of their era. Abby thought they were the ugliest part of the kitchen. She wanted to replace them with granite, but that wasn't in her budget either. Soon, she told herself. She wasn't lazy, and she was patient. In time, not only would she have her little home in tip-top shape, she'd also own and operate her own tabloid. Sometimes dreams came true.

She wasn't sure on the details, but she knew it would happen because when she wanted something, no matter how hard it might be to obtain, she set her mind solely on her goal and always achieved what she set out to accomplish. At least in her dreams.

A quitter Abby Simpson was not. Like her parents, she believed in hard work and self-discipline. With those inherited traits, Abby knew she was destined for success. Her dreams were all the proof she needed that it could and would happen.

Two hours later, after she'd polished the large picture window in her living room, she sat down on her sumptuous red sofa and fell into a deep sleep.

Upstairs in Toots's guest room, Ida concluded that taking that first step to control her obsessiveness was the hardest task she had ever attempted in her entire sixty-four years. Removing the bacteria-filtering mask had left her shaken and uneasy, her normal routine completely disrupted by making this trip. It had taken all the willpower she could muster to hire a limo to drive her to the airport. Knowing there had been hundreds of other passengers in the vehicle before her had almost sent her racing back to the safety and hygiene of her penthouse apartment on Park Avenue. The flight had been equally horrendous, with its airborne germs recirculating throughout the plane. She'd persevered because she wanted to see her friends, and she knew that she needed help. Badly. However, at this precise moment, her hands shook, and her stomach was in knots, her palms damp with perspiration, her throat tight and dry. Knowing that the symptoms were the precursor to a full-blown panic attack, Ida removed a small brown paper bag from the zippered compartment inside one of her bags. Sitting on the edge of the bed, she scrunched up the end of the bag, leaving a small hole where she then placed her mouth and inhaled and exhaled slowly. This procedure usually kept her from hyperventilating, even if it was not a surefire method.

Ida inhaled and exhaled into the paper bag for the next ten minutes. While doing so, she took in the room Toots had prepared for her, hoping it would distract her from having a major attack. An antique four-poster walnut bed with a matching armoire and vanity took up one half of the room. Two comfortable-looking chairs were placed strategically in front of a fireplace. Rose- and cream-colored walls gave off a warm and cozy glow. Green plants were placed throughout the room, bringing a feeling of the outdoors inside. Toots was well known for her good taste. Ida was sure the room had not been touched by a professional decorator.

When she felt as though she could stand on her own two feet without passing out, she tossed the brown paper bag aside, praying she wouldn't need to use it again. At least not that night.

To distract herself from further negative thoughts, she took the germ-zapping light Toots had purchased for her and began her odd—yet comforting—routine. Inch by inch she scanned the guest room. First the doorknobs. After each scan, she removed a Clorox wipe from its container and thoroughly wiped any area that showed the slightest amount of germs. She would then scan each area a second time, making sure she'd removed as many of the deadly microbes as humanly possible.

She scanned the night table, the lamp, the alarm clock. Anything that required touching, she scanned. Seeing that these items were virtually germ-free, she then scanned the crisp white sheets. Upon her arrival, Bernice had explained that she had washed the sheets in hot water and plenty of bleach. Ida was grateful for this because sleeping on the same sheets two nights in a row was nearly impossible for her. Toots had certainly catered to her strange ways, and, sadly, Ida knew she was asking her friends to also act as enablers, but at that point she couldn't help herself. Removing the mask and breathing unfiltered air was a giant step and a testament to her determination to conquer her phobia.

When she was satisfied that her room was as germ-free as possible, she repeated the same process in the guest bathroom. She wiped the knobs on the sink, the handle on the toilet, and the inside doorknob.

She removed antibacterial soap, small and medium garbage bags, and a nailbrush from the drawer where Bernice had placed them. Next she carefully removed her latex gloves. While telling herself she was avoiding contamination when she wore them, she couldn't deny that she also wore them to hide her hands. Constant hand washing with harsh antibacterial soaps had left her once soft and delicate hands red and chapped. She carefully removed the gloves, dropping them into a small plastic bag. She placed the plastic bag inside another bag, this one being a medium-size and antibacterial, or so the company claimed, garbage bag. Taking a wipe from the container, she used it as protection as she turned water on. Allowing it to get as hot as possible, with her free hand she opened a fresh bar of soap. She could never use the same bar of soap more than once because it, too, would be covered with germs from her last washing.

Taking a deep breath, Ida held both hands beneath the warm water. Lathering up, careful of her tender hands, she used a new soft buff pad to scrub imaginary germs from her hands ten times. Thomas died on the tenth of October. From that day forward, ten had become her magic number.

Next she massaged an antibiotic pain-relieving cream into her hands. After Ida completed this part of her routine, she replaced her latex gloves with a fresh pair. From there she stripped down, placed her clothing in another bag before turning on the shower. With a new loofa and another fresh bar of disinfecting soap, she scrubbed her body until it was pink. Ten times. Always ten times. Then her hair. She used Prell, a harsh detergent shampoo, to wash her hair. Again she repeated the process ten times.

When she finished, she used the white bath towels Bernice again swore had been washed in bleach and hot water. She rubbed her skin until she couldn't stand it a minute longer. This bizarre routine provided her a few hours of mental relief, only to be repeated in the morning and as many times as her daily schedule would allow.

Fearing she would stay awake worrying about the upcoming trip, Ida took a sleeping pill before carefully sliding into bed. Her last conscious thought before drifting off to sleep was that she was one goddamn sick puppy to go through what she had just gone through.

Some nights she prayed she wouldn't wake up.

Chapter 11

In the room across the hall, Sophie was engrossed in reading the pile of tabloids Toots had left by her bed. After perusing most of them, she was hit by a sudden pang of guilt. "Damn that man!" she said to no one.

Near death, Walter still held her in his grip. A choking *death* grip.

Tossing the tabloids aside, Sophie had to practically jump off the bed, it was so high. Toots and her decorating. Sophie had to admit the room was inviting in every sense of the word. An oak bedroom set with a headboard that reached nearly halfway up the celery-colored walls was beyond comfortable, the mattress plush, and sheets at least a thousand-thread count. A box of chocolates lay on the night table. A minifridge held bottled water, small frosted bottles of Coke and Dr Pepper. A basket in the bathroom contained every toiletry known to woman. Shampoo, toothpaste, mouthwash, and gardenia-scented body lotion. Sophie felt as though she were at a luxury resort instead of her best friend's home. Toots had spared no expense to make this visit memorable.

She walked over to the open window that overlooked the backyard, if you could call it a yard. Sweet-smelling bushes, Confederate jasmine, she thought, filled the late-night air with a delicious scent. It reminded her of bubble gum. A cool breeze wafting through the open window sent her racing back to the bed and beneath the covers. She was tired of the chill. Anything cold reminded her of Walter.

At that precise moment in time, Sophie was happier than she'd been in years. Being with Toots always had that effect on her. It was always that way even when they were in their teens. Maybe it was nothing more than feeling safe and secure. Whatever the feeling was, she liked it.

Snuggling beneath the warm covers, Sophie allowed herself to recall the past, something she tried not to do very often. Life with Walter hadn't been without difficulty. Hell on earth was a much better description.

Being on her own in Manhattan had been scarier than she'd ever imagined. She'd just finished nursing school and was sharing an apartment with a former classmate who did nothing but complain. Life in the big city wasn't all it was cracked up to be until she met Walter.

She recalled the first time they met. She had just opened a new checking account at the Bank of Manhattan, where Walter had just been promoted to assistant branch manager. He was charming and handsome, and she'd been completely and pleasantly surprised when he invited her to dinner to celebrate his new promotion.

Their romance had been hot and heavy, virtually consuming her every waking moment. Since he was ten years her senior, she'd been impressed with his knowledge, admired his wit. After a whirl-wind courtship that lasted three months, he proposed, and Sophie accepted with-out a second thought.

For the first four years of marriage, she'd put her career as a nurse on hold. Walter hadn't wanted her to work. When Walter became obsessed with his job at the bank and began to work eighteen-hour days, she couldn't cope with the empti-ness or the boredom. With too much time on her hands, Sophie took a job at a pedi-atrician's office in Brooklyn. She'd loved the doctor she worked with and adored the children she cared for. After three years of surrounding herself with sick kids, Sophie decided she'd waited long enough for a child of her own. Walter wasn't get-ting any younger, and she hadn't wanted to wait, fearing she'd become one of those "older moms" the girls in the office talked about.

For the next two years, she tried every trick in the book and then some to get preg-nant. When each month rolled around with no results, Sophie gave up on having a child of her own. Walter did, too. Disappointed that she was unable to bear a child, Walter began taking his anger and frustration out on her. It started with little things. His steak was overcooked. Her hair looked messy. Their apartment wasn't as clean as he felt it should be.

Walter demanded she give up her job, letting it be known in no uncertain terms that she needed to concentrate on him, their home, and nothing more. As the Bank of Manhattan's newest branch manager, having a wife who worked outside the home was not an asset. Walter referred to her career as nothing more than an embarrassment, going as far as to suggest friends and colleagues looked down on him, insinuating he didn't earn enough money to support her.

For the first time in almost ten years of marriage, Sophie stood up to him. No way would she give up her career. Without it, she had nothing. She thought his reasoning ludicrous and told him so.

Sophie recalled the first time he struck her.

They'd just returned from the bank's annual Christmas party. As was becoming the norm, Walter had drunk too much, flirted too much, and spoken to her as though she were nothing more than his servant. On the taxi ride home, Sophie refused to speak to him. When they arrived at their Manhattan apartment, Walter began ranting and raving, telling her she was no good and he'd made a mistake by marrying her. She was low-class. She didn't fit in with the other bank executives' wives. Tired of fighting, Sophie had told Walter she would file for a divorce as soon as the holidays were over. She'd barely gotten the words out of her mouth when he backhanded her, ripping open her lip. Shocked and humiliated, with the salty taste of her own blood filling her mouth, Sophie had tried to leave the apartment, knowing that when her husband sobered up, he'd apologize. Walter restrained her and, in doing so, broke her arm.

After the third or fourth beating, Sophie gave up on any hopes she'd had of happily-ever-after. At one point, Walter actually convinced her the beatings were her fault. Sadly, she had believed him until Toots made an unannounced visit to New York and found her bruised and battered. Enraged that she would allow her husband to hit her, Toots went directly to Walter's superior. Two weeks later, he had been asked to resign his position as branch manager.

She'd promised Toots then that she would leave Walter. However, deep-rooted Catholic beliefs ingrained in her since she was a little girl prevented her from walking out on a man whom she'd sworn to love, honor, and obey. She spent the rest of her life supporting Walter and his drinking habit.

And now here she was, almost thirty years later, anxiously waiting for the old bastard to die. At sixty-five, her life was finally her own. Just thinking about the possibilities sent butterflies buzzing to her stomach. Sophie fell asleep with a smile as wide as the Grand Canyon on her face.

Chapter 12

As usual, Toots woke up at five A.M. even though it'd been after three when she went to bed. *Old habits die hard*, she thought as she switched on the bedside lamp. With Bernice due to arrive any minute, Toots reached for the well-worn blue chenille robe at the foot of the bed. She'd left the window open, and her room was downright chilly. Summer would bring sultry breezes and blazing heat soon enough. California would be deliciously warm without the mugginess South Carolina was so well known for. Toots couldn't wait to begin her bicoastal lifestyle. Having her three best friends along for the ride was better than good sex and sugar. Seeing Abby almost whenever she wanted was decadent piles of pink puffy icing on a very large cake. She laughed at her thoughts as she entered the enormous bathroom, where she turned on the shower and stepped under its warm spray.

As the water sluiced over her shoulders and down her back, Toots turned her head from left to right to release the tightness in her neck. She'd noticed over the past few months a stiffness to her joints when she first got up in the morning. Arthritis and old age knocking at the door. Screw that, she was only sixty-five! Wasn't that the new fifty? Sort of? Sort of? Pushing aside further negative thoughts, Toots finished her shower in record time. Wrapping herself in a giant bath sheet, she rummaged through her ample closet and found her favorite ancient pair of jeans, the ones she had purchased right after Abby was born. She dried off quickly, rummaged in her drawer for her lacy undies, then slipped on her jeans. They still fit like a glove. She topped them off with a bright orange blouse. She pulled her thick hair up in her usual top-knot, dabbed a bit of blush on her cheeks and a pale pink bit of shimmer on her lips. Gazing at herself in the mirror, Toots had to admit she looked pretty darn good for an old broad. She'd aged well in spite of her nasty habit of smoking and her sugar addiction. Maybe she'd give one of them up when she got settled in California. Maybe.

"Oh, bull, you're not going to give up your vices any more than Joe's going to retire," she mumbled to herself before her guilty conscience assaulted her. She was asking her best friends to give up bad habits; shouldn't she be practicing what she preached? Yes, said the little devil perched on her shoulder. She should and she would. Soon. Maybe. Not.

Without another thought, Toots hurried downstairs to the kitchen. She readied a pot of coffee for Bernice. While the machine gurgled, Toots stepped outside for her first cigarette of the day. Cool air smacked her squarely in the face. "Damn weather. Figures it would cool off when I'm about to leave." Toots inhaled another puff of nicotine. When she heard the front door open, she crushed her cigarette out in the giant ashtray she'd left on the porch before going to bed.

"Morning, Bernice. You look bright and shiny," Toots said to her housekeeper.

Bernice cleared her throat with such force that Toots expected to see her esophagus fly out of her mouth right through the wall.

"Are you ill?" Toots asked in amazement. "You sound terrible."

"Just my early-morning allergies," Bernice said. She poured two cups of coffee and took them to the table.

Bernice looked to be in one of her cranky-sassy moods that day. If she was right, then Bernice had about five minutes to get over it because the day was young, and she had a to-do list a mile long. Worrying about Bernice wasn't on her list.

"Whatever you say, boss. Will the ladies be wanting their breakfast anytime soon?"

"Fix a plate of fruit and some of those steel-cut oats for Mavis. I expect her to come downstairs any minute since she's always been an early riser. Sophie can share my Froot Loops. I'm not sure about

Ida, maybe a boiled egg?" Toots knew whatever went in Ida's mouth had better be as germ-free as humanly possible. She was just itching to succeed in helping Ida overcome her phobia.

"I'm on it, boss," Bernice said. "Any tea drinkers in the group?"

"Not that I know, but don't worry. I can nuke a cup of water if need be." Toots wasn't worth a grain of salt in the kitchen, but she was more than efficient when it came to the microwave.

"Whatever you say, you're the boss." Toots grimaced as she watched Bernice remove oranges, grapefruit, and strawberries from the refrigerator and place them on a cutting board. "Do you want me to fix you a bowl of Froot Loops, too?"

"Oh, hush, Bernice! You never fix my cereal. I don't know what in the world has gotten into you the past few days." Toots knew Bernice was ticked off because of all the extra work, but it wasn't like she didn't pitch in and help her wherever she could. Bernice was simply getting too old to work so hard. Toots had a nice retirement account set up for her. Maybe it was time to consider telling her to slow down or to out-and-out retire. Toots felt sad at the thought. As soon as she knew what her duties would be as the new owner of *The Informer,* she would give some serious thought to Bernice's retirement.

Before Bernice had a chance to come back with a snappy reply, Sophie entered the kitchen, wearing a red-and-blue-plaid robe that had seen better days. "Is that coffee I smell?" she asked of no one in particular.

Toots watched as Bernice quickly looked up, then genuflected. "Does it *smell* like coffee?" Toots asked with a grin.

"Oh, you witch! It's early. Every person I know says the same thing first thing in the morning." Sophie filled a bright orange mug with coffee before finding her place at the table.

Toots refilled her own cup and sat in the chair across from her. "If you say so. Listen, I spoke with Abby before I went to bed. She's thrilled to death at the prospect of seeing her godmothers. She's offered to let us stay at her place, but I told her I took care of our temporary living arrangements."

"You never were one to procrastinate.

What did you do, buy a house?" Sophie asked between sips of the dark brew.

"No, but I'm sure I will sooner or later. I can't live at the Beverly Hills Hotel forever. I heard Aaron Spelling's mansion is on the market."

"Lord help us all," Bernice tossed out as she sliced a pink grapefruit.

"I hope He does because I'm going to need all the help I can get once we're in LA. Sophie, how do you feel about living in a Hollywood bungalow for a few weeks? LA isn't New York, so I don't know how you'll feel about having more than ten square feet of living space." Toots was forever joking about Sophie and Walter's cracker-box apartment. Before he and Sophie had married, Walter had purchased the eight-hundred-square-foot apartment for a pittance, and they'd remained there for almost forty years. Toots wasn't sure how Sophie would react to large open spaces.

"Woof! Woof!" Coco, all five pounds of her, with nails click-clacking against the wood floors, made her grand entrance, with Mavis at her heels. "Sorry, she's so noisy in the morning. She needs her caffeine. Did I tell you that? I share my coffee with her. I don't think she'll do so well going cold turkey," Mavis huffed.

Sophie and Toots laughed.

"A Chihuahua on caffeine. I should have known." Toots got up from the table and went to the cupboard, where she took out a small cup that she filled with milk and a splash of coffee. She set it down on the floor next to the table. "That should keep her happy."

"She likes sugar, too," Mavis added.

"Well, tough. She's going to have to learn to live without it, just the way you are. Aren't you the one who said if it was good enough for you, it was good enough for your dog?" Toots poured Mavis a cup of black coffee. "No milk or sugar, okay?" Toots raised her brows, and Mavis nodded.

"I can do this. I will do this." It was said with such grim determination, Toots believed her old friend. "I can't wait for the girls to see all those gorgeous clothes you bought for me."

Toots reminded Mavis that she had an eight o'clock appointment for the stress test. Luckily, it would take less than an hour.

"I can't wait either," Sophie announced drily. "Maybe when we get to LA, where there's all that *open space,* we can all hire a makeup artist to do our faces. I've always wanted to do that but never had a reason to. Seeing how my future is looking so bright and shiny with Walter barely clinging to life, I've never had a reason until now. Maybe I'll do it for the funeral. I'm sure all of Walter's friends from the bank will attend. They think I'm a bitch, or so he always said. If I look ten years younger and plaster a smile on my face, I think that might give all the old codgers something to talk about. Yes"—Sophie took a big gulp of her coffee—"that's exactly what I'm going to do. Women hate seeing other women look good, especially when they're grieving."

"Sadly, that's true. I remember John's funeral as the only time I ever truly felt like a grieving widow. John was the love of my life." Tears welled in Toots's eyes as she remembered Abby's father.

"Look, before we get completely morbid, let's talk about something else. I don't do grief this early in the morning," Sophie said.

Toots sniffed and dabbed at her eyes with her napkin. "You're right. We have too much to look forward to in the next few weeks to spend even one unhappy minute moaning about the past. I've been to one too many pity parties lately." Toots paused while Bernice placed a platter of fruit in the center of the table, followed by a heaping bowl of oats. "Though I have to admit that I was truly sad when each of my husbands passed. More or less." She shrugged.

Mavis and Sophie looked at Toots, their expressions laughable. "Well, except for Leland. He was so mean and cheap. I was shocked when he stated in his will that he wanted that seven-piece string band to play at his funeral. He really did spring for an expensive send-off, I'll say that for him. I don't even know why I was so shocked, since it was for himself even though he was dead."

Sophie held her mug high in the air. "Here's to Walter! May he suffer greatly and die soon!"

Toots clinked her mug. "That's not the way to toast one's soon-to-be-departed husband." Inside the pantry, Toots had a

stash of booze she saved for special occasions, very *special* occasions, such
as the death of a husband. She got up
from the table and was back in a matter of
seconds with an extremely rare bottle of
Glenfiddich that was known to have ma-
tured in its cask for more than sixty years
before bottling. Leland had paid almost
fifty thousand dollars for one bottle. It
was the one request he'd made in his will
that she denied him. No way in hell was
she going to bury him with such a fine,
such a *rare* bottle of booze, as he'd requested. Now seemed like as good a
time as any to open it up and make
a toast to her future. And to Walter's imminent demise.

"Here." Toots opened the bottle of
liquor before she raced to the hutch in the
dining room, where she removed four
crystal whiskey tumblers. At fifty grand a
bottle, if they were going to drink Leland's
high-priced whiskey, they were *not* going
to drink it out of coffee mugs. She placed
the tumblers in the middle of the table,
pouring a liberal dollop of scotch into
each one. "This is the best money can
buy. One of Leland's splurges. He wanted

me to bury this with him, but I couldn't bring myself to do something that stupid."

"As if he would know," Sophie said smartly.

"Well, there is the afterlife and all. He might be a tad ticked when you meet up again," Mavis gurgled as she agreed to only a small nip, given the upcoming test.

"Mavis, I know without a doubt that Leland is roasting in the fires of hell by now, and I do not think we will be meeting up in the afterlife. At least I hope not," Toots said.

Ida chose that moment to make an entrance, stopping just short of the kitchen table. She was freshly showered and dressed to kill, in black slacks and a cream-colored blouse and not a hair out of place. "Who's roasting in the fires of hell?"

"Toots's last dearly departed," Sophie said. "We're preparing to make a toast to Walter's demise. Want to join us?"

Ida took a step forward, closing the distance between herself and the table. She nodded and reached for one of the tumblers. This was the first time in a very long time she'd actually touched something without making sure it was as germ-free as humanly possible. *One step at a time*, she thought as she held the glass in her latex-covered hands. "Why not?"

For the second time in less than twenty-four hours, the women gathered around the kitchen table and made a toast.

"To new beginnings," Toots said, raising her glass high in the air.

Ida, Sophie, and Mavis clicked their glasses against Toots's tumbler. Except for the clinking of the glasses, the kitchen went completely silent as each woman silently wondered what their new future would bring to each of them.

When Mavis returned, the four of them would embark on the greatest, and unlikeliest, adventure of their lives.

Chapter 13

Ten million bucks! By the time he paid off the mortgage on *The Informer* plus his gambling debts, he'd still be in the hole for two million.

Rodwell Archibald Godfrey III was in deep doo-doo. Big-time. Unless . . .

Rag's brain kicked into overdrive. Part of him wanted to take the money and run. He could head down to the Cayman Islands, where he'd heard there were dozens of banks that didn't ask questions about large deposits. A new identity, a new lifestyle. Maybe if he played his cards right, he could pull off a disappearing act without losing his ass, or his life. He had a few connections who were as unscrupulous as he was. He'd need a birth certificate, driver's license, credit card, and passport. He knew in his gut he would never have another opportunity to literally disappear with ten million smackeroos. In the blink of an eye, he decided to go for the whole enchilada. Another part of him, the stubborn stupid part that he hated, said to stay and fight it out. He also knew his biggest failing in life was that he lived for the moment and never thought things through to a satisfactory conclusion. He'd get an itch, scratch it, and worry about the consequences later. That was what had gotten him into this mess in the first place. He squeezed his eyes shut for a moment and took a deep breath as he weighed option one and option two. A no-brainer for sure. He was going to grab the ball and run with option one, and the devil take the hindmost.

Removing the BlackBerry from his pocket, Rag used the mini roller ball to scroll through his address book. When he saw the name and number he was searching for, he removed a TAC phone from his other pocket and punched in the number.

The phone rang as Rag paced the length of his office, raking a hand through his thinning brown hair. His comb-over was way too obvious, worse than Donald Trump's because he could feel the slick bald spot at the top of his head. Maybe he'd invest in some hair plugs sometime in the near future. If he was able to keep most of the ten million dollars some crazy person had offered for *The Informer.*

Rag took a moment to wonder if the crazy buyer was an alien from outer space. Nothing else made sense to him. He knew a thing or two about space aliens because he published articles about them at least once a month.

Because he was so antsy, Rag started to think seriously about the hair plugs. Maybe he'd get a face-lift, too. At fifty-two, he wasn't getting any younger. The women who hit on him now were middle-aged, with brittle bleached blond hair, with skin tanned so dark it resembled a wrinkled cigar, and they wore their eyeliner too thick and their lipstick too bright. They were all pretty much the same. When he tried to puff himself up and told them he owned a newspaper, they thought he was Mr. Moneybags and threw themselves at him. Once they learned he owned a third-rate tabloid and was knee-deep in debt, they moved on to the next willing sucker. Rodwell, *Rag,* as he was referred to in tabloid journalism, thought it time to move on to greener and younger pastures. Ten million bucks almost guaranteed success in all areas. Oh, yeah.

"Yeah?" said a rough-sounding voice.

"I need to speak to Micky," Rag growled.

"Yeah, so does half the world. He ain't here."

"When do you expect him?" Rag growled again. He hadn't even considered this part, that Micky wouldn't be available. Shit!

A moment of silence. "Who the hell are you to ask where my boss is? The president? *When do I expect him?*" The last sentence sounded so ominous, Rag felt the fine hairs on the back of his neck move.

Time to suck up. Micky was a good contact he couldn't afford to lose or mess with. Rag wasn't sure, but he rather thought Micky had Mafia ties. Shit, that was a lie. He *knew* Micky had mob ties. "It's urgent that I speak with him; otherwise, I wouldn't be calling his private number. Tell him there is a very large sum of money involved. He can call this number if he's interested." Rag rattled off his cell number, the one he used to call his bookies and other unsavory friends. He hung up, and ten seconds later, his cell rang.

He looked at the caller ID. Micky.

"Hello."

"You called me. I'm returnin' the call." The deep voice sent a chill up Rag's spine.

Tough guy. Rag felt a whole second's worth of guilt hit him before he pushed it aside. This was a once-in-a-lifetime chance to start over. He wasn't going to let anything get in his way if he could help it.

"I need some documents. Fast. Like in instant *fast*! Birth certificate, passport, driver's license, credit card, the whole megillah. How soon can you get them?"

"Wait a minute . . . we ain't discussed my fee yet. We always gotta discuss my fee first," Micky said.

Rag thought him as crass and tacky as the guy who had answered the phone seconds ago. He knew crass and tacky, he lived and worked in Hollywood. What happened to manners in the mob? He also knew if he wanted a class act, he should have gone to JPMorgan Chase and borrowed ten million dollars. "I'll pay the going rate." He had no clue what the going rate was, but he wasn't stupid enough to name a price.

"A hundred grand," Micky said, then added, "each."

"Four hundred thousand dollars! You must be out of your mind. I can get fake documents on the Internet for a thousand." There was no way in hell he was forking over four hundred grand for a new identity.

"Sure ya can, but will they pass customs? I don't think so. It's your life and your nickel. Do what you want."

Damn! "Okay, let's negotiate. I'll give you fifty grand for everything. That's all I have. Deal or no deal?" Wasn't that the name of a new game show? Rag held his breath, waiting to see if his offer would be accepted.

Silence. "Yeah, for you I guess I can bend the rules a bit, seein' as we've done business before. When do ya want 'em?"

"As quick as you can get them, like as in an hour ago," Rag said, suddenly more excited than he'd been in a *very* long time. Screw Los Angeles. He was sick of all the phony stars who thought they were royalty, even sicker of chasing after some damned story that wasn't really a story just so he could one-up his competition, a ploy that never worked anyway. Screw it, he was on his way to bigger and better things, he could feel it. Hell, he could *smell* it.

Christopher Lee Clay, Chris to his friends, had a nagging suspicion something was wrong with the pending sale of *The Informer*. Something wasn't right, but he couldn't put his finger on exactly what it was. Rodwell Godfrey had a nasty reputation for being a con man. Chris had drawn up the papers for the sale of *The Informer* for Toots just as she'd asked him to. Was that when he started to rethink the whole deal, or was it when she'd wired the money to the required bank and he knew it was official? He'd gone over the paperwork numerous times; then, as an extra precaution, he'd faxed the papers to one of his tennis buddies, a corporate attorney, just to make sure all the *t*'s were crossed and all the *i*'s were dotted properly. Yes, said his buddy, all appeared to be on the up-and-up. Still, Chris felt something was off. He hadn't told Toots yet, figuring he would wait until she and her friends arrived later that afternoon. Maybe he was just being overly cautious where his stepmom was concerned. Though she had millions, he'd hate to see her bilked out of them unnecessarily. Hoping his paranoia was unfounded, Chris scrutinized the legal documents one last time. It all looked good on paper, but there was something nagging him. Godfrey was making out big-time, that much he was sure of. Maybe it was the outlandish price Toots had paid. Of course she *had* asked him to double any offer that had already been made. Sure, that was what it was, it had to be. Chris knew the paper was worth a pile of dung, but he also knew when Toots set her mind on doing something, there was no stopping her. Her daughter, Abby, was the same way.

Speaking of Abby. Chris remembered when he'd first met his new stepsister.

She'd been in her early teens, and he'd just finished his last year of high school. They'd hit it off immediately, but after that one visit, it seemed his visits to Charleston rarely coincided with hers, so they hardly saw one another. After his father died, he'd remained close to Toots but hadn't seen enough of Abby to have any real genuine brotherly feelings toward her. Toots practically begged him to come home for Abby's college graduation. Chris figured it was the least he could do for a stepsister that he really liked. Though when he saw her after the ceremony, when she'd removed her cap and gown, she about knocked his socks off. No longer the skinny little girl with towheaded curls. Abby Simpson was a knockout. Pure and simple. From that moment on, Chris never looked at her the same way again. The few times they'd been together, he'd always teased her about being so small, telling her she would never grow up. Well, grow up she had. Abby was gorgeous, much more so than the starlets who clung to his arm seven days a week.

When Abby moved to LA, they got together occasionally for lunch or dinner and usually at his suggestion. Each time they saw one another, Chris felt drawn to Abby in a way that was anything but brotherly. He suspected Typhoon Toots would kill him if she knew, so he kept up the big-brother act. There had been a few times he'd caught Abby looking at him in a way that he was sure wasn't sisterly love either, though he'd never pursued a relationship with her because it didn't feel right.

He dated his share of Hollywood starlets. Being an entertainment attorney had its benefits. He'd negotiated tons of contracts for Hollywood's finest and was paid out the yin-yang for his services. And then there were those special stars who always liked to give him more than his 20 percent share of their earnings, a little added bonus, as they put it. If he was truthful, and truthful he was, at least to himself, he was tiring of LA's fast-paced lifestyle. The glitter and glamour had worn off a long time ago. At thirty-three, he longed for something more, something real, which always brought him back to Abby.

Abby had made no bones about it, she loved LA, loved her job as a tabloid reporter, and made no excuses for her choices. He'd admired her for her honesty and guts. Compact loveliness, he thought, even though he knew it sounded old-fashioned and silly. When it was time to settle down, Chris knew he wanted a woman like Abby, someone sure of herself and secure with her choices. Sadly, he'd probably have to relocate to someplace like North Dakota if he wanted to find a woman as real as Abby, because real wasn't something LA was noted for.

Clutching the legal documents in his hand, Chris meandered out to the kitchen for a bottle of Perrier before settling himself on the terrace, which overlooked the ocean. He'd paid a small fortune for the beachfront house, and now he wondered why. It had never felt like a real home to him. Certainly nothing like Toots's Southern mansion or Abby's little ranch house. His place was modern with wall-to-wall glass, white pine floors, and absolutely no personality at all. No throw pillows tossed about to lounge on, no stack of magazines placed casually on a side table, no family photos, no green plants growing wildly. Chris reasoned that when he left this behind, all he would need to do would be to pack his clothes and toothbrush and leave. He didn't really like the furniture, the dishes, the drapes; he didn't like the pictures on the walls. Actually, he hadn't liked much of anything about this place since purchasing it five years ago. He blamed the decorator and his own lack of input. He'd given her carte blanche because he was too damn busy negotiating all those nice fat contracts and collecting his equally fat fees. After all, he did little more than sleep here, and with his eyes closed, he didn't have to look at anything.

He'd hosted a few client dinners with the help of a catering service, and nothing more. No friends came to visit, no Sunday football days with the guys, nothing. To him, his house was simply a place to sleep and shower. Since he didn't have an office, he spent most of his workdays at various hot spots and clubs, doing business with clients and potential clients who wanted to "be seen." As he had been voted one of LA's top ten bachelors, women both young and old hankered to be seen with him. Chris didn't think it much of an accomplishment in his shallow world of see-and-be-seen. Though there were those who would contradict him, who would trade places with him in a heartbeat.

Maybe with Toots coming to town, he'd actually find time to enjoy himself for a change.

Chapter 14

As soon as the plane landed and it was permissible to turn cell phones on, Toots called Abby, and just as she'd promised, Abby had a limo waiting for them on the tarmac at LAX. Toots couldn't wait to see her daughter and take the girls to the Beverly Hills Hotel, where they would all be in need of a bit of pampering. She was so excited she was giddy with the feeling.

The flight had been smooth, and Toots was glad she'd hired a private jet for the trip. She could not imagine Ida on a commercial flight. White-knuckled the entire flight, Ida had remained quietly in her seat.

Toots was sure it wasn't out of a fear of flying. More like a fear of touching. Poor Ida. She had her first appointment with the shrink specializing in OCD tomorrow afternoon. And if the appointment wasn't productive, then Ida was going to go it cold turkey.

Before leaving Charleston, Toots had made arrangements with Henry Whitmore to wire ten million dollars to Chris's escrow account for the purchase of *The Informer.* Henry sputtered and snarled, asking her if she'd lost her mind when she'd told him what she was buying. When she spoke to Chris about the pending sale, he hadn't sounded as confident as usual. She felt a tinge of worry. What if she had to tell Abby she was the new owner of *The Informer*? Would Abby want to work for her *mother*? Toots didn't think so. But if it came down to it, she would confess to Abby and risk whatever the fallout was.

Putting her concerns aside, Toots waited for the limo driver to secure their luggage in the trunk. Once he'd finished, she stepped aside, allowing Mavis to get in first since she would take up an entire section of the U-shaped seats. Joe had given Mavis a clean bill of health just this morning. The stress test indicated she could start a reasonable exercise program anytime she wanted. Mavis was another one who was going to go cold turkey if she didn't perform and live up to the promises she'd made to lose her extra weight.

With Mavis seated and Coco snug in the carrier next to her, Sophie piled inside. "I can't believe it. After all these years, I'm finally riding in a stretch limousine. I see them around the city all the time." She smoothed her skirt and patted the place next to her. "Come on, Ida. I don't have cooties." Sophie laughed, and Toots couldn't help but join in.

As though she were about to enter a minefield, Ida carefully eased herself into the seat beside Sophie. Toots climbed inside, sitting across from the trio.

A bottle of champagne chilled in an ice bucket with four crystal glasses placed beside it beckoned the ladies. Someone had propped a note card next to the ice bucket. Toots opened it. "This is from Abby." She pointed to the champagne and scanned the note. "She says welcome to

LA and that she will meet us at the Polo Lounge for dinner at seven. Seven will be ten our time, so we'll have to take a nap, or at least rest a bit. What do you say?" Toots heard the excitement in her own voice, something she hadn't felt in a while. Not since she'd up and married Leland. Well, Leland was six feet under, and she was alive and well and about to embark on a new adventure. Nothing could stop her from enjoying her life now, not that anything ever had. She'd just been a little more reserved back in the day— sometimes, anyway. Well, this was a whole new day! Toots was simply thrilled to be footloose and fancy-free. And she was damn well going to remain free this time around. No more men for her. Well, no more *marriages,* at least; she hadn't completely sworn off men. Besides, eight husbands was enough of a track record.

"I say we go for it! I want to get that full-body massage you always rave about. I could use a cut, color, and a wax job, too," Sophie said with a grin.

"What parts do you wax?" Mavis asked curiously.

"What parts do you think I wax?" Sophie shot back.

"I don't know, that's why I asked. I see on TV where women wax everything these days. And I mean *everything*."

"Well, I don't go that far. It kills me to get my eyebrows done. I can't imagine what it would feel like . . . you know"—Sophie looked at her lap—"down there."

Toots burst out laughing. Mavis and Sophie were so naive. She knew that before Ida's phobia, she'd done all those things. She looked over at her old friend and was surprised at the grin on her face. Maybe there was some hope for Ida after all.

"She asked," Sophie commented drily. "What about it, Toots, have you ever gotten a full-body wax job?"

"Of course I have."

"Where?" Sophie persisted.

"Oh, for God's sake, stop asking questions like a teenager. No, I haven't had anything below the belt waxed, okay? And if I had, I wouldn't tell you."

"You don't have to get all pissy on me. I was just curious. Since I never had a full-body wax job, what's wrong with asking questions. What about it, Ida? You live in the big wicked city. You ever go to one of those fancy salons for a wax job?"

"Sophie!" Toots chastised.

"I meant before she got all wacky with her germ thing."

"Sophie Manchester, I'll have you know that I have had that area waxed more than once. Actually, Thomas suggested it after he watched *The Jerry Springer Show* once. It's not too painful." Ida had a glazed look in her eyes.

The women stared at Ida in surprise. Coco woke up, barked at the high-volume discussion, her tiny tail straight in the air. Ida had been virtually silent the entire trip. They all tried to envision the Ida sitting across from them admitting to getting a bikini wax.

"I think that's more than we need to know, Ida," Mavis mumbled. "I don't know about the rest of you, but I am starving. Are we planning a snack before dinner?"

Coco barked again. *The dog must know that the word* dinner *means food*, Toots thought.

"Of course. I've arranged for each of our bungalows to be fully stocked with food and alcoholic beverages as well as diet soft drinks. We'll have a light snack at my place before we have our massages. I even have a dog sitter lined up for Coco." Toots stopped talking to gaze out the window. "Look at this! All this sunshine, the exotic flowers, it's simply beautiful here. I'm so glad you girls came along. I say we make a toast." Toots popped the cork on the bottle of champagne and poured each one of them a glass of the pale bubbly. She had a visitor's view of the city, she knew, but she was just so damn happy, she wanted to shout it to the world.

"What are we toasting now? Not that I mind. It's just that I don't want to get drunk until later. That scotch threw me for a loop this morning. I haven't had this much since nursing school," Sophie said.

Toots held up her glass. "I'd like to make a toast to my best friends and to the best three godmothers a girl could ask for."

For the second time that day, the foursome clinked their glasses together.

Traffic was unusually light, Toots thought, as they arrived at the Beverly Hills Hotel within an hour of their landing. Toots was impressed. As far as she was concerned, this was the way to travel. Top of the line, first class all the way. She had enough money, so why not spend it and enjoy herself? At the same time, she was treating her friends to a wonderful vacation. If something more materialized, all the better. If not, the girls would have a great memory to take back home. If nothing else, Toots was realistic. She knew a thing or two about the best-laid plans of mice and men—women, that is.

Amidst sprawling green shrubbery and a kaleidoscope of lush flowers blossoming from every direction, Toots felt like Dorothy entering the land of Oz as they passed through the private gates and entered the hotel grounds. Toots couldn't remember ever seeing so many brilliant plants and flowers in one place, and Charleston was known for its flora. Her own grounds as well as her veranda were awash in a rainbow of color, but it was nothing like what she was seeing right at that moment.

"Would you look at this?" Sophie peered out the window as the limo crawled toward the entrance. "I don't even want to know how much it cost to stay in a place like this."

Mavis tried to peek out of the tinted window behind her, but she was too heavy to turn around. "Darn, I'm too fat to look! Oh, Toots, I can't wait to rid myself of this blubber. I'm almost too embarrassed to enter the hotel. I'm sure it's full of movie stars and Hollywood types."

Toots saw real fear in her friend's eyes. "Listen, Mavis, you are as good, no, you're better than those people. So what if you've gained a few pounds? We're here, and you're going to enjoy yourself. You deserve this. And if anyone gives you one second of grief, they'll have to deal with me."

Mavis's eyes glistened with tears. "Okay, okay, I can handle this," she muttered over and over under her breath.

"Remember what you just said when I won't let you off the treadmill or when I give you a plate of sprouts with a slice of lemon." Toots grinned.

"I'll do my best, I promise," Mavis said. Toots knew her old friend meant it.

"I know you will. Now wipe off those tears, and let's see a smile on your face. You, my friend, are in Hollywood now. God, isn't it wonderful! And on top of that, we're on a mission to make Abby's life as perfect as we can."

"And everyone in Hollywood smiles or else." Sophie grinned as an example.

When the car came to a complete stop, the driver hopped out and opened the passenger door. One by one, the ladies stepped out of the limousine into the bright midafternoon California sunshine.

"Welcome to the Beverly Hills Hotel." A young man dressed in white from head to toe smiled. "If you will, follow me, please."

The Beverly Hills Hotel, located on Sunset Boulevard, was *the* hotel where movie stars could be seen on a daily basis, according to Toots's travel agent, and that's why she'd okayed the reservation. That, and because she wanted to sleep where Elizabeth Taylor had slept. As the new owner and publisher of *The Informer,* she wasn't going to miss an opportunity for any news stories about Hollywood. If she had to make them up herself, she was prepared to do so. Abby was not going to lose her job to that gambling, womanizing idiot she worked for. Not as long as Toots had breath left in her body.

"Come on, Toots, we're waiting," Mavis called.

Lost in thought, Toots didn't realize the others were already inside the van that would deliver them to their private bunga-lows. She climbed inside for the short ride. "I got lost there for a minute. Sorry. Must be all the sunshine," she said hap-pily.

"And you really want to live here?" So-phie queried.

"Not all the time. At least not at this stage of the game. I plan on spending the next two weeks learning how to run a tabloid. I don't think the actual running of the paper will be that hard since we'll hire people to do that. I think it will be more overseeing things than actually operating the paper. What's going to be difficult is staying undercover and pulling it off with-out Abby's suspecting anything."

Had she bitten off more than she could chew? She certainly hoped not.

"I don't understand why you don't just tell her you bought the paper," Ida said out of the blue. "It's not like she won't find out eventually."

"Get that thought out of your mind right

now. And since you've been known to be a little too chatty on occasion, you better not tell her, or I will personally dunk your hand minus the latex glove in the nastiest garbage can I can find," Sophie said.

"I didn't say I was going to tell Abby. Of course I would never say or do anything to upset her. I just don't understand why it all has to be kept secret. I'm for being up front and honest. You get into less trouble that way. Don't threaten me, Sophie."

Toots put her finger over her lips and nodded toward the hotel driver. "We'll talk about this later. Right now I want to relax, enjoy the scenery, and have a drink to celebrate our visit. It's almost a blessing to be out from under Bernice's watchful eye. She's wonderful, but she's way too protective and a tad nosy. Normally, I don't mind. Crap, yes, I do mind."

"Oh, that's not true! Nosy just means she cares about you. Admit it, you love her as much as the rest of us. You told me so yourself in an e-mail," Sophie said tartly.

"True, but nonetheless it's good to be on my own with no one hovering over me."

"I totally understand. When I was teaching, I used to pray for the summers. By the end of the school year, the kids were antsy, and I would get really tired of being the English teacher. I just wanted to go home and relax, not have to worry about someone else. Of course, when Herbert died, I was so lonely I almost considered signing up to substitute. I don't know why I changed my mind. Maybe if I had continued working, I wouldn't have gotten so fat!" Mavis laughed at herself. Toots thought the laughter was a good sign.

"Well, you know what they say: The past is prologue. It's time to move on to bigger and better things," Toots announced.

"I already have the bigger, but I'm more than willing to take a chance on the better," Mavis said, smiling from ear to ear.

"That's the spirit!" Sophie encouraged. "Something tells me we're all about to experience the ride of our life."

Toots nodded. "Let's just hope it's a smooth one."

"Teresa, do you really think I can overcome this . . . this *issue* I have?" Ida looked down at her latex-covered hands. "I know

this is crazy, but I can't seem to help myself. I'll do anything humanly possible to get
back to a normal life. If you help me with
this . . . this problem, I'll forgive you for
stealing Jerry away from me."

"You've already taken the first step.
And of course I plan to be with you every
step of the way until you can dunk your
hand in a garbage can just like Sophie
said. That's what friends are for. We stick
together. And, Ida, I did you a favor by
marrying old Jerry. How many times do I
have to tell you that? He couldn't even . . .
well, let's just say that most of our married
years, we had nothing more than a pla-
tonic relationship."

"I suppose I should thank you, then,"
Ida said, with a slight tilt to her lips.

"Forget Jerry, Ida, and move forward
with your life. The past is gone. We aren't
getting any younger, and I, for one, intend
to savor my so-called twilight years."

The van stopped at a discreet parking
area near the bungalows. The driver
stepped out and spoke to another young
man wearing a matching uniform. Two
more young men appeared and removed
their luggage from the back of the van.

The driver opened the passenger door and offered up a sweeping gesture with his arm. "Ladies, welcome to the Pink Palace." It was so dramatic that, as one, the women burst out in laughter.

Chapter 15

Before she could change her mind, Abby dialed Chris's cell phone number. She hadn't seen him in ages, and she was sure he'd want to see her mom while she was in town. As far as excuses went, it was as good as any. She had a rule. No matter how much she wanted to see Chris or talk to him, she never called without a reason.

"Chris Clay," he said.

"Whatever happened to hello?" Abby teased.

"I'll be damned, you do come out of your cave once in a while, don't you?" Chris said. Abby heard the laughter in his voice, could imagine the twinkle in his sexy blue eyes. Damn, she shouldn't be having these kinds of thoughts. Then again, why shouldn't she? She wasn't a nun.

She laughed. "I do, and if Rag has anything to say about it, I'll soon be looking for another place to hide. He's put the paper up for sale, and rumor has it he's found someone stupid enough to buy it. While it's just a rumor, there is usually a kernel of truth in most rumors, especially when they concern Rag."

Chris was quick to say, "I heard that rumor."

"News travels fast, but that's not why I called. You won't believe this, but Mother and my three godmothers are in town. They're staying at the Pink Palace. I plan on having dinner with them tonight at the Polo Lounge. I thought you might like to join us."

"I think I can manage that. I haven't seen Typhoon Toots in a while myself. Want me to pick you up?"

Abby pondered the offer for a few seconds. Her car was dirty, Chester had slobbered all over the windows, and she hadn't cleaned them yet. Probably wouldn't look good to the valet parking guys at the Polo Lounge. "Sure, pick me up. The ride will give us a chance to play catch-up without Mom hovering over us. Is six o'clock too early? By the way, which movie star are you dating this week?" she asked bluntly. She was glad Chris couldn't see how childish she was with her crossed fingers.

"Six o'clock works for me. I'll see you then, and thanks for the invitation. No stars this week. My hair is starting to fall out; that might be the reason they're losing interest." He laughed at his own witticism before he broke the connection.

Abby looked at the phone for a long minute as she congratulated herself for getting Chris to accept her invitation. She knew his reputation with the ladies, and it was a rare night that Chris Clay wasn't seen escorting a female star to any number of LA's hottest nightspots. She'd had the opportunity more than once to write a story about him; but, as family, he was totally off-limits, no matter who graced his arm. She'd missed a lot of stories because of her loyalty to family.

Abby could just imagine her mother

soaking in her giant Jacuzzi with a glass of wine and a tall stack of tabloids. If she ever came across a story about Chris, she would've fainted right on the spot simply because her mother considered him to be as much her son as Abby was her daughter. Her mother would never allow anyone to trample on their reputations, warranted or not. And if anyone did, Abby knew there would be hell to pay. She laughed as she visualized her mother, the transplanted Southern belle, kicking ass and taking names later.

With time to spare and the fact that she would be out for the evening, Abby decided to take Chester for a long walk. Chester, all ninety-seven pounds of him, came leaping off the sofa and raced to the front door. "Come on, boy. We need some fresh air."

An hour later, Abby and Chester returned home, both energized from their long walk. Chester's tongue lolled to one side as he followed her to the kitchen, where his water bowl was full of fresh water. It only took him a minute to lap it all up. Thirsty herself, Abby reached for a bottle of water and chugged it down. Glancing at the clock on the stove, she saw she had an hour to shower and dress before Chris arrived.

Not one to waste time, Abby sprinted to the bathroom, turned on the shower, and stepped beneath the spray. She washed her hair with grapefruit-scented shampoo, filled a mesh shower sponge with a gardenia-scented body wash, scrubbed down, then stood under the spray, letting the soap bubbles spiral down the drain.

Turbaning her wet hair in a towel and wrapping another around her body, Abby stepped inside her closet to find something appropriate to wear for the evening. She spied a black Versace sheath dress, a birthday gift from her mother last year. Removing it from the hanger, she draped it in front of her, then stood in front of the full-length mirror on the back of her closet door. Not bad, but Chris might view her as prissy and uptight in a dress like that. A good-girl dress. She tossed the dress on the bed. A good girl she was not, at least not tonight. She didn't want Chris to think of her as his sassy-ass little stepsister. She wanted him to look at her as though she were one of those starlets who clung to him all the time. Just not in a *bimboish* way. Damn, what the hell was she thinking? She was preparing to have dinner with her mother and godmothers, and here she was worrying about what she should wear. Actually, the black dress was perfect. She'd wear her pearls and open-toed high-heeled sandals. The decision made, Abby made fast work of blow-drying her hair. For once, she went full glamour girl and applied makeup with a professional hand. When she'd finished, she stepped back to admire her handiwork. Her coworkers often said she was a mirror image of Meg Ryan. Bullshit. She made Meg Ryan look like an old warhorse trying to play an ingenue.

Chapter 16

Toots decked herself out in a teal skirt with a matching blouse and silver sandals. She piled her thick chestnut hair on top of her head and clipped a pair of diamond studs on her ears before adding a touch of cover-up to hide the circles forming beneath her eyes. She finished up by dusting blush across her high cheekbones. She looked at the shimmering bronze lipstick, then smacked her lips in satisfaction. The mirror told her this was as good as it was going to get. At the sterling age of sixty-five, she felt like she had traveled into another time zone. She didn't expect to look like Kate

Hudson; well, maybe her mother, Goldie Hawn. She promised herself she would try to sleep in tomorrow but knew her biological clock wouldn't care if it was two in the morning or not. Didn't matter. She was here where she wanted to be, surrounded by those she loved most.

Mavis, Sophie, and she had spent an hour getting a massage and a facial. Ida had opted to remain behind, cleaning and disinfecting everything in the room. She'd called room service twice, asking them for fresh sheets and towels. Toots tried to convince her the ones on the bed were clean, but Ida wouldn't back down. When Toots had returned from her massage, she made a point to call the front desk, where she spoke to the manager and explained Ida's problem. While she hated to betray her friend, Toots was afraid if she didn't explain Ida's obsessive compulsive disorder, management would get fed up and throw Ida out of the hotel or have her carted straight to the nearest loony bin.

The manager had been more than gracious, saying Ida could have all the fresh linens she needed, and if she wanted to watch while they were being washed, she was welcome to do so. Toots hoped it wouldn't come to that.

Toots picked up her small, sparkly clutch purse, which was supposed to be one of the current fashion trends in Los Angeles, and left the bedroom. The Polo Lounge! How wonderful was that?

Toots took a deep breath and looked around, really seeing the decor for the first time. Her bungalow was elegantly decorated in greens and pinks. The furniture throughout her suite had been custom-made, or so said her housemaid, who came with the package. She had her own private entrance, a formal living room and dining room, a wood-burning fireplace that she was sure had never seen a fire, a kitchen large enough to satisfy anyone with a love of cooking. The appliances were all top of the line, the dishes exquisite. Her bathroom had double sinks, a large Jacuzzi, and the shower was pink Grecian marble. Plush pink towels and luxurious terry bathrobes with matching slippers were in an armoire just waiting to be used. Amenities were placed neatly on the marble countertop. Bath gel, shampoo, and conditioner, along with hand and body lotion. There were even pink tooth-brushes and toothpaste with a pink fluo-ride mouthwash. Pink everything.

The Beverly Hills Hotel was lavish, and so were its prices, but again, she had more money than she knew what to do with, so if she wanted to plunk out five thousand bucks a night, she could. *Times four*, she thought as she stepped out into the courtyard.

Sophie was waiting for her outside of her own bungalow. "I've never seen such luxury. Pinch me. I can't believe this is real."

Toots laughed and linked her arm through Sophie's as they strolled to Mavis's bungalow. "This is the land of make-believe, remember?"

"I do, and I can't thank you enough. No one would ever suspect I have a husband at home on his deathbed." Sophie looked off in the distance.

Toots knew where this was headed. "Sophie, don't start laying a guilt trip on yourself. I know where you're coming from, trust me. Guilt does terrible things, and I don't need to remind you of all the 'terrible things' you've been through the past thirty years. It's me, Toots, remember? I want you to relax and enjoy your time here. Who knows when you'll have to race back to New York to take care of Walter's final arrangements." She removed a tissue from her tiny purse and handed it to Sophie.

"I know, but I can't help thinking about him lying there just waiting to . . . die. He's so feebleminded and old. All those years of hard, fast living and the drinking aged him before his time. He was a mean old bastard, wasn't he?" Sophie asked, tears glistening in her warm brown eyes.

"Yes, he was, and that's one more reason why I want you to put him out of your mind. At least for tonight. It's been a long and tiring day for all of us. I think we've earned a night of fun. Abby's bringing Chris with her. I can't wait for you and the others to meet him. You want a cigarette?"

"I'm dying for one," Sophie said. Toots removed two Marlboro Lights from her purse, lit them, and gave one to Sophie. How classy was *that*? Toots burst out laughing.

They continued down the private

walkway, the path quiet and tranquil. Surrounded by lush tropical gardens, heavenly scented early-evening air, and glowing from an hour of pampering, Toots wanted to wrap her arms around the moment and hold on tightly for fear it would disappear and she would never experience such bliss again. And there wasn't a man in sight. Her happiness at this very moment was so great, tears filled her eyes. She took another tissue from her bag and blotted her own eyes.

"Look at you! Crying like a baby. Your mascara's running." With her cigarette dangling from the corner of her mouth, Sophie took the tissue from her hand and wiped the black streaks off Toots's face. "There. Now let's stop bawling like two babies. Look at her, would you?" Sophie pointed to Mavis waiting outside her own bungalow. She hurried to greet her.

"I don't think I've ever seen you look so . . . stunning! My God, your hair and makeup are perfect. Well, maybe when you were eighteen! You don't look like the Mavis I know, you look like a movie star!" Sophie grinned.

Clumsily, Mavis twirled around, showing off her new hairstyle and makeup. "I wouldn't go that far, but I do kind of feel like Cinderella. I know I've said that a hundred times, but I really do feel that way. When I saw myself in the mirror, I wanted to cry. Coco hardly recognized me. I haven't felt or looked this good in twenty years. I can't wait to exercise. My housemaid is going to show me the gym tomorrow. She said someone had arranged for me to work with a private trainer. I can't imagine who would do such a thing." Mavis's clear blue eyes sparkled like two shiny sapphires. She looked at both women. "I had no clue they made such nice clothes for fat women. I feel . . ." She tipped her head, blushing. "Sexy." The last word was barely a whisper.

"You are the sexiest retired English teacher I've ever seen. The dark green looks fabulous on you," Sophie commented, then ground her cigarette out on the sidewalk. She picked up the discarded cigarette and stuffed it in her skirt pocket. Toots blinked. When in Rome. Her discarded cigarette went into Sophie's pocket, too. "We have to think about giving up these things. No one smokes anymore. We're pariahs."

"*You* think about it, and *you* quit. Don't include me," Sophie said sharply.

"Yes, ma'am," Toots replied meekly.

Mavis ignored the two old friends' dialogue. "Liz, the woman at the dress shop, knew what would and what wouldn't work for me. I'll be forever in her debt." Mavis wore a deep green tunic top with wide-legged hostess slacks that trimmed at least thirty pounds from her frame. Her new caramel-colored hair and peachy makeup complemented her fair coloring. Toots could see the transformation taking place already.

"Well, I think you both look fantastic." Toots looked at the slim diamond watch on her wrist. "Let's see if Ida is ready to venture outside her Clorox cocoon. I don't want to keep Abby waiting."

The threesome, dressed in the latest casual finery, promenaded through the winding path leading to Ida's bungalow, which was situated between towering palm trees and bright pink floral blossoms.

"I've never seen such gardens," Sophie

said in awe. "In New York, the only flowers I see are at Joanne's Market. I'm sure they're at least three days old when she gets them; she's an old tightwad if ever there was one. She repackages old meat. It was in all the papers. I wonder if that's where Ida's Thomas got hold of that tainted meat that killed him?" Sophie continued to stare at the landscaping. "I wish I had my camera."

"I'm sure we can purchase one of those throwaways in the gift shop," Toots offered. "And I can't see Ida shopping for her own groceries, so I think we can safely rule out Joanne's Market as the source of Thomas's poison even though it sounds good. Whatever you do, don't mention it to Ida. We have enough going on tonight without setting her off."

Sophie shrugged but promised. Sophie was known to break most of her offhand promises. Toots tried to squelch the prickle of alarm she was feeling.

"Poor Ida. I wish there was some way I could help her," Mavis said out of the blue. "I want her to feel as good about herself as I do right now. I'm being realistic here."

"She will. It will just take some time and

patience on our part. Now," Toots said in a low voice, "let's try to focus on Ida's positive attributes tonight." Toots had a mean thought; what exactly *were* Ida's positive attributes? They'd never been as close as she, Sophie, and Mavis. Dear departed Jerry, the dud, had always stood between them.

Sophie rapped lightly on the door. Toots and Mavis stood behind her. Sophie was more successful in dealing with Ida than the others for some reason. Another light knock.

"Ida, we know you're in there. Open up, or I'm going to spit in my hand and force you to hold it," Sophie snarled.

"Well, *that* should certainly convince her to open the door," Toots hissed.

The door opened barely an inch. One blue eye peeked out. "I can't go. Tell Abby I'm sorry; just go without me." Ida closed the door. They heard the lock engage.

"It's her loss," Sophie stated as she whipped around. "I'm not going to force her to do anything she's not comfortable doing. At least not yet."

"Getting her out of New York was a major hurdle, so let's give her a little more time before we lower the boom on her. She'll come around," Toots said. "I don't know about the rest of you, but I'm starving."

Proudly, Mavis declared, "I'm not the least bit hungry."

"You have to eat, dear. We're just going to make sure what you put in your mouth is healthful." Toots would give anything for a big bowl of Froot Loops, but she'd wait until breakfast. Somehow she couldn't see asking the waiters at the Polo Lounge for a bowl of cereal as her entrée.

In her usual no-nonsense-straight-to-the-point way, Sophie said, "I am frigging starving. Can't you two walk any faster?" she hollered as she raced ahead of them. Mavis plodded along as quickly as her bulk allowed, with Toots trailing closely on her heels. Toots scanned the walkway, making sure no one could see her before she gave Sophie the finger. Mavis laughed at the juvenile display.

When they reached the entrance to the restaurant, Toots entered first since the reservations were in her name. At the hostess stand, she was greeted by a beautiful young Latina with hair as black as night. When she spoke, her accent only added to her dark, sultry beauty. "If you will follow me, please."

Mavis whispered to Sophie, "I bet she's a movie star."

Sophie rolled her eyes. "I don't think so. If she were, she wouldn't be working here."

"Maybe it's for a role."

"Mavis, get real. Actresses don't practice for their roles working at the Polo Lounge. I'm sure they work here hoping some big-wig movie producer will spot them and make them Hollywood's next big star. Or they're looking for rich husbands." Sophie rolled her eyes. "You need to start reading the tabloids like Toots. Just don't get addicted."

"Wasn't Lana Turner discovered that way?" Toots tossed over her shoulder.

"I think she was drinking a Coke at a drugstore," Mavis offered.

They followed the hostess outside to the patio. White wrought-iron tables with forest green cushions and color-coordinated tablecloths were placed closely together across the brickwork. Giant urns held bright pink azaleas. In the center, an old Brazilian pepper tree shadowed several groups of diners. The friends were seated right in the center, where they had a bird's-eye view of anyone entering the patio. They'd just been seated when Toots saw Abby and Chris heading to their table.

Chapter 17

Toots embraced her daughter in a tight hug, then latched on to Chris. "I'm so thrilled you're here. I'd like for you to meet Abby's godmothers."

Both Mavis and Sophie greeted Chris with enthusiasm. "I've heard so much about you through the years," Mavis said.

"Me, too, but I didn't realize you were *this* good-looking," Sophie gushed as she evaluated Chris.

Chris laughed, a shivery, husky sound, and thanked the ladies for their compliments, his pearly whites glistening.

Chris waited until the women were

seated before taking his seat next to Abby. Finding it hard to focus on the here and now with Abby sitting so close to him that he could smell her perfume, something floral and light, he had to force himself to pay attention to the conversation going on around him. He was still trying to deal with the way his heartbeat had quadrupled when Abby had answered the door earlier. He hoped he wasn't too obvious when he'd sized her up. He'd gone from sweating palms to a burning neck all in two seconds. Abby could hold her own and, compared to the women he'd been dating lately, she was the prize of prizes. He wondered if she knew the effect she had on him. Probably not, since she treated him like a brother. Her dog, Chester, loved him.

"Ida couldn't force herself to come out of her room. She has OCD," Toots explained to Chris when Abby asked if her third godmother would be joining them for dinner. "I've arranged for her to see a doctor tomorrow. If that doesn't work, we're just going to hog-tie her and make her go cold turkey."

"Everyone is OCD in Hollywood these days. Makes for good tabloid reading."

Chris winked at Abby to show he was teasing. He wished he'd had a chance to have a moment alone with Toots before he picked up Abby. Before leaving his house, he'd received a rather strange message. He didn't want to alarm Toots or cause her any unnecessary anxiety, but he had a gut feeling she wasn't going to be happy when he told her of his suspicions. All along he'd had a bad feeling that the purchase of *The Informer* was not going to be as simple as he'd originally thought. He wished now he had acted on those feelings, but feelings were just that, not facts. As a lawyer, he dealt in facts.

A waiter brought the wine list to their table. Chris quickly scanned the selections before settling on a bottle of Pinot Grigio from the Napa Valley.

When the wine was poured, the toasts taken care of, they ordered dinner. Chris did his best to relax and enjoy Abby's company and Toots's zany friends. An impossible feat, with Abby sitting so close. Damn, she smelled good, like the first scent of summer. He felt light-headed at her nearness. He did wonder if any of the women suspected what he was feeling.

Chris was only half aware of the typical subdued dinner chatter, glasses clinking, stifled laughter, and the occasional sound of dropped silverware. He did his best to shift into a neutral zone so he could enjoy himself. He couldn't remember the last time he'd felt so amused by three older women. They each took turns sharing stories of their youth. He thought it was funny when he saw Abby kicking her mother under the table when Toots brought up her daughter's first prom.

"Let's not go there, Mom," Abby said sharply, then softened her tone. "Please."

"Oh, come on, Abs, we're all adults. What happened, Toots?" Chris cajoled. He'd always thought Abby was so totally in control, and the possibility that she wasn't quite perfect intrigued him.

Toots shook her head. "I'd better not. If Abby wants you to know, she'll have to be the one to tell you."

"Thank you, Mom. Now can we talk about something else? By the way, Chris knew the paper was up for sale, can you believe that?"

"LA is like a small town in that respect. News travels fast, gossip even faster,"

Chris said as he gazed around the crowded room. He was afraid to look in Toots's eyes or in her friends' direction for fear Abby would pick up on his expression.

Toots spoke quickly, her words running together. "Uh . . . oh, yes, I'm sure everyone in the newspaper business knows about the impending sale even if it's a tabloid. That's how it goes, the papers go up for sale, then create their own news. Absolutely amazing," she said airily.

"True, but the funny thing is, you usually know who the buyer is. Word has it the new owner wants to remain anonymous. I heard the poor sucker paid triple what it's worth. I can't imagine anyone throwing their money away on a tabloid like *The Informer,* but I have to admit, I considered making an offer myself. With all my funds tied up in the house, I couldn't swing it, and you know what, I'm glad I didn't. Because with my luck, I would end up losing my shirt. It's going to take years for *The Informer* to become a force to reckon with, at least in the tabloid market." Abby stopped to take a sip of wine. "We've been third-rate as long as I've worked there. I suppose there is the possibility the new owner can pull it out of the sludge pile, but I doubt it."

Triple the price! Shit!

If Toots hadn't been sitting down, she would've fallen flat on her face. She cleared her throat, cast a wary glance at Chris before speaking. She wished she had a cigarette to fiddle with. "Are you planning on leaving the paper, Abby?" She hoped her voice sounded nonchalant.

Abby took a deep breath. "I'm not sure. I haven't had any job offers, not that I'm looking, and I really don't want to go back to regular boring reporting, so I guess that means I'll stay until I see how the new ownership works out. If they turn out to be anything at all like Rag, I'll probably move on, because he screwed me over too many times. I don't see myself allowing that to continue under new ownership, and this time around I'm going to ask for a contract. Chris can make sure it's bullet-proof."

"I'm sure that won't happen," Toots said matter-of-factly. "You were never fired, so that has to mean you're good at what you do."

Abby grinned. "Flattery will get you

everywhere unless you know something I don't know. Do you?" she asked quietly.

Chris made a mental note that Abby liked flattery. Well, who the hell didn't?

In a voice laced with anxiety, Toots asked, "Why would you ask something like that, dear? I know as much about the newspaper business as you know about the Ladies Guild back in Charleston."

"I'm joking, Mom."

Before any of them could utter another word, pro or con, their waiter appeared with their dinners. Toots thought she couldn't have timed it better if she had tried. Open mouth, insert foot. Hoping to turn Abby's mind in a different direction, she waited until the waiter left before speaking. "You know, Mavis is on a new diet." *Lame,* Toots thought. Just lame, but she had to say something.

"That's fantastic, Aunt Mavis! I'm very proud of you," Abby said.

"Thanks, sweetie. It was your mother who convinced me that it was time, and we all know how persuasive she can be. I'm glad she did. Though it's only been two days, I think it's something I can stick with. I'm going to give it my best shot. I haven't been tempted with a pint of Cherry Garcia yet. Or as your mother so quaintly put it, 'You don't want to be a walking heart attack, now, do you?'"

"One day at a time," Abby said, smiling.

"Isn't that what they tell the drunks at Alcoholics Anonymous?" Sophie asked between bites of food.

Chris burst out laughing. "I believe it is."

"My husband was . . . is an alcoholic," Sophie retorted. "I know a thing or two about Al-Anon and the steps program. He used to tell me he was going to those meetings, but he kept coming home drunk. He had the audacity to tell me the coffee was spiked."

"I'm sorry," Chris said, not knowing what else to say.

"Don't be. I'm not. My husband in name only is dying. Can you guess what he's dying of?" Sophie bit down into a crunchy roll and then rolled her eyes. She sounded like she was discussing the weather and didn't much care if it was going to rain or not.

"Cirrhosis of the liver?" Chris asked.

Sophie watched Chris. She realized her bluntness was making him uncomfortable.

"Yep, that's it. Look, you're as good as family. You might as well know. I'm just waiting for the old coot to kick the bucket so I can collect his life insurance. Ours was not a marriage made in heaven, as I said. If my words offend you, I'm sorry, but you haven't walked in my shoes all these years." She speared a baby carrot and popped it into her mouth, her expression guileless.

"Sophie, do you think we could move on to something a little more appropriate for dinner conversation. Remember, we're supposed to be enjoying ourselves tonight," Toots admonished.

"Who says I'm not enjoying myself? Just for the record, I am."

"Well, just for the record, I would like to hear more about the tabloid business. You know what I'm thinking?" Toots held her hand in front of Sophie's face. "Don't say another word, or I'll push you right off that chair you're sitting in. I was thinking we should all go back to my bungalow for dessert and coffee. Or drinks, whatever you prefer."

"As much as I'd like to, I'll have to pass. Chester's home, and I don't want to leave him any longer than necessary. He doesn't like it when I leave him alone for long periods of time. Besides, I want to see if I can find out the name of the new owner. I still have a few decent sources, and with the Internet, nothing is sacred anymore."

Toots's stomach did a belly flop as she jumped right in, anything to take Abby's mind away from *The Informer.* "Oh, that doesn't matter, dear, that's work. Tonight is for family. You really should've brought Chester along. Coco, that's Mavis's Chihuahua, came with us. I hired a dog sitter. He works with Cesar Millan, too, so you know the dogs are being well taken care of. I've been thinking about getting a dog myself. Or maybe a cat. Bernice will complain or threaten to quit, but I don't really care. I heard people who own animals have lower blood pressure than those who don't own a pet. Mavis, Joe said your blood pressure was perfect. I think I'll check into getting a pet as soon as I return to Charleston." Toots babbled until she was out of breath. What she really needed just then was a cigarette. And a stiff slug of whiskey.

"Mom, slow down! Chester's close to a

hundred pounds now. I don't know how he would act around a tiny little dog. He'd probably think it was a bug or something," Abby said. "But before you leave to go back home, you should bring Coco to the house so they can get acquainted. We could have a love match in the making."

Mavis nodded. "I'd like that, and I know Coco would, too. She's used to being around animals, both large and small. My neighbor Phyllis has two golden retrievers and a dachshund. They're all best friends, too."

"Then it's settled. We're going to Abby's with the dog before we leave." Toots forked a bite of her now-cold quiche lorraine, wishing they could get through the rest of dinner without any more talk of *The Informer.* Suddenly she had doubts about remaining anonymous, and she wasn't sure that she could still pull it off without Abby's discovering that *she* was the sucker who'd paid triple for a third-rate rag. What would she do if Abby used her excellent investigative skills in her quest to find the name of the new owner even though Chris had assured her he'd buried everything deep. Although she trusted Chris implicitly, she needed assurances that deep was really *deep.*

Conversation dwindled as the diners concentrated on the meals in front of them. Mavis picked at her free-range rotisserie chicken, Toots forced herself to eat the bland quiche, while Sophie stuffed her petite prime rib down as though she were attending the Last Supper. Abby munched on the famous sirloin burger, and Chris expertly twirled the linguini pomodoro around his fork.

When they finished dinner, Abby promised she would spend more time with them soon, apologizing for the short evening. Chris walked Abby out to get her a taxi. He came back to escort the ladies back to their bungalows.

Sophie reached for Mavis's hand, suggesting a walk to work off their dinner. And it was definitely time for a cigarette. Toots was grateful the two women were leaving, because she wanted to speak to Chris alone even though she was dying for a cigarette. When they arrived back at her bungalow, Toots poured them each a shot of whiskey before they settled themselves on the sofa.

"Okay, Mr. Clay, spit it out. I know something is going on with you, and you'd better tell your dear old stepmom what it is. You were as fidgety as a two-year-old during dinner. What gives?"

Chris leaned in as close as he could without invading Toots's personal space. "Just before I left to pick up Abby, I received a phone call from Emmanuel Rodriguez. He's the vice president of the Bank of Los Angeles, where I have my escrow account."

"And?" Toots said tightly.

"The wire transfer from your bank in Charleston went through just fine, all the paperwork is just as it should be." Chris paused, not for dramatic effect but because he wanted to break the news as gently as possible.

"Then what's the problem? I don't understand. I've been dealing with Henry Whitmore at my bank in Charleston for twenty years; we haven't had a problem yet, and I do wire transfers all the time." Toots reached for her cigarettes and lit up, even though Chris was only two feet away from her. She inhaled deeply, then blew the smoke out in one long whoosh.

Chris looked at his stepmother, trying to figure the best way to say what he had to say.

"Will you please get to the damn point already." Toots took another puff, blowing the smoke over her shoulder.

"It appears that your ten million dollars has disappeared," Chris said.

Toots took a whole ten seconds before she finally found her tongue. Shaking her head from left to right so hard her topknot came loose, she crushed out her cigarette in a crystal bowl sitting on the coffee table. She immediately lit another before downing the rest of her whiskey. "Say that again, because I know I misunderstood you. My money is *gone*? All of it? That's impossible! You said it arrived in your account. If it arrived, it can't be gone! I don't fucking believe this, ten million dollars gone! I hope you know where the president of that bank lives, because I want to go there right now! Now, as in *now*!"

Chris took a deep breath. "No, you didn't misunderstand me, Toots. It's just like I said. Rodriguez explained that as soon as the money was deposited in my escrow account, before he could inform me so that I could transfer the money to *The Informer*'s bank account, it was gone. After some investigation, he managed to ascertain that it had been transferred to another bank, the Bank of Bermuda. In the Cayman Islands. Since I did not authorize the transfer, someone obviously hacked into the account and arranged to remove the money."

Chris hated giving his stepmom such ugly news her first night in town, but it couldn't be helped. He paused to give Toots time to come to terms with what he'd just told her.

Toots thought she was going to faint. "The bank is insured. They had my money in the account; if someone took it, that means they have to replace it. If someone hacked into their bank, that is not my problem. I want my money! Do not tell me the bank is going to fight me." Her hands started to shake so badly she felt like she was Katharine Hepburn during her final stages of dealing with Parkinson's. "Chris, these things only happen in the movies. There has to be some kind of mistake."

"That's what I said, but it's not the case.

I trust Emmanuel, I've dealt with him on many occasions, and if he says the money isn't there, it isn't there."

Toots refused to accept Chris's explanation. It was simply too stupid even to consider—ten million dollars of her money gone, just like that. "The bank has to be liable for it, doesn't it?" Chris's dour expression was all she needed to see to know that the bank was *not* liable. Toots took a deep breath. "Then we need to find out who took it. Isn't there a paper trail we can follow? And what about the ownership of *The Informer*? Who's going to oversee the day-to-day operations? There has to be someone at the helm. We both know a tabloid doesn't run itself."

Toots lost it then as she screamed at her stepson. "What the hell am I supposed to do, roll over and play dead? I want my goddamn money, and somebody better come up with it. The police! Did you call the police, the FBI? Hell, call in the CIA while you're at it." Toots wound down like a pricked balloon as the tears started to roll down her cheeks, and she started wringing her hands in despair and frustration.

Chris wished the floor would open up and swallow him. He hated it when women cried, because it made him feel inadequate. Especially now, because he was the person responsible for making his beloved stepmother cry. He put his arms around her, a clumsy gesture, and did his best to console her. "I'm going to do my best to make this right. Right now, this minute, we're going to consider this a blip on our radar screen. Just so you know, there is no paper trail. There is a trail, but it's an electronic one. You don't have to be a rocket scientist to hack into a bank's computer system. Any savvy computer geek can do it. Stealing ten million dollars takes a bit more skill than your average hacker has, so someone really good was involved. I have a friend of a friend who knows everything there is to know about hacking into any system. He could hack into the CIA's computer if he wanted to, but he has no desire to go to the federal pen. The only way to contact him is by e-mail. Just to be on the safe side, I sent him a quick message from my cell phone on the drive over. If anyone can help us, he's the one."

On the edge of the sofa, Toots could hardly get the words past her trembling lips. "What did he say? Promise him anything, Chris. Well, within reason you can promise him anything."

Chris pulled out his cell phone, punched in a few numbers and letters before answering Toots. "He hasn't gotten back to me yet."

"What about Abby? Does she know or suspect anything?" Toots hiccuped. This could really blow her plans to hell and back. She'd just lost ten million dollars and she was worrying about her daughter finding out how stupid she had been. Toots sighed as she wiped at her eyes.

"No, but it's only a matter of time before she figures it out. She is your daughter, Toots. How long do you think it will take?"

Toots shrugged. "We can't let that happen even if it means I have to pay out another ten million dollars to buy the paper. She'll never forgive me for deceiving her if she finds out, so we can't let that happen. No mother worth her salt, regardless of her intentions, wants her daughter to know said mother is devious, an old fool who got snookered in a business deal."

Chris shook his head. "I won't let that happen, Toots, but there is no way I will let you fork out another ten million dollars. That's damn near blackmail."

"Then what do you suggest I do?" Toots stood and began to pace in front of the fireplace. She fired up another cigarette. She'd always thought she was smart, one step ahead of everyone else, and here she was behind the proverbial eight ball, and she didn't like the feeling, not one damn little bit. And she was fighting mad.

"As much as you don't want to hear this, for now we wait. I don't want to do anything until I hear from my friend. The paper is covered for the next week at least. You know those stories go to press days, sometimes weeks, ahead of schedule."

"And if Abby finds out," Toots asked. "Then what?"

"That's a good question, Toots, but one I'm afraid I can't answer."

Chapter 18

Michael "Micky" Constantine opened the
locker for the umpteenth time. He peered
inside—empty. He hadn't made a mistake.
The envelope containing the new identity
papers for Rag was definitely gone, along
with the envelope of cash that should have
been left in its place. He stuck his hand inside the metal square again, feeling both
sides, the back, and even running his hand
along the top. Nothing. Nada. Zip. Zilch!

Fifty grand. Gone. He'd kill the slimy
bastard when he found whoever it was
that took his money. No one put one over

on Micky Constantine and got away with it. Glancing over his shoulder to make sure no one watched him, he adjusted the Glock stuffed in his waistband. If he saw the son of a bitch, he'd blow his ass away right here in the middle of Los Angeles International Airport. He corrected his thought; at least he'd make the son of a bitch think he'd blow him away. He wasn't *that* stupid. His boss, the big man, would have him tarred and feathered for sure if he pulled a stunt like that. But Micky was gonna make damn sure his boss didn't find out. Besides *the corrupter,* the dude who made all their phony documents, they were the only two people who knew of Rag's new identity, and he knew that neither of them had taken his money. That left only old Rag.

Slamming the locker door shut, Micky jerked the key out of the lock and placed it in his hip pocket. He glanced at his watch, a knockoff of a Rolex that was so good he'd almost pawned it for ten grand. He hustled outside to his Corvette, which he'd left in short-term parking. Once inside the car, he zoomed through the parking lot, zigzagging his way out of the airport. He needed to think about his next move, needed to plan everything out to the last detail. Rodwell Godfrey thought he'd pulled one over on him. He laughed, raised the volume on the CD player, jamming to Marilyn Manson's latest. When he reached the interstate, he stomped down on the gas, the odometer jumping to one hundred miles per hour in less than a minute. He glanced in his rearview mirror, making sure no cops were on his ass, then jerked from the left lane to the right lane several times before slowing down. Man, he loved the power beneath the hood. In his spare time, he tinkered with cars, loved the smell of fuel and oil. His dream was to sponsor a NASCAR driver. He could see it all now, his name displayed in bright red letters, MICKY CONSTANTINE. Someday, but not today. Now he had to concentrate on finding Rag. When he did, he'd make him regret he'd ever laid eyes on Micky.

Rodwell Archibald Godfrey, now Richard Allen Goodwin, couldn't keep the shit-eating grin off his face. He smiled at the passengers as they formed a line in front of customs. He slung the leather carry-on personalized with his old and new initials from one shoulder to the other. Using his real initials had been a stretch, but he convinced himself this was necessary since he owned too many monogrammed possessions that he refused to part with. He'd invested thousands through the years and saw no reason to toss them now. He was in another country, where no one knew about him or of his past.

Ripping off *The Informer*'s buyer had been easy. Almost too easy. He knew enough about computers and their systems to set up an account here in George Town in the Cayman Islands under his new name. From there he'd used a top-flight hacker who owed him a favor for keeping his name out of a nasty divorce action and had him hack the lawyer's escrow account before the money could be transferred to *The Informer*'s account. The hacker had the money deposited in the Goodwin account in the Bank of Bermuda in the Cayman Islands. It was like taking candy from a baby.

Rag, *Richard*, was sure the hacker had covered his tracks. And there he was in the sunny Cayman Islands with ten million dollars, plus the fifty thousand he had *forgotten* to leave in the locker where he'd arranged to pick up his new documents. He'd been impressed with the excellent quality of his documents. Driver's license, birth certificate, passport, credit card, and a social security card all in his new name. He'd had his age listed as forty-eight, knocking off a few years. Why not? He was a free man, and he could do anything his heart desired. He could certainly afford anything; price didn't matter. He felt so powerful he thought he was going to black out.

Richard had made reservations in Grand Cayman at the Westin Casuarina Resort. Though not as luxurious as he would have liked, it would do until he made other plans. At least he had requested the presidential suite. Tomorrow he would introduce himself to the president of the Bank of Bermuda. When they saw his balance,

he just knew he would be treated like royalty, certainly not the down-and-out tabloid
owner of his past.

Yes, Richard Allen Goodwin thought
as he moved through customs, life was
good.

And he was just getting started.

Chapter 19

For the first time in years, Toots didn't feel like eating her morning bowl of Froot Loops. Sitting on the terrace overlooking the colorful plant-filled lawn and watching the sunrise was so peaceful. She loved hearing the various birds as they cawed to one another, just like back home. But the early-morning magic wasn't working that morning. She wondered if it would ever work for her again. At that moment, all she wanted was an excuse to crawl back under the covers and forget her conversation with Chris.

Never a quitter, Toots squared her

shoulders as she lit her fifth cigarette, and it was only six in the morning, which meant it was nine at home, so five smokes was right on her daily schedule. She'd barely slept a wink, and she knew it showed on her face. She had showered and dressed in a bright yellow skirt and orange blouse, hoping the sunshiny colors would brighten her dull mood, but as yet, they hadn't done a damn thing but depress her. Sophie, Mavis, and Ida, or so she hoped for the latter, were due for breakfast at seven. Toots wanted to remain cheerful and positive for her friends, who were all going through crises of their own. More than anything, she didn't want them to discover she'd been taken for a fool. An old widow fooled by some computer-savvy jerk who was laughing at her. All the way to the bank.

Well, she might be old, but she sure as hell wasn't a fossil, and she was a widow many times over, so what? Maybe she wasn't as computer-savvy as some, but she could maneuver her way around a laptop as well as anyone else her age. What she couldn't tolerate was the thought of some schmuck like Tod, or whatever the hell his name was, laughing

at her behind her back. That was incom-
prehensible and damn well unacceptable.
Call it pride or an old woman getting
pissed to the teeth. Either way, she intended to find out who was behind the
loss of her ten million dollars, and *when*
she did find out, she was personally going
to make his life a living hell. There was
the money factor, for sure, but in her heart
of hearts she knew it truly wasn't about
the money, even though it was about the
money. It wasn't even the fact that she
could very well lose the opportunity to run
her own tabloid, although that was going
to sting big-time. It was Abby. As a mother,
she would do whatever it took, albeit on
the sly or not, to make sure Abby was
happy. And working elsewhere just wasn't
going to cut it for her daughter. So, as her
mother, the sucker who'd paid triple what
the paper was worth, she intended to do
something about it.

A light tap on the patio window jarred
her from further plotting the downfall of
her newfound yet unknown enemy.

Sophie, wearing her old plaid robe,
stood inside Toots's bungalow with a mug
of coffee in her hand and an unlit cigarette

in the other. She slid the patio door closed. "You didn't lock your door. What if I was some pervert just waiting to jump your bones?"

Toots blinked. After Chris had left, she'd been so upset she apparently forgot to lock up. "Like some pervert is going to attack an old lady," Toots grumbled. "Get real."

Sophie lit her cigarette and gave Toots the evil eye before she even took a sip of coffee. "I've known you too long not to know when there's a problem. So, do you want to tell me, or do I have to drag it out of you as usual? I'd rather you just spit it out because Mavis will be here any minute, and Ida's supposed to grace us with her presence this morning. If we're to have a smidgen of privacy, it's now or later. The choice is yours. The easy way or the hard way." She stubbed out her cigarette and reached for another.

"Has anyone ever told you you're nosy, and you smoke too much?" Toots asked before reaching for another cigarette. Number six. She might smoke the entire carton before the day was over. She was too old to give a good rat's ass what was good for her or not. She'd smoked since she was in high school, when it was all the rage. Before all those terrible warnings were on the boxes. Didn't matter, because Toots had no plans to quit anytime in the near future. They could bury her with a carton tucked under her arm and a cigarette hanging from her lips. She visualized the scene and laughed. She'd try and remember to have that added to her will. Sort of like Leland and his fifty-thousand-dollar bottle of scotch and his damn string band.

"You have on more than one occasion. Stop trying to change the subject. Either you want to discuss what's eating at you, or you don't." Sophie stared at her until Toots squirmed in her cushioned chair.

Toots glanced over her shoulder. "If I tell you, you have to swear on Abby's life you won't tell a soul. Not even Mavis or Ida. No one. This has to stay between us."

"I can keep a secret, Toots. You of all people should know that. How long was I married to Walter before you found out he was knocking me around?"

Toots nodded. "Of course I know that, it's just that this is . . . shameful. I'm almost too embarrassed to admit what a fool I was. Am."

A smile as wide as a football field lit up Sophie's thin face. "You had a one-night stand?"

"Oh, for God's sake, that's the last thing I want to do. I don't want to end up with a damned STD. You always revert to sex. Why is that, Sophie?"

"You sound like Ida. Truthfully, I haven't had a decent lay since I was in my forties. Do the math. And don't you dare repeat what I just said."

Toots couldn't help but laugh. Crazy-ass Sophie, truly her best friend in the world minus Mavis and sometimes Ida, always had the power to put a smile on her face no matter what the situation.

"See? You're smiling, so it can't be all that bad. Now spit it out before the girls arrive."

"I thought the deal with the paper had gone through. I signed the papers Chris faxed, sent all the proper paperwork to Henry at my bank in Charleston. Henry wired the funds to the bank here, and it was supposed to be a done deal." Toots sighed, suddenly feeling each and every one of her sixty-five years. "Last night Chris told me the money for the sale of *The Informer* had been transferred to an account in the Cayman Islands. Someone ripped me off for ten million bucks, and I do not own the paper."

"Holy shit! What are you going to do, Toots? Isn't that where rich people have offshore accounts so they don't have to pay taxes on them?" Sophie lit up again.

"I'm not sure, something like that. But the kicker is, whoever took the money from Chris's escrow account had to know that the money for the purchase of *The Informer* was supposed to arrive yesterday. The money no sooner arrived than it was gone. I have to think that whoever arranged the disappearance knew about what was going down with *The Informer*. The money is simply gone. Chris is working on finding out who our thief is, but my biggest concern is Abby. What if she finds this out? What will she think of her old mom then?"

"Toots, you worry too much. Even if Abby does manage to find out somehow, what's the big deal? So her mom owns the paper she works for. So what? Is the world going to come to an end. I don't think so. End of story.

"Assuming Abby does find out, if she doesn't want to work for you, she gets a job elsewhere. Again, end of story. I'd be more concerned with finding out the whos and whys. Abby loves you, no matter what, Toots. You should know that. You didn't raise a stupid kid."

"I know, but I did raise her to be self-reliant and independent, and that's the problem. If she thought I'd purchased *The Informer* just so she could keep her job, she'd do whatever she had to just to prove to herself that she could make it on her own without help from me or anyone else."

Sophie smiled. "Sounds like she's as stubborn as her mother."

"True."

"So what are we going to do about this besides wait around for Chris to discover the culprit?" Sophie rubbed the palms of her hands together. "This could be fun, you know, kind of like Angela Lansbury on *Murder, She Wrote.* Looks like we've got a genuine mystery to solve. I recall an e-mail from someone saying she needed some excitement in her life. If this isn't excitement, I don't know what is. Other than a decent roll in the hay, of course. Which, at this late date in my life, the odds of ever happening are slim to none."

Toots swallowed hard as she remembered how antsy she had been and how she wanted to stir up some trouble. Being ripped off to the tune of ten million dollars definitely fell into the category of trouble. Now all she had to do was smooth it out. She had Sophie's support. Toots loved that Sophie had said *we*. Maybe she could get through this without Abby discovering what a sneaky mother she was. Maybe this is just the kind of distraction she needed, though she wasn't sure what she needed to be distracted from. Either way, she had a problem, a big problem. One way or another, she had to resolve it.

"If Abby wasn't involved, I'd welcome the challenge." Toots stood up, took both of their cups, and went into the kitchen, Sophie following her. Deciding Sophie had a point, a spark of an idea started to form. "What would you say if I asked you to help set a trap for this . . . rip-off artist? It would have to remain between the two of us.

I don't want Ida or Mavis to get involved. We both know they aren't made of the same stuff we are. They're too . . . ah . . . delicate. If either one of them ever had any gusto, it's gone now." Toots smiled, thinking Ida was anything but delicate. What she was, was a griping, complaining germophobe with extreme jealousy issues. Not to mention a king-size pain in the ass. And Mavis was simply too sweet to taint with this scandal.

Sophie refilled their cups from the Krups coffeemaker. "I'd say yes, and when do we get started?"

"Soon, maybe tomorrow. Today we need to focus on getting Ida to the shrink and Mavis to the gym just as we planned. Chris said if he learned anything new, he would call me on my cell. I need some downtime to think, too."

"Think all you want, but the bottom line is, you've been ripped off for ten million bucks. If you weren't so gung ho on keeping this from Abby, I'd say let's go to the police or the feds. I bet the FBI would find it interesting to know someone stole your money and transferred it to a bank in another country. That's a crime," Sophie said virtuously.

"If it comes down to that, I suppose I won't have a choice. Fortunately, I've got more money than I know what to do with, so recovering the ten million dollars isn't life or death for me, but it is for the lowlife who had the nerve to steal from me. Did I ever tell you how much I dislike a thief? A thief and a liar usually go hand in hand." Toots turned her back to Sophie, who sat on one of the barstools at the kitchen's island.

"When Ida and Mavis get here, let's just try to act normal, like nothing is out of the ordinary. I've got to fix something for them to eat besides Froot Loops." Toots opened and closed several cabinets, removing three boxes of cereal along with a five-pound bag of sugar. From the refrigerator she took whole milk, fat-free milk, English muffins, butter, strawberry jam, and a grapefruit, placing them on the counter next to the stove.

"I hope Mavis doesn't go gaga over the jam and butter. I made sure to have plenty of Special K and fat-free milk on hand.

I want her to get some of that weight off before she goes back to Maine. Just think how surprised her neighbors will be when they see the new Mavis."

Glad for the change of subject, feeling more upbeat than she had an hour ago, Toots took three pink bowls from the cabinet and spoons from the drawer, placing them on the counter next to the cereal. Taking a serrated knife, she cut the muffins in half and put them in the stainless-steel toaster next to the Wolf range. "That's it for breakfast. I hope no one was expecting eggs Benedict or French toast. I've never been one to waste time in the kitchen."

A loud rap on the door sent Sophie scurrying. "I'm coming," she called out.

Toots started a fresh pot of coffee. She'd need megadoses of caffeine to get through whatever the day held in store for her and the others.

She heard Ida crying and Coco yapping in Mavis's arms as they entered the bungalow. Toots sighed. For one very long minute, she wished she was back in Charleston. She just knew it was going to be a *very* long and *very* tiring day.

Chapter 20

Abby gathered up the papers containing the sliver of information she'd printed off the Internet last night. She stuffed them into the pocket of her well-worn leather briefcase, a graduation gift from Chris. At the time, she'd thought it a dull, boring gift, but now that she was a full-fledged tabloid reporter, she never went anywhere without it slung over her shoulder. In the kitchen, she scooped a handful of doggie treats from a canister that read CHESTER'S DELIGHT into a Ziploc bag. Never knowing when she'd need to keep Chester calm and quiet, she always carried a supply with her wherever she went. In a true emergency, she was known to whip out one of several stuffed dachshunds she kept safely stored away in her trunk. Chester loved the colored weenie dogs with the squeakers inside. His record for dismantling and dismembering one of the cuddly creatures was 38.2 seconds.

She grabbed Chester's leash off its hook, checked her appearance in the mirror one last time, then whistled, her sign to Chester that they were about to leave. She'd been taking him to work with her since he was a puppy. One of the few benefits of working for Rag. Rag, too, was an avid animal lover; in her opinion, his only saving grace. He'd told her to use the dog to gain access to the stars who were active supporters of PETA, People for the Ethical Treatment of Animals. With Rag, there was always an ulterior motive. So far, Chester's biggest challenge on the job had been a pesky poodle belonging to Hollywood's current star of the month, Lori Locks. Abby interviewed her after she'd won the People's Choice Award for her role as a ditzy blonde in the comedic movie *Blondes Have More Dumb*. It was the perfect part for the collagen-filled, silicone-inflated twenty-three-year-old. Abby was sure it had been created exclusively for her. Personally, she thought the acting was atrocious. Abby joked to anyone who listened that Lori simply played herself.

Chester nudged her hand with his nose, startling her. "Okay, boy. Let's not get in such a hurry. Rag is nowhere to be found this morning. We can take our time." She fluffed him between the ears, then opened the front door. The big German shepherd shot out like a rocket, stopping next to the passenger door. Once he was inside, she strapped him securely in his seat belt, closing the door and locking it before sliding into the driver's seat.

The ignition turned over on the first try, for which Abby was grateful. Last week, when she'd learned through a sometimes reliable source that George Mellow, an aging Hollywood hunk, was falling-down drunk at Grauman's Chinese Theatre, where his current sci-fi flick had premiered, she'd intended to break all speed limits to make front-page news. It hadn't happened. Her MINI Cooper parked in its usual spot at the office was dead as a doornail when she'd tried to start it. Just her luck Mr. Not-So-Mellow's face was splashed across the front page of *The Enquirer* the next day. Abby wasn't so sure her car's dead battery hadn't involved a little sabotaging from her rival at *The Enquirer,* Jane Kane. Did anyone in Hollywood use their real names anymore? Jane Kane's real name was Gertrude Marquett. Actually, if Abby had a name that silly, she would have resorted to using a pseudonym as well.

Speaking of names, Abby hadn't found diddly-squat on the new owner of *The Informer* in her research. She had stayed up until the wee hours scouring the Internet for documents related to the transaction. She thought it more than odd the two other major tabloids made no mention of its sale. Also strange was the fact that Rag hadn't sent her a dozen e-mails or called her ten times already. On a normal day, he'd have had her running all over Los Angeles searching for the latest scoop. Maybe he'd called in sick again. He did that quite often, especially on Mondays after he'd spent the weekend boozing and gambling in Vegas. Maybe one of his bookies had called in a marker, and old Rag was in seclusion. If so, it was fine by her. She hated the slimeball. *The Informer* functioned just fine without his input. Really, all they needed him for was his signature on their bimonthly pay-checks. And that, too, was about to be history. She just prayed the new owner or owners had some scruples and a great deal of business ethics. Maybe with a pro-fessional at the helm, *The Informer* might have a fighting chance at becoming more than a laughingstock in the world of tabloid journalism.

Abby arrived at the offices, located in Hollywood on Santa Monica Boulevard. Driving through the usual throngs of tourists, monkeys playing cymbals, and stargazers, and any other oddity that Cal-ifornians considered normal, Abby care-fully steered the MINI Cooper toward the back of the office building. Parking in her usual space, she grabbed her briefcase before letting Chester out. He raced to the back door, waiting for her to catch up. Good old Chester, there wasn't a more loyal and protective animal alive. At least none she'd ever owned. Occasionally she would pull a twenty-four-hour shift, with Chester remaining faithfully by her side. She felt guilty for keeping him cooped up but always made sure to reward him with a trip to the beach, where he would run until he collapsed from exhaustion. They were both due for a break. Maybe she would ask her mother and godmothers if they wanted to spend a day at the beach with her. It would give Chester and Coco a chance to play and get acquainted.

Inside the building, she crept down a narrow hall leading to her office, which was situated directly across from Rag's. Before she got involved in her next story, she stopped by Rag's office. The door was closed as usual. She put her ear to the door to see if she could hear muted conversation, meaning he was chewing someone out on the phone, but she couldn't hear a thing. She tapped on the door, waiting for his usual rude reply. Two more loud knocks and still nothing. Taking a chance, she twisted the doorknob, finding it unlocked. That was unusual. Rag always kept his office door locked when he was out of the building. She stepped inside and looked around, but there was no sign of her boss, and there was no sign that he'd been in earlier and left. There was no smell of burnt coffee emanating from the outdated Mr. Coffee machine, and all six of his televisions were turned off. The computer was black and silent. This couldn't be good. Rag *never* turned off his computer. And everyone at the paper knew he was tuned to the E! Networks for all their infamous gossip twenty-four/seven. Something was very wrong.

Abby whirled around when she heard Chester growling in the doorway. Even her dog disliked Rag. "Shhh, it's okay, boy. Come on, let's get out of here. This place is suddenly giving me the creeps." She closed the door, wondering if she was the only reporter in the office. Crossing the hall to her own office, she went inside and turned on her computer. She then turned on her TV to FOX News, dropped her briefcase on top of her desk, and opened the shutters to allow for a bit of light in the dank old building. Though her office space was somewhat on the shabby side, Abby had taken extra pains to make her work environment pleasing to her eye. She'd painted the once gunmetal gray walls a soft beige, replaced the old-fashioned metal blinds with plantation shutters, and added a variety of green plants. In a fit of something she couldn't define, she'd brought her antique cherry desk, which had once belonged to her father, to the office at her own expense, placing it squarely in the center of the room. Plush green throw rugs she'd paid for herself hid the scarred wood floors. Framed pictures of the few covers she'd made hung in matching wood frames on the wall opposite her window. As the light from her single window reflected off them, the actors and actresses appeared pale and distorted, with sun slashing across them.

Abby was usually the first to arrive in the morning. Even though her job required late hours on the nights she had to hit the nightclubs, she still managed to get to the office no later than nine.

She filled Chester's water bowl, hung his leash over the back of a chair before plopping down in her well-worn office chair. "Okay, Chester, you can relax now."

Religiously she went through this same routine. As soon as she told Chester he could relax, he left his post by her door and curled up in an old recliner she'd brought to the office when he was a pup. Dogs liked routine, and Chester was no exception.

Remembering the papers she'd stuck in her briefcase, she removed them, scanning their content once again. Other than discovering that *The Informer* had sold for an outrageous sum of money, she'd gained little from her Internet search. She still thought it odd, though, that the other papers hadn't run with the news. Then again, maybe it wasn't so odd, since they all hated Rag.

Where the hell is my boss? Maybe since he sold the paper, he's flown the coop. Vegas most likely. Abby guessed if that was the case, then it was only a matter of time before he went through every bit of the money he'd made from the sale. She doubted he'd even turned a profit. Rag made no bones about reminding the staff the paper was knee-deep in debt. She'd always assumed he was lying to keep them on their toes for fear of losing their jobs. Now she wasn't so sure. Putting her boss's financial woes aside for the moment, she read through her e-mail, answered those requiring an answer, then began her search of the latest celebrity haunts. In the past she'd gotten some great leads off the Web sites, but as usual, right when she thought she had a scoop, one of the other papers seemed to beat her to it.

An hour of searching and finding no new information on any of Hollywood's current top ten stars, she leaned back in her chair and allowed her mind to stray to last night's dinner with her mother and two of the three Gs, as she thought of them. Of course she couldn't forget Chris. Even though she'd pretended otherwise, he'd pissed her off big-time when he'd arranged for a taxi to take her home. Or was it her idea? Profusely apologetic, he said he had forgotten an earlier engagement and couldn't take her home. *Bullshit,* she thought. More than likely he'd received a text message from some bimbo on that high-tech cell phone he kept glancing at when he thought no one was watching. Meow! Why did she care? she asked herself. It was more than obvious Chris was a player. He hadn't been voted one of LA's top ten bachelors for nothing. Though she had an unwritten rule about how she received information, the unwritten rule being she would never ask Chris for an inside scoop, news was slow that day and she told herself she was truly desperate, so she decided to break her rule. Kind of. Sort of. Before she could change her mind, she punched in Chris's personal cell phone number.

One ring, two, then three. She heard his voice mail. "Hey, this is Chris, you know what to do."

"Yes, I know what to do. That has to be the lamest message ever to come out of Hollywood. I can cram this phone down your throat and hope you choke on it, that's what I can do." Abby pushed the END button. Chester's ears perked up at Abby's tone. "Never mind," she said to the dog. "That wasn't one of my better ideas. I'll find a damn story, I always do."

"Woof!" Having voiced his opinion, Chester went back to sleep.

"That's right. Christopher Clay is a jerk. I don't need him even though I'd cut off my left foot to get him." Chester opened one eye and decided no comment was called for.

Yeah, right, she thought. What she really needed, no, what she really *wanted* him for didn't have a thing to do with writing a story for *The Informer.*

Nope, not a thing. Her needs where Mr. Chris Clay was concerned had nothing to do with work. *If only the feeling were mutual.* Abby knew she'd never be more to Chris than his annoying stepsister.

Chapter 21

Though Chris knew that the missing ten million dollars was in an account in the Bank of Bermuda in the Cayman Islands, now he was up against a stone wall. Neither he nor his private investigator ever imagined a hurricane would impede their investigation.

According to the latest news on The Weather Channel, tropical storm Deborah had been upgraded to hurricane status. What were the odds of that happening? Eighty-mile-an-hour winds were being reported, with waves as high as ten feet

battering the smaller barrier islands. Fore-
casters were predicting a minimum of ten
inches of rain. All flights coming in and out
of Owen Roberts International Airport were
canceled. Areas of Grand Cayman were
already reporting a loss of power.

Any thoughts of flying to the island to
investigate further were dead in the
water—so to speak—at least temporarily.
Chris called a friend of a friend who knew
the hacker to see if he'd learned anything
new via the Internet. Nothing. They were
right back where they had started. He re-
gretted involving himself in the whole
transaction, but it'd always been hard for
him to say no to anything that concerned
Toots. She was the only mother he'd ever
known. Toots had always treated him
fairly, kindly, and, most important of all,
she'd shown him unconditional love. That
alone was reason enough to help her
when she'd asked. Chris couldn't wait to
get his hands on the bastard who had
screwed her over. Ripping off old ladies
was as low as whale shit, lower actually. It
didn't matter that this particular old lady
was a multimillionaire. As usual, Typhoon
Toots was trying to save the day, some-

thing she did quite often, though this time it'd bounced back, biting her in the ass.

Chris finished his cup of coffee, placing the delicate china cup in the dishwasher next to three others from a matching set of sixteen. There were two bowls on the bottom rack, each with a ring of pale green mint-chocolate-chip ice cream hardened around the edges. Two spoons and a single solitary butter knife comprised a week's worth of dishes. He debated if he should run the dishwasher now or wait another week. Who was he kidding? He could wait an entire month before running the damned thing. It wasn't as though he had dinner parties and friends over to use the dishes in the first place. A sad testament to his life as one of LA's top ten bachelors. Lately, single life had lost its glow more than he really cared to admit. He had no desire to endure another evening with another wannabe star. Chris yearned for a relationship with a real woman, not the plumped-up, dyed-haired, bronzed space cadets he usually escorted for an evening of seen and be seen. When his thoughts headed down this path, he knew exactly where they were leading. Straight to dear little Abby. He'd made her angry last night at dinner, but it couldn't be helped. Unknown to her, Toots had sent him a text message asking him to come to her bungalow to discuss the sale of the paper. He'd seen her watching him out of the corner of her eye, saw the smart-ass look she'd cast his way when she thought he wasn't looking. It is what it is, he thought before filling the dishwasher's compartment with detergent and turning the knob to the wash cycle. There! He felt like he'd just accomplished a major feat.

With nothing more on his immediate agenda, Chris was about to take a long, hot shower when he heard his cell phone buzzing. He didn't want to answer, but given Toots's current situation, he wasn't about to let his voice mail pick up.

"Chris Clay," he said, using his most professional tone on the slim chance it was the bank calling.

"I don't believe you've ever used the word *hello* in your life."

Abby.

"We both know that's not true." Chris leaned against the kitchen counter, grinning from ear to ear, his heart pumping furiously. Damn, he felt light-headed.

"Well, I, for one, have never heard you say hello. So there."

"Maybe in your off-hours, you can stop by to instruct me on proper telephone etiquette, then I could instruct you on a few ways to use that mouth of yours."

Did I actually just say what I think I did? Yes, you stupid idiot, you did!

"What did you just say?" He heard the surprise in her voice.

"Nothing. I talk to myself sometimes. So, have you seen your mother today? I really enjoyed meeting your godmothers last night. I can see why you're so crazy about them." *Well, that should go down as the most titillating dialogue of the day.*

"Wait until you meet Ida, you might have a change of heart. I love her to death, even though she's . . . different from the others."

"You know what they say," Chris stated. "Variety is the spice of life."

Shit! Shit! Shit!

"Not for everyone," Abby shot back.

"And what is that supposed to mean?" Chris asked. He really enjoyed sparring with Abby on the rare occasions when they spoke on the phone. He loved her quick wit and her *smart-assness,* if there was such a word.

"Stop it! You always do this to me when I call you. Then you have the nerve to ask why I never come over to visit you. You know exactly what I'm talking about, too," Abby snapped.

"You're a poor sport, Abigail Simpson."

"Takes one to know one. I didn't say you could call me Abigail, either. My father is the only man who's ever had the privilege. Just so you know," Abby snapped again.

"Yes, you did tell me that a few times, *Abby.* I was trying to inject some levity into the conversation."

"Look, cut the crap, okay?" *Oh, God, why am I being so . . . so . . . bitchy?* "I called you on . . . a professional matter."

"Well well well! Am I hearing Abby Simpson asking me for a favor? I seem to recall your saying you would never, and I mean *never,* resort to using my professional services. I remember you saying something to the tune of how you despised bloodsucking lawyers, and that their version of the First Amendment was extremely warped. Not that I want to bust your bubble, sweetheart, but I am a member, and still in good standing, I might add, of that bloodsucking society. So what can I do for you?" Chris asked. He hadn't had this much fun since . . . since he'd sat next to her at dinner last night, if you could call sitting on pins and needles fun. Just thinking about Abby always made him smile.

"Forget it, Mr. Clay. I'd rather—"

"Just say it, Ab." Whatever he had was hers for the asking. Didn't she know that?

He heard her suck in her breath, then exhale. He knew she was already regretting the call.

"IneedastoryandIneeditnow."   She blurted out the words so fast, he thought at first he had misunderstood her.

I need a story and I need it now. Hmmmm.

He wanted to ask what it was worth to her but knew how much professional and familial pride it'd taken for her to make the call, let alone follow through with her request.

"I'm all yours, Abby. Anything you need," Chris said, realizing he'd never uttered more truthful words in his entire life.

The fact was, dear old—*well, I'm not* that *old*—Christopher Lee Clay, was/is totally, completely, madly in love with Abigail Simpson.

"Anything, huh?" Chris heard the humor in her voice.

"Anything, Abby. I'd go to the ends of the earth for you, you know that." If she didn't know he was more than a little bit in love with her, surely she would know it, given what he'd just blurted out. Dickweed that he was, he knew he would have to say the actual words out loud before he could hope for any kind of reaction from Abby. Even then, she'd probably stomp him to death.

"Thanks, but you don't need to go that far. Just to the Buzz Club with me tonight. Like I said, I need a story."

Chris had a date with a potential client, another airhead. He couldn't wait to call and cancel.

"What time would you like me to pick you up?" In the blink of an eye, they were back on a professional level.

"I'll meet you there. Just in case . . . something comes up. Is ten o'clock too late?"

"Ten o'clock is perfect, Abby. Just perfect." *Perfect like you*, he wanted to add, but figured he'd gone too far already.

"I'll see you there."

With bells on, Chris thought. With a lightness to his step, Chris practically danced to the shower. Once inside, with the hot spray sluicing down his well-muscled back, he started to sing at the top of his lungs. It was turning into the best day he'd had in a long, long time.

Chapter 22

"I promise you won't die, Ida. If I thought that for a skinny minute, do you think I'd subject myself to such an environment? Remember, I have a daughter to consider, and hopefully one day grandchildren. You and the others will be surrogate great-godmothers if Abby has a child. This is the last time I am going to ask you to open the door and come outside. If you don't . . . if you don't, I will not be responsible for the consequences. Do you hear me, Ida?" Toots said in a soft, soothing tone as she stood outside Ida's door. A soft soothing voice that was a hair away from turning into a snarl.

"For God's sake already, enough is enough. Let me inside, and I'll drag her ass to the car." Sophie shoved Toots to the side before she pushed Ida's door wide open to see her cowering behind it when she entered the room. Seeing her old friend in such a state brought tears to her eyes. Ida was decked out in something that covered her person from head to toe, including latex gloves and a surgeon's mask. Even from where she was standing, she could see Ida trembling. "Ida, I know this is hard for you. You have to trust us. There is no germ out here that's going to kill you. Now get your ass to the car. If you don't, I'm going to find a sweaty construction worker and have him toss you over his shoulder and haul you out to the car. Is that what you want?" Sophie asked, all traces of her normal silliness gone.

Ida blinked rapidly, shaking her head from side to side. "Thomas died from a germ," she whispered.

"For God's sake, the whole world knows

Thomas died of E. coli. The chances of you picking up *any* kind of life-threatening germ is so slim, it doesn't bear thinking about. Do you really want Toots to think you're a wimp? She spent all that money to get us out here, and this is how you pay her back. You *SAID* you were *IN* on this caper. It means you do your share. We all agreed to make this trip believing you were going to be part of it. Now, enough of this goddamn bullshit. Move your ass, and I mean move your ass. Like fucking now, Ida!" Sophie screeched.

"Sophie, stop it!" Toots hissed from the other side of the door.

"Kiss my ass, Toots. Listen, Ida, it's now or never. Do you really want to spend the rest of your life disinfecting yourself and anything you might have to touch? I don't think you do, so what I am about to do is for your own good." Without another word, Sophie grabbed Ida by her latex-covered hands and dragged her out the door. Once they were outside, Sophie slammed the door to the bungalow, knowing Ida would fight her and try to run back inside. Pulling and shoving Ida like a reluctant child, she wrapped one arm around her shoulder and motioned for Toots to do the same. Dragging their friend, they ran as fast as they could to Mavis's bungalow, where she was waiting outside with Coco on her leash.

Mavis scooped Coco up in her arms. "What's wrong with her? Did she have a spell? What?" she asked as she waddled along, trying to catch up with them.

"Does she look all right?" Sophie snapped. "Of course she's not all right. She's off in the Twilight Zone at the moment."

"Yip, yip!"

"Good Lord, Sophie, do you always have to be so blunt?" Toots asked as they pulled Ida down the pathway toward the exit, where a limo waited.

"Listen to the damn dog. Even she knows Ida isn't playing with a full deck. And, yes, I suppose I could phrase it better, but that's not my style. All of you, just handle it, or I'm outta here. I mean it. We agreed to come here at your insistence to try and do something good for Abby, and this *schmuck*," Sophie said, pointing to Ida, "is screwing up the works. I'm too old for this shit, and so are the rest of you, so let's get it in gear and make things happen."

"Maybe you should consider a new style," Toots said, but her tone left a lot to be desired. Secretly, she applauded Sophie's in-your-face attitude.

"I will when hell freezes over, okay? Now, let's get Mrs. Clean to the car. You can worry about my style later."

With Mavis and Coco lagging behind, Sophie and Toots half dragged a protesting Ida toward the hotel's exit.

Toots grappled for something to say. "I know you don't like us very much right now, Ida, but at some point I know you'll thank both of us when we get you back up to snuff. Try to remember what life was like before you went nuts. Right now, speaking strictly for myself, I don't give a good rat's ass if you ever speak to me again or not. I'm going to get you back to functioning the way you did then if it kills me. Are you listening to me, Ida? Just nod if you want your old life back."

A spark from Ida. "Yes, I would like that. Very much. It's just . . . *hard*."

"There's hard, then there's *hard*," Mavis said breathlessly. "Do you have any idea how hard it is for me to resist calling room service and ordering up a giant hot fudge sundae? But I want to live, so I just ask myself, what's more important, my life or a hot fudge sundae? That's why I went to the gym this morning, where I met a wonderful young lady who promises to help me lose weight. I did seven whole minutes on the treadmill. Seven minutes! Tomorrow my goal is nine minutes," she said proudly. "All you have to do, Ida, is to take off all that crap and fucking do what we all tell you!"

Toots and Sophie gasped at Mavis's choice of words. Mavis never, as in *never,* said a bad word; it was the schoolteacher in her.

"Unlike you, I have nothing to live for," Ida said without a trace of emotion. "When Thomas died, I died."

Sophie chimed right in. "If that isn't the biggest crock of shit, I don't know what is! How many times have you been married? I've heard that song and dance from you so many times I've lost count. Has it ever occurred to you that you might be better off alone? Don't answer that, Ida."

With more venom than necessary,

Sophie continued, "I've known you for fifty years, and not once in all these years have you ever been without a man. I think it's time you got your act together and stopped depending on other people, especially men, and toss your daily RSVP to your own damned pity party. You know something, Ida? You just might find out that life isn't all about you! Stand on your own two feet for a change. I can't believe what a pathetic old woman you've allowed yourself to become!" Out of breath, Sophie clamped her jaw tight, angrier than she'd ever been. She decided she wasn't finished. "Where do you get off thinking the world is your personal oyster? As far as I'm concerned, and I think I speak for Toots and Mavis, you, Ida, are a failure as a woman, as a godmother, and as a friend. I refuse to play your stupid 'poor me' game anymore."

Toots took a deep breath. "I guess we all know how you really feel now."

"It's just the uncensored version of what I see. You know I call it like it is. What's the point of adding all the niceties if you're lying? I don't do lies, Toots. Not anymore."

The limo, a white Lincoln Town Car, waited beneath the portico as they forced Ida ahead. "I don't want to do this. I've changed my mind."

"Tough," said Sophie. "You're going to do it whether you want to or not. Right, Toots?" Sophie gave her the evil eye, daring Toots not to support her.

"Ida, Sophie is right. You know what else? Sophie did speak for me, and, by the way Mavis is nodding, she spoke for her, too. Resign yourself to the fact that you are going to the doctor today. One more word out of you, and I will personally slug you."

Toots mouthed "she's gone" to Sophie and Mavis. This was getting old fast.

The limo driver walked around to the passenger side to open the door. "Can I assist you?" he asked, looking at Ida, who was trying to wiggle free.

"No, we're fine. Just get ready to burn rubber when we get her inside," Sophie said. "She might try to jump out, so you'd better keep your speed up, too."

Arms flailing and flapping, Toots and Sophie managed to force Ida into the backseat. "Get in, Mavis," Sophie shouted. "Mavis, sit on her if you have to."

Mavis waddled as fast as her sausage legs would go. With a surprisingly new speed, she and Coco climbed into the car without any assistance. Toots crawled in next, then Sophie.

"Tromp on it," Sophie shouted to the driver.

"Oh"—Mavis clapped her pudgy hands—"this is just like in the movies!"

"Well, I, for one, wouldn't pay a dime to see this movie," Toots commented drily.

Ida sat scrunched in the corner, staring listlessly out the window as they raced down Beverly Hills Boulevard to the Center for Mind and Body, where she had an appointment with renowned psychiatrist Dr. Benjamin Sameer, courtesy of Dr. Joe Pauley. He'd made sure Toots knew what he had done was above and beyond the call of duty. What it also meant was Toots was now on the hook for his wife's next do-good project.

"Me, either," Sophie added, never missing an opportunity to get her two cents' worth in. "Can we smoke in here? I need a cigarette."

"Me, too, and no, we can't smoke. It says so right there." Toots pointed to a

small rectangular sign displaying a cigarette within a circle and a forward slash
running through it.

Fifteen minutes later, they passed
through the gates leading to the Center for
Mind and Body. Sophie strained to look out
the window. "Look at this place, Ida, it's all
white and clean-looking."

Ida dared a glimpse out her window.

"This place looks like the Taj Mahal,"
Toots said. "I think Dr. Sameer is from
India."

"I don't care if he's from Timbuktu, as
long as he can do something to help Ida.
If not, I'll go nuts, and you'll have to bury
Walter," Sophie said as she admired the
manicured lawns, the bright white build-
ings scattered throughout the pristine
grounds. "Aren't people from India really
clean? Or are they really dirty? I can't recall which it is."

"I wouldn't know, Sophie. I believe I've
heard somewhere that they bathe before
a meal, a purification sort of thing among
Hindus," Toots said.

"That's wonderful. Isn't that wonderful,
Ida? The doctor will understand exactly
where you're coming from," Mavis said.

Sophie rolled her eyes. Toots grinned.

"Do I have to do this?" Ida asked, as the limo came to a stop.

Toots cast Sophie a "not-now" look before answering. "Yes, you do have to do it, Ida. All your options just ran out. Just think of the freedom you'll have before you know it."

"And all the money you'll save when you don't have to buy those gloves and bleach and soap and that other crap you use to make *your* world a better place," Sophie sniped.

"Snap to it, Ida, we have to go inside. We certainly don't want to keep Dr. Sameer waiting, especially since he's seeing you as a special favor," Toots said.

Their driver, ever the gentleman, opened the door, stepping aside as the women crawled out of the limousine. Toots reached inside her clutch bag, removed a hundred-dollar bill, and tucked it in the driver's hand. "Would you mind waiting here?" Though she'd hired the limo indefinitely, she wasn't sure if she had clarified that she wanted the driver to wait for them.

The driver glanced at the bill Toots had

thrust in his hand before he answered. "Not at all."

"Fine, then let's get started. Show-time, girls!" Typhoon Toots said dramatically.

Together, they assisted Ida as she walked up the stairs, her head lolling to the side like a rag doll's. "Cooperate, Ida, or I will strip you naked right here in front of the door. That means pick up your damn feet and pretend you're alive."

Inside the office, they were greeted by a pleasant young woman wearing a red-and-gold sari made of silk. She had soulful brown eyes, honey-colored skin, and a welcoming smile that lit up the room and put them all at ease.

"You must be Mrs. McGullicutty. I'm Amala. The doctor will be with you very soon." She clasped her hands together as though in prayer. "May I offer you ladies a cool drink, some tea?" Toots looked at Sophie, daring her to open her mouth.

"I am dying for a cigarette. Is there a smoking area around here?"

The young woman smiled. "As a matter of fact, we have a specially ventilated smoking room because Dr. Sameer smokes cigars. He says it helps him think. If you'll follow me, I'll take you there."

Sophie flipped the bird to Toots before she and Mavis, leading Coco on her leash, followed Amala to a door located in the rear of the building. "My father, Dr. Sameer, enjoys having his cigars out here." She gestured to a beautiful courtyard of sorts. Stone benches beneath a vaulted ceiling made of marble did indeed make it seem like a room. The area looked like something out of an Indiana Jones movie. Lush, colorful flowers in giant urns, palm trees as high as the clouds, and verdant shrubbery created a calm, relaxing atmosphere.

"I'm almost afraid to light up out here," Sophie said.

"Over here." Amala motioned for her to follow. "You place ashes and discard your cigar or cigarette inside this urn."

Sophie eyed the urn with a smidgen of alarm. It looked like it held ashes all right, but not the kind that came from tobacco. More like human cremains, in her opinion the worst word anyone had ever invented. For a split second, Sophie had doubts about Dr. Sameer. Maybe he torched his patients and disposed of their ashes while taking a quick smoke break. Amala left her alone, saying she had to return to a patient.

"Oh . . . sure, that's why we're here." Sophie waited until Amala was inside before lighting up.

Mavis and Coco waddled along outside, keeping their distance. "Sophie, I wish you would stop smoking. I hate to see what it does to you. You are so dependent on those things. You could have waited." This last was said in such an accusing tone, Sophie felt ashamed. She *should* have waited.

"Isn't that kind of like the pot calling the kettle black?" Sophie shot back, then wished she had kept quiet. At least Mavis was trying and sticking to her diet. She made a mental note to quit smoking the first of the year. A wonderful New Year's resolution. Ha!

Mavis put Coco down, and the little Chihuahua proceeded to pee all over the sidewalk. "You're right it is, but at least I'm trying to do something about it. That's more than I can say for you and Toots. I don't mean to come off as an old stick-in-the-mud, but it is a nasty habit, and you know it. You can't smoke anywhere in public anymore, so that should tell you something. And your fingers are turning yellow from the nicotine, and so are your teeth."

"I know it's nasty, and I might quit someday, but not now. I enjoy it too much to give it up. I might make it my New Year's resolution." There, that was a verbal confirmation that she was seriously considering giving up the terrible habit.

Toots barreled through the door, digging inside her purse for a cigarette the second she stepped outside. She lit up, then walked over and sat down beside Sophie.

"The doctor just took Ida into his office. If he can't help her, or if Ida refuses the help, I think we better prepare to commit ourselves—maybe *really* commit ourselves if this keeps up. That scene at the hotel wore me out."

"Yeah, I hear you. I'm not going to pamper her ass anymore," Sophie said.

"Try and be nice to her," Mavis pleaded.

Toots glanced over at Sophie to see her reaction.

All three women burst out laughing at the same time.

Chapter 23

An hour later, Dr. Sameer and Toots escorted Ida to the waiting limo, Sophie and Mavis trailing behind. "The doctor said this is going to be much easier to cure than you think. He really wants you to take the medication, says it will speed up the healing process, sort of a boost type of thing. I know how you feel about taking medication, but you have to try, Ida. At the risk of repeating myself, this is no way to live."

"I know, Teresa. I'm just so *afraid,*" Ida said. "I'll take the medication if you think I should."

"It doesn't matter what I think, it's what the doctor thinks that matters. I told you, the man is the best in his field. If it was me, I'd move heaven and earth to get my old life back, but it's all up to you, Ida. I did my share. You're on your own now. In other words, girlfriend, this is where the rubber meets the road." Toots stood aside while the driver opened the door.

Careful not to touch anything, Ida, tears dripping down her cheeks, slipped inside the limo. Toots followed, then Sophie and Mavis. Coco curled up on her mistress's lap.

They were barely out of the parking lot before Sophie made an announcement. "Ida, listen, I owe you an apology for the way I spoke to you earlier. I don't know what you're going through, but I've been down a few unpleasant roads myself, so I just want you to know that you will get well. I have a lot of faith in you. Bad times don't last forever. Right, Toots?"

Toots knew Sophie referred to the many years of abuse she'd suffered. She shrugged.

Ida smiled, a genuine smile. "Thank you for saying that."

"I'm not the ogre I make myself out to be at times." Sophie grinned. "But sometimes, Ida, like now, you irritate the shit out of me. Toots is right, you need to get with the program here."

"Bullshit, you're worse," Toots quipped.

"Now, girls, that will be enough of that," Mavis chastised in a loud, firm voice. "Oh, goodness, I sounded just like Sister Mary Elizabeth, didn't I?"

Sister Mary Elizabeth was the meanest nun in the whole world, or so they'd thought their freshman year.

"No one sounds like Sister Mary Elizabeth. I really hated her. I wonder what happened to her?" Toots asked.

"I used to think she'd scare the devil right out of hell. I'm sure she's dead and gone by now. Remember how she used to tell us men, not money, were the root of all evil? I think she might have been onto something even back then. She had to be at least a hundred and ten when we were in high school." Sophie cackled.

They all laughed, Ida included.

"We sure do have some great memories," Mavis said.

"Some of us don't. Remember the

prom, Ida? When you were chosen prom queen?"

Ida laughed, actually *laughed.* "I do, and I don't want to be reminded of it. It was the worst day of my life."

"That can't be. You said when Toots snatched Jerry away from you, *that* was the worst day of your life."

"Sophie, zip it up! I swear you are the biggest troublemaker I've ever seen. Do you get some kind of sick delight out of tormenting us? Now be quiet and let's enjoy the scenery. I'm tired of arguing with you," Toots said in a tone that meant it was final and there would be no more talk of Ida's night at the prom.

"Well, *excuse* me, Your Royal Highness. Leave it to you to rain on my parade," Sophie shot back.

Toots's cell phone rang, saving her from further discussion. She pulled the little black square out of her clutch bag. "Hello. Abby! Of course, we'd love to. Hang on a minute." Toots looked over at Ida. "Ida, are you up to taking a tour of *The Informer*?"

Toots saw fear rearrange Ida's perfectly defined features. "No, no. I'm not ready for that yet, but tell Abby I will someday."

"Toots, do you think I can bring Coco with us? I would hate to leave her at the bungalow. She gets so lonely."

"Abby, Ida isn't feeling up to a tour just now. But Mavis wants to know if it's all right if she brings Coco along."

"Absolutely. Chester is in my office as we speak. This will give the two of them a chance to get acquainted."

"Then we'll be there as soon as we drop Ida off at the hotel. I'm so excited, Abby, you know how much I love your tabloid!"

"Yes, I do. I'll see you in about an hour, then," Abby said. "Ask your driver if he knows where we're located."

"Of course, hold on." More muffled sounds. "Yes, he says everyone in LA knows where *The Informer* is. I'll see you soon."

"Okay, Mom. Bye."

Toots put the phone back inside her purse.

Abby hit the END button on the phone.

Since she now had time to kill before her guests arrived, Abby decided to go back online. She did a few searches, hoping something new would appear on the sale of the paper. When nothing new came up, she used her cell phone to call Rag for the hundredth time. This definitely wasn't normal. While Rag was a bona fide jerk, it wasn't like him not to let anyone know he wasn't coming into the office. Even on the days when he was suffering from a hangover and his weekend jaunts to Vegas, he always called with some kind of cockamamie excuse. For the umpteenth time, she got his voice mail and left another message that was unlike any message she'd ever left before: "This is Abby. Look, dammit, if you're going to skip out, you need to let one of us know. I hope to hell you didn't spend the payroll yesterday because this is the week we're supposed to get paid. Call me as soon as you get this message." Abby tossed the phone on top of her desk. Maybe she should take a ride to Rag's apartment, just to make sure he was alive. It was entirely possible that he could have fallen, especially given the fact that he drank so much.

Abby looked at the clock on the wall. She had enough time to race over to his apartment and get back before her mother and the others arrived. A morbid thought hit her. She called her mother a second time and told her what she was going to do.

"Mom, sorry to bug you. I just realized I have an errand that I can't put off. Can you wait a couple of hours before coming by?"

"No problem, Abby. Actually, it works out just fine, and we'll have enough time to freshen up. We'll see you in a little while."

Abby grabbed her briefcase, wondering what she'd ever done to deserve such a wonderful parent. Though she'd grown up with more stepfathers than the norm, her mother had never neglected her in any way. If anything, when it came to her needs, she usually told whomever she was married to at the time that Abby was more important than he was. She meant it, too. Her mother often swore she jinxed the men she married, even going so far as telling the third or fourth that all her previous husbands had died, and if he wanted to bow out gracefully, do it before the wedding because there was no way

Teresa Amelia Loudenberry was going to be humiliated by being left at the altar.

Abby grabbed Chester's leash. "Let's go for a ride."

Hearing the magic words, Chester bolted for the door and stood waiting. Chester walked out the door and down the dark hallway, stopping when he reached the exit stairs to the door. Abby swore he was smarter than most of the men she'd dated. Actually, she was sure of it. Those idiots didn't bother to stop and wait for her at the door. "You're a good guy, Chester. Maybe you'll meet the girl of your dreams today. Something tells me in your case, size won't matter."

The shepherd cocked his head to the side to look at his mistress. Abby knew he understood every word she said. On the ground floor, Abby stopped to buy a bottle of water from the soda machine.

Abby's yellow MINI Cooper looked like a ray of sunshine after she had been inside the dark office. The main reason she bought the car in the first place was because it reminded her of a big golden sun. Her thoughts took her back to the office as she wondered if the new owners, if she ever learned who they were, would spring for a remodeling job. A few windows and some fresh paint would make all the difference in the world to the grimy interior.

"Inside, Chester." She unlocked the passenger door, strapped Chester into his seat belt, then scurried around to the driver's side.

Traffic was terrible on Santa Monica Boulevard, nothing new there. She watched the tourists while waiting at a traffic light. They were young, old, large, small, and of every nationality in the world. Some carried book bags filled to the brim, others had huge cameras strapped around their necks, and without fail she spotted several older gentlemen wearing the proverbial flowered shirt. She smiled. It was just like in the movies. Sometimes.

A loud beep from the car behind her sent her foot to the accelerator faster than normal, causing Chester to lunge forward. "Sorry, boy. Everybody seems to be in a hurry these days." She cast a glance in her rearview mirror. Typical Hollywood smart-ass, she thought. Black BMW convertible, designer shades, a cell phone stuck to the side of his face. She was tempted to flip the driver the bird, something she'd seen her mother do on more than one occasion, but stopped herself just in time. There was probably some law against it anyway. She made a mental note to check into it, and, if so, make sure her mother kept her finger to herself, at least while she was in town.

Rag lived in an older section of LA that always made Abby feel as though she were entering a time warp. Flat ranch-style houses similar to hers minus all the updates. Scattered tree-lined streets. Bicycles that had seen better days, Big Wheels that had spent too much time in the sun, and rusting swing sets littered several browning lawns. In one yard she spied an old Volkswagen van with big, faded orange flowers that looked as though it'd taken one too many flower-power trips. A stray dog stood on the corner as though waiting for traffic. It always broke Abby's heart to see homeless animals. She slowed down, then on a whim turned around to see if the dog wore a collar. If not, well, she'd take it from there. She was relieved to see a bright red collar around its neck. Its owners were probably too busy to take it for a walk, so the dog decided to go on its own. The thought made her smile.

Abby turned left on Sable Street, following it to Greenlawn Drive, where it dead-ended at Rag's apartment complex. The Timberland Apartments, vintage 1960s, were an ugly shade of green, with black shutters. A low-pitched roof with a two-foot wooden overhang, which she supposed was some kind of sixties cornice, reminded her of a box. Frankly, Abby thought they were the ugliest apartments in the city. She pulled in front of apartment B-2. Rag's new Chrysler wasn't in its usual parking space, which really didn't surprise her. She hadn't expected to find him at home waiting for company. Chester whined to get out.

"Come on, boy. Let's take a break." Abby opened the passenger door. "Stay close, Chester."

With the dog trailing her, Abby walked across the small parking area to Rag's apartment. She knocked loudly, hoping he was inside and that he was alive. She knocked again. "Shit!" Crossing the sidewalk to the side of the single-story apartment, Abby hoped no one was watching her. All she needed was the police to come and tag her as a prowler or a peeping Tom. Then again, she rather thought this was one of those mind-your-own-business kinds of apartment complexes.

Abby rapped on the glass a second time. If Rag was inside and alive, he would have made himself known by now. Worried and ticked at herself for being worried and ticked at her boss, she went back to the front of the apartment, where she proceeded to pound on the door again. "If you're in there and not answering because you're hung over, a hangover is going to be a blessing after I get through kicking your nuts between your ears," she shouted, not caring if the neighbors heard her or not. She grimaced at the visual.

Finally convinced that Rag wasn't at home, Abby turned the doorknob and was stunned to discover that the door was unlocked. As she motioned for Chester to follow her inside, she observed, "I am not getting a good feeling here, Chester."

The inside of Rag's apartment was as ugly as the outside. Orange vinyl chairs were pushed back from a round glass table. In the center was a wine caddy with six matching glasses that had brownish-gold leaves painted on them. A two-tiered modern-looking end table was placed at one end of a zebra-patterned sofa.

Decorating 101 it wasn't.

Abby made her way to Rag's bedroom at the end of a short hallway. She contemplated the odds of her ever being inside Rag's bedroom and didn't like them.

As she entered the room, what she saw stunned her. The single closet door hung open, revealing a few empty wire hangers. Why did it not surprise her that her boss still used wire hangers? Abby glanced at the floor of the closet, where she saw a pair of well-worn Nikes. Opposite the closet was an armoire, its drawers pulled all the way out. She looked inside, but they were as empty as the closet. Hurrying, she stepped inside the old-fashioned green-and-white-tiled bathroom. An old claw-foot tub with a huge rust stain. A showerhead poking out from the Sheetrock, the shower curtain grimy at the bottom. A freestanding sink and a toilet with a black seat were crammed so close together, Abby had a horrible vision of Rag using the john, soaking his feet in the tub, and brushing his teeth at the same time. Quickly she opened the medicine cabinet. It was as empty as the closet and armoire.

Abby had a sneaky feeling dear old Rag had gotten himself into a very deep and smelly mess this time and, with no options, had cut and run.

Chapter 24

Richard Allen Goodwin remained a betting man even though in the past the odds rarely went in his favor. Upon his arrival in Grand Cayman, it appeared Lady Luck was making up for lost time. He'd had rotten luck for most of his fifty-two years—now forty-eight, according to his new credentials. It was high time he hit a winning streak.

His change of luck almost frightened him. There he was in Grand Cayman starting over, relishing the second chance he'd been given or, in his case, taken. What none of those assholes at the paper understood was if they wanted front-page news, they had to be willing to get out there and take a chance instead of whining about how someone always beat them to it. In this day and age, people had to be on their toes. And he'd been twirling on his tiptoes for days.

He was a multimillionaire. He could gamble all night if he wanted to. He could drink until he passed out. He could do whatever he damn well pleased.

"If they only knew," he said out loud. Walking over to the floor-to-ceiling window overlooking the aqua blue water of the Caribbean, he couldn't believe how his fortune had changed in just a matter of hours. He stared out at the beach as waves slammed against the shore. Palm trees, bent over like ballerinas, swayed as if dancing. Rain splashing against the windows sounded like pebbles being tossed against the glass.

Stuck in the middle of a fucking hurricane! He'd already heard that half of the island had lost power. He'd called the airport, pretending to schedule a flight. He'd been told by a woman with a lovely accent that all flights were canceled. A damn shame.

He then checked with the concierge, asking if any of the casinos downstairs would remain open in spite of the weather. He'd been assured that they would remain open for the guests.

After a shower and shave, he dressed in khaki slacks and a light blue shirt. He looked at himself in the full-length mirror. He needed to lose thirty pounds, but with his money, he could get some lipo. He slid a comb through his thinning hair and decided he would check into hair plugs as soon as the storm was over. He pinched the excess skin beneath his chin. That had to go, too. In a couple of months, he'd be a new man. Literally.

For the rest of the evening he would enjoy himself in the casino. Yes, life was good.

Back in California, Micky observed the hot young reporter as she drove off in her bright yellow car with a dog that looked like Rin Tin Tin. He carefully made his way to the back entrance of *The Informer.* Pushing the door aside, he entered quietly, unsure if anyone else was inside the office.

"Hey, anyone in here?" he called out. Like they'd answer if they were there at this hour. Sometimes he was stupid.

Taking care to walk softly down the long, dark hallway that he knew led to the offices, Micky pushed a door aside. Nothing. A metal desk with a cheap office chair and an outdated computer. No wonder this piece-of-shit paper was in the hole. Look at the antiquated crap they had to use. Probably still had dial-up Internet. He stepped back out into the hallway. He opened the next door and saw more of the same. This was supposed to be a newspaper, a rag? *Fuck, my home office beats this dump to hell and back.* He shook his head as he peeked around into the office next door. More of the same stuff. Desk, chair, no computer. Must use pencil and paper. He laughed at his own wit.

As soon as he stepped out of the office back into the hall, he heard voices.

Son of a bitch! Maybe Rag has decided to come to work today after all. If so, he was about to get a major, major ass whipping.

Micky stepped inside the office directly across from him.

Bingo! It was the boss's office. He turned on the lights, took a seat in the lumpy chair behind the desk. He was a patient man. Kind of. He had nothing better to do that day.

Yesiree, he was going to sit there in that damn office until Mr. Newspaper Owner himself showed up. Yep, for fifty grand, he had all the time in the world.

Chapter 25

Unsure what to make of Rag's sudden disappearance, Abby decided to shelve the man's departure for the moment. More than likely he was holed up in some seedy hotel, sleeping off his latest drunk. She had more important issues at hand, like her mother and her godmothers and the promised tour of *The Informer.* She raced back to the office in record time.

Parking in her assigned space, before getting out of her car, Abby scanned the parking lot, searching for Rag's Chrysler, on the off chance that he might have miraculously shown up while she was out looking for him. *No such luck,* she thought, before she corrected herself. Any workday without Rag on her case was a lucky day. Reaching for her briefcase in the backseat, she pulled it over the top of the seat, searching for Chester's leash at the same time. Sure she had tucked it in there earlier, she rummaged through until she found it.

"Come on, boy, let me loop this around your neck. I don't want anyone saying I don't respect the leash law." Once, Rag had seen her and Chester in the parking lot without a leash. He'd come down on her like a ton of bricks, saying it was a lawsuit waiting to happen and from now on, when the dog was on *Informer* property, he had better be leashed or else. It was the "or else" that had made her hate him more than ever.

"Chester! What are you growling at?" Abby looped the leash around the dog's neck before getting out and opening the passenger door. "I know you don't like Rag. I don't like him either. The sad truth is, I don't think anyone likes him."

With her briefcase tucked under her right arm, Abby held the leash with her left hand, then used her right hand to open Chester's door and release him from his seat belt. Dogs were like kids and needed just as much protection.

As soon as she clipped Chester's leash to his collar, she made a mental note to call Precious Paws and arrange a spa day for Chester. Maybe she'd invite Coco, too. Chester wasn't too hip on spa days, but he might make an exception if he had company. Especially a sweet little Chihuahua.

Walking across the parking lot with Chester jutting out in front of her as far as his leash extended, Abby jumped when she heard someone shout her name. She turned around in time to see a sleek white limousine pulling into the parking lot. Sophie hung out the back window, waving a cigarette in the air. Laughing, Abby simply shook her head.

"Chester, stay!" The huge dog immediately sat down on his hind legs.

Abby hurried over to the vehicle, anxious to take her mother and godmothers on a tour of her workplace. She glanced at her watch. She had at least another two or three hours before any of the stringers were due to report in for the day.

One by one, the women spilled out of the limousine. First Sophie, then Toots, and lastly Mavis, who clutched a small dog that couldn't weigh more than three or four pounds, possessively cradled against her ample chest.

"Yip, yip!"

Mavis trundled over to where Abby stood with Chester.

"This must be Coco." Abby held her hand out for the little dog to sniff. Coco growled, revealing tiny sharp teeth.

"She's afraid." Mavis glanced at the large dog sitting at attention. Chester was as still as a statue.

"Don't worry, Mavis, Chester is harmless."

"It's true, Mavis. When it's called for, Chester is a killer dog, but he's as lovable as a kitten other times," Toots said as she leaned in for a quick hug from her daughter. Toots ruffled her grandson/dog between the ears.

"He's the best of the best. Don't know how I'd manage without him. Let's go inside. I want to show you around before anyone else shows up." Abby reached for Chester's leash and led him to the back door. "Just follow me," she tossed over her shoulder.

"I can't believe we're really here! It's so exciting! Do you have any new issues I haven't seen?" Toots asked, as they entered the decrepit building through the back door.

"I think we've got a couple. We print seven issues every other week. That gives us every other day to assemble our stories for the press, then another day to collect new information."

First Abby showed them her office. "It's not much, but it's the nicest office in this dank old building. I'm hoping when and if I ever learn who the new owners are, I can get them to spring for a remodeling job. This building used to house the *Los Angeles Examiner*. It's more than a hundred years old. Sadly, not much has changed since then, other than we're now a third-rate rag. I don't know if that's a good or a bad thing anymore."

Abby noticed that Mavis's pale skin was flushed. She motioned to a chair. "Take a load off, Mavis," she said cheerfully.

"Thank you, dear. I am a bit overheated."

Toots and Sophie gazed in awe at the framed covers of *The Informer* that graced all the walls.

"I must have missed some of these," Toots said, continuing to scan the front-page news her daughter had reported on.

"Maybe you just forgot about them. Now, if you're all ready for a tour, we might as well get started."

"We're ready, Abby. I hope we're not keeping you from your work. If you'd rather schedule this for a later time, I'm sure that would be fine with Mavis and Sophie." Toots glanced at the women to see their reaction. They both nodded.

"Now is perfect because Rag isn't here. Actually, I haven't heard from him. I'm starting to get worried."

Toots sucked in a deep breath. "Is this unusual?"

Abby thought about her words before she spoke. It *wasn't* unusual, that was just it. Why she suddenly started worrying about him wasn't normal. It was just a feeling she had. "Not really. He's probably locked up in some sleazy hotel out in Vegas with one of his bimbos."

"Sounds like you admire and respect

your boss," Sophie muttered. She had been hoping for a little more glitz and glamour, and what she was getting was pure sleaze.

Abby laughed. "In his dreams. Rag wasn't so bad until he started gambling. I think that's what led to his drinking, and the rest . . . needless to say, I can't stand the sight of him. No one else can either. What's left of the staff stays out of the office as much as they can. I'm the only reporter besides Rag who shows up in the mornings. When he decides to show up. Come on, let's get this tour started," Abby called to Chester. Apparently, Coco was going to take direction from the shepherd. As soon as he trotted to the door, she followed.

"Why don't you quit?" Mavis asked, trailing behind, her gaze glued to her little dog, who was more intent on Chester than on her owner.

Smiling at the thought, Abby said, "I can't do that. In spite of Rag, I love my job. I know it doesn't come with a lot of respect, but someone has to do it." Abby led them down the hallway to a door on her left.

"Once we're downstairs in the basement, it's pitch-black, so don't do anything until I give you the word. There's a problem with the electricity in this old building. The lights don't always work."

Once Abby reached the door to the basement, she turned around to make sure her mother and godmothers were behind her. "The steps are steep, but there's a handrail, just be careful." She fumbled with the light switch, and a second later, the basement lit up.

The German-engineered printing press stood like a ghostly monument in the middle of the basement. Different-size round gears with hundreds of metal teeth meshed with precision even a fine watchmaker would envy. Abby could almost imagine the deafening noise emanating from the machine of days long past. Other than the frayed wiring hanging from an electrical workbox, the machine appeared in pristine condition. Operational status would be only minutes away were a qualified electrician hired.

Rolls of paper stacked floor to ceiling beside several fifty-five-gallon drums of ink lay in waiting for the next breaking story.

Off to the right was a small office where the typesetters had toiled endlessly with the tedious task of setting the small typeface backward from right to left.

Multiple dye-setting tools on ink-stained workbenches lay in military precision, as if keeping a vigilant watch over their domain.

The women gathered at the foot of the printing press, where Abby briefly explained how the massive machine worked.

"Why is this junk still here?" Sophie asked. "How can you be competitive if you don't keep up with the times?"

"It's not junk. When William Randolph Hearst purchased this machinery in the early 1900s, it was top of the line and could still produce a paper to this day if need be," Abby explained.

Across the large room, Chester and Coco waited patiently at the foot of the stairs.

Mavis toddled over to stand next to the two canines.

"The dogs are getting antsy. Let's go back upstairs, and I'll show you all the rest of the building," Abby said.

At the top of the stairs, they waited as Mavis struggled to catch her breath mid-

way up. "Sorry, this is just one more reason for me to lose weight."

"Why don't you take the dogs and wait
in my office while I show Mom and Sophie the remaining three floors. That will
cover the mailroom, distribution, sales,
and marketing. You won't be missing a
thing."

"Thanks, dear. I think I'll do that."

Twenty minutes later, the trio returned
to Abby's office. The scene that greeted
them caused all three to burst out laughing. In front of Abby's desk, Chester and
Coco lay cuddled closely side by side,
with Chester's baby toy wedged between
them. Mavis was grinning from ear to ear,
pleased with her canine accomplishment.

Bewildered, Toots asked, "How in the
world did you ever manage that?" she
asked, pointing to the two dogs.

"What can I say, dogs love me."

"With good reason. We all love you,"
Abby said with a smile.

"We better be going, we've taken up
enough of your time today. I'm sure you
have dozens of stories to write." Toots
gave her daughter a quick hug. "I'll call
you later."

"Sounds like a plan," Abby said, returning her mother's hug. "Didn't you mention to me one time, way back when, that you'd like to own a newspaper?"

Toots stopped in her tracks and whirled around, caught off guard by her daughter's unexpected question. She thought about the question before she answered, "I may have said that, but I don't remember. What was that, a hundred years ago? Why are you asking, dear?" she inquired nonchalantly.

"Just a thought, nothing important," Abby said.

Toots felt a ripple of apprehension course through her body. She did not give birth to or raise a stupid daughter. Abby *smelled* something.

"Whatever. This is way above my pay grade," Toots said. "Mavis, if you're ready, we'd better get back to the bungalows. I want to check on Ida, make sure she took her medication."

Reluctantly, Mavis reached for Coco, hating to end her reign of victory over the canine duo.

As they made their way to the waiting limousine, Toots promised a get-together later in the day. Abby waved to them until the long white stretch was out of sight.

Micky heard voices coming from the hallway. He drew in a deep breath, releasing it as he heard the group exit the building. With the coast clear, he carefully made his way outside, racing down the block to where he'd parked his royal blue Corvette in an alley behind a Japanese restaurant. He circled the vehicle, making sure there were no scratches or dings. Satisfied, he slid into the driver's seat before taking his cell phone out of his pocket to check his voice mail. He listened to a message from the pal who'd made the documents for Rag. All he could hear was a string of profanity.

"Rodwell Godfrey had better have nine lives because I'm planning to take eight of them the second I lay eyes on the lowlife slimeball. Old Rag has messed with the wrong man."

Barreling down the alley, Micky almost lost control of his wheels as he skidded onto Santa Monica Boulevard. Slamming on the brakes, merging with the rest of the slow-moving traffic, he contemplated what he was going to do to the SOB who had ripped him off. It wasn't pretty. He envisioned scalping the hair off Rag's head, at least what little hair the con artist had left, then one at a time he would remove his shiny fake white crowns with a pair of dirty pliers. Yeah, he liked that visual.

No one, and he meant *no one,* got away with ripping off Micky Constantine. The asshole Rag had moved up to number one on his very long shit list.

When all was said and done, Rodwell Godfrey would be begging to give him the fifty thousand dollars he'd screwed him out of.

Chapter 26

Chris checked his watch for the hundredth time. Twenty-eight seconds since he'd checked it the last time. Today seemed like the longest day of his life. It kind of reminded him of being a kid at Christmas. He remembered as a child he was positive Christmas only rolled around every other year because it took so long to arrive. Smiling, he remembered his father telling him to wait until he was older, then it would come and go so fast, it would seem as though it never even happened. Dad had been right.

Waiting for his big night out with Abby was like waiting for Christmas morning all those years ago, when he'd barreled out of his bed and raced downstairs to tackle the pile of presents placed beneath the tree. Always anxious, excited, butterflies dancing in the pit of his stomach in anticipation of the big event.

He pictured tackling Abby in the middle of a pile of presents beneath a giant blue spruce. What a present that would be! And it wasn't even close to Christmastime. He thought back to the many Christmases he'd spent with Toots growing up. She'd always made sure he felt as special as Abby even though he and Abby didn't spend much time together. He didn't know how he knew that, it was just one of those things that he knew.

Suddenly, thinking about Typhoon Toots put a damper on any fantasy he'd ever had about her daughter. She'd wring his neck if she knew his feelings for Abby were not of a brotherly nature, but he didn't have to worry about that because she would never find out, simply because there was nothing to find out.

He glanced at his watch again. One minute sixteen seconds. At this rate he'd be an old man before it was time to meet Abby at the Buzz Club. The reason she'd asked him out for the evening did nothing to advance his status as one of LA's top ten bachelors either; he felt like she was doing *him* a favor.

However, Chris knew if Abby needed him for a story, a scoop, about any of the starlets he'd dated, as long as he didn't have a legal contract with them, he'd spill his guts in a heartbeat. Anything for Abby. Maybe he wouldn't provide all of the sordid details, but he would come to her rescue this time because he knew how hard it was for her to ask for help. Her fierce independence was something he'd always admired about her, but there were times when he didn't care for it at all. He wanted Abby to *need* him, to *want* him as much as he needed and wanted her. He told himself to forget about it because it wasn't going to happen anytime in the near future or ever for that matter.

With two hours to kill before he had to

leave, he whipped out his laptop. Accessing the Internet, he checked his e-mail, hoping for some news on *The Informer.* He scanned through sixty-four e-mails, answered three that were business-related, then sent his friend of a friend's hacker friend an e-mail inquiring into the status of his investigation. Chris had a bad feeling about the entire transaction. Toots just might have to write this one off as a loss, a lesson learned, and move on. He cringed at a ten-million-dollar write-off. If the paper failed, which he expected, which he would bet money on, Abby could get another job as a reporter. She was good. Any of the metropolitan papers would hire her, but he knew that wasn't where her passion lay. She loved tabloid reporting, and Chris didn't think she was going to switch one style for another anytime soon. He didn't blame her either. Hell, if anything, he admired her for her determination despite the rotten reputation the paparazzi had. Abby was the consummate professional, he had to give her that. She didn't stalk the celebrities she wrote about, didn't force herself on them if she just happened to "bump into them"

while out and about. No, Abby took everything seriously.

Except him.

Abby turned the lights off in her office,
packed her briefcase with three lighthearted articles she'd found on the Internet
concerning a certain celebrity she planned
to interview down the road, then called her
dog. "It's time to go, Chester. I have a hot
date this evening."

As she made her way down the hallway,
Abby could have sworn she smelled Rag's
cheap cologne. She knew for a fact Rag
wore three-dollar-a-bottle Brut because
she remembered giving Chris a bottle of
the smelly stuff for Christmas light-years
ago. Maybe he'd slipped inside while she'd
been engrossed in her reading. She
paused outside his office, thinking that if
he was inside, she would hear all the televisions blaring. Nothing. As she did earlier,
she tried the knob, and the door opened
immediately. She entered Rag's nasty office and noticed right away that something
was different. Chester emitted a low growl
from his position at the door. Abby twisted
around to look at her dog. That was not

a happy growl. That was Chester's *alert* growl.

"What is it, boy?"

Tail tucked between his legs, ears flat against his head, Chester growled again, the sound ominous in the quiet room.

"Shhh!" Abby whispered. Something was wrong.

Her gaze ricocheted around Rag's office, searching for something, anything that might be different from hours ago. She drew in a sharp breath when she realized what it was. When she peeked inside earlier, she recalled, the desk chair had been far away from the desk, which was nothing unusual because Rag usually got up and never bothered to push his chair back under the desk. Someone had pushed the chair so close to the desk, the wheels were stuck on the edge of the hard-plastic floor mat. Maybe Mavis had wandered off while she'd been showing her mother and Sophie around. But Mavis hadn't smelled of Brut. The rest of the staff had come and gone while she'd been in her office. If anyone had been in the hallway, Chester would've alerted her. It was one of many reasons she liked having the big dog with her at all times. The building had its creaks and cracks, but she had worked there long enough to become familiar with them. Someone had definitely been inside Rag's office. Abby was positive it hadn't been her boss. Chester appeared to be just as sure as she was.

Fearing one of his gambling buddies had come looking for Rag to collect a debt, Abby hurried out of his office.

"Let's go, Chester! I don't want to be around when Rag gets his ass beat." She led Chester to the exit, practically running to her MINI Cooper. Inside, she secured hers and Chester's seat belts before careening out of the parking lot.

Abby was grateful that traffic wasn't a total washout, which was extremely unusual for that time of day. She made it to Brentwood in record time. She pulled into the driveway beneath the small carport on the side of the garage. Someday she planned to empty the garage of the last owner's possessions so she could park in it, but for the time being, this worked. She removed her keys from the ignition, grabbed her briefcase, then released Chester from his seat belt. She glanced at her watch. She had exactly ninety minutes to shower and change for her date with Chris.

Inside, Abby tossed her keys along with her briefcase on a side table in the foyer. She hung Chester's leash on its hook. Kicking her shoes off, one flying left and the other right before she headed to the kitchen for a bottle of cold water.

"Woof!" Chester's signal that it was dinnertime.

"I know you're hungry." Abby filled his bowl with fresh water and scooped out three cups of kibble from a plastic container in the pantry. She added a few tablespoons of homemade gravy to the bowl, gave it a stir, and set it down on the floor. "Okay, buddy, you're on your own for a bit."

While Chester dined in private, Abby hurried to her bedroom, where she spent fifteen minutes searching for an outfit. Nothing too dressy, though she *could* dress knockout hot if she chose because she was going out on the town for work. She didn't want Chris to think she'd dressed up for him, so she settled on a pair of skinny black jeans with a shiny silver tank top. She'd wear her slut shoes, the silver ones. Chris always called her Shorty. She'd show him *shorty.*

Abby took a long, hot shower, relishing the feel of the water as it ran down her neck and back. She lathered up, washing her hair twice with a fragrant, sweet green-apple shampoo. Wrapping a giant bath sheet around her, she combed out her hair, deciding to go "au naturelle," curls and all. She applied a smoky eye shadow, lined her eyes with kohl eyeliner. Blush and a sheer pink lip gloss and she was good to go. She didn't want to glam up too much. Maybe later at some point in time she'd glam it up and blow old Chris's socks off. Ha!

Abby rummaged through her drawer, finding a pink lacy bra with matching panties. Before she could change her mind, she slipped on the sexy lingerie, telling herself she simply wanted to feel feminine tonight. Who knew? Maybe she'd meet the man of her dreams.

Right.

The man of *her* dreams was off-limits.

Chapter 27

The Buzz was the current hot spot for celebrities in Hollywood, or so said the Style Network. Twenty minutes early, Chris scanned the crowd, hoping he wouldn't see any clients or any female who could possibly be dangerous to his bachelor status. Couples, both gay and straight, were stacked against one another like sardines. He inched his way through the crowd, hoping to find an empty table. Rock music blared from speakers the size of small houses. Chris wanted to stick his finger in his ears, but that would not be the cool LA thing to do.

Not that he followed LA's so-called socially accepted rules, but he always seemed to manage to fit in with just about any group while remaining true to himself. More or less.

Spotting a tall table with two empty barstools across from the bar, Chris bee-lined to claim it. He'd just sat down when a leggy cocktail waitress with pillow lips greeted him.

"Just you?" she asked in a low, kitten-ish purr, nudging him with her voluptuous breasts. Chris hated the place already. It reminded him of why he was so burned out on the party scene.

"Actually, I'm meeting my wife here. I hired a sitter for the night to give her a break. Four kids isn't a walk in the park, you know?" The waitress went from kitten to mountain lion in 0.2 seconds because husband-wife teams were not known for big tips.

"What will it be?" she asked, impatient now that she knew the tip would be the standard 20 percent. Four kids more than likely meant 10 percent. If she was lucky.

"I'll have a Coke, and my wife will have a . . . water with a slice of lemon."

The waitress scribbled something on a napkin, and dropped two cardboard coasters on the table before racing over to three older men who looked like big tippers.

Chris checked his watch. Ten o'clock. Abby should be here any minute. He knew for a fact that she was punctual, hated when anyone showed up late, because she made it a point either to be early or right on time. Maybe his watch was a bit fast. He continued to search the crowd for a petite woman with long blond curly hair.

"Who are you looking for? Your latest bimbo?"

Chris whirled around. "You sly little devil, sneaking up on me." He offered up a grin as wide as the Pacific Ocean. "Take a load off, Shorty." He got up and pulled the barstool out for her. "You want me to help you, is that what this is all about? So spit it out, Miss Reporter."

"No, I don't want your help. Well, I did, but now I don't. I'm just short, Chris, not helpless," Abby snapped. Why was she always so . . . persnickety with him? She suddenly felt like she was sixteen years old again.

"Actually, I think you've grown"—
he peered at her spike heels—"about four
inches. How in the hell do you women
walk in those things?"

Abby smiled. Chris, of all people, would
notice her heels. "They're three inches,
and I walk *very* carefully. I had to practice
with them at home before I was comfortable walking in them in the great outdoors. Just for the record, they give me
low-back pain. Bet that was more than
you wanted or needed to know, huh?" A
sound came out of her throat that Chris
thought was a giggle. A *giggle*!

The supercilious waitress brought their
drinks, plopping his Coke down so hard it
splashed over the rim of the glass.

"What did you do to piss her off?" Abby
asked, not caring if the waitress heard
her.

"I think it had something to do with the
fact I told her I was meeting my wife, giving her the night off from our four kids."
Chris winked at her.

"She probably recognizes you from that
billboard, you know, one of LA's top ten
bachelors, and knows you're lying."

"I didn't ask for that title, and, for the

record, it's embarrassing," Chris said. At first he'd had fun with the title, women hitting on him constantly, then it got old real fast.

Abby watched Chris out of the corner of her eye as she tried to see which bad boys and girls were on the prowl. "I'm sure you didn't, but I don't know of any red-blooded American male who would toss that particular crown. I imagine it has its . . . fringe benefits."

Did it ever, but he wasn't about to discuss his past relationships with Abby. Not now, not ever. The only relationship Chris wanted to discuss with Abby was his future relationship with her. But that was not going to happen. No way, no how.

All of a sudden, Chris's mouth went as dry as the Mojave. He took a drink of Coke before replying. "It does, did."

"Pick one," Abby said. "Either it does or not."

"Abby, if you must know I . . . never mind." *What the hell came over me? I almost made a very big slip of the tongue.* "I'm done with that title, Abby. I'm not surprised you've been ragging on me about it. I gave it up a long while back. I had my fun, and it didn't take that long finally to figure out the fast-paced lifestyle isn't what it's cracked up to be. We all make mistakes from time to time, even you, Miss Perfect!"

"Should I take that to mean the glitz and glamour is fading?" she asked in a teasing tone. *Please let him say it's so.*

"Like I said, that life is not all it's cracked up to be, Abby. I want more from life than a night out with a woman who only wants to be with me because she wants to use me to advance her career." Once the words were out, he couldn't take them back. But this was Abby and she wasn't like other women.

"If I didn't know you so well, Chris, I'd be offended, but I happen to agree with you. Just for the record, I didn't come here tonight to advance my career. When I called and asked you for a story, at the time I needed a tip, a bit of gossip, something, but I've changed my mind. I don't need anything from you." *Liar liar, pants on fire. I want everything you could possibly offer me. Me, Abby.*

Slapping his face would have had the same effect as her words. He wished he had the guts to come clean with Abby, but he couldn't. All he could do was to up the sparring, play his usual role of cocky friend.

"Good, because if I told you all of my secrets, then I'd have to kill you," he bantered. Why couldn't she see that it was killing him to sit there and pretend she meant nothing more to him than a good friend, but if that was all he was going to get, he'd live with it.

Abby's blue eyes met his, intent and unwavering. Chris had that kid-on-Christmas-morning feeling again. His stomach muscles took on a life of their own, and his ears felt hot; so did his neck. Shit, he felt hot all over, who the hell was he kidding. He wanted to tear his gaze from hers, but he couldn't make his eyeballs work. Abby broke the stare first, looking down at the table and tracing her finger through a minipuddle of spilled Coke. She started to speak, then stopped, glanced around the bar as though seeing it for the first time and not liking what she was seeing.

"You want to go somewhere else?

Someplace . . . real?" Abby asked out of the blue.

Chris didn't know what to say, so he just shook his head up and down, indicating he was okay with a move.

"Have you had dinner?"

"Does a pint of mint-chocolate-chip ice cream count as dinner?" he quipped.

"Depends on whom you ask. Me, I say it does. But I've had this hankering for a Pink's chili dog for days. It's heartburn on a bun, but they are sooo good."

Chris laughed, remembering how much Abby loved their chili dogs. He did, too. "Pink's it is. I'm game if you are." He pulled a twenty out of his wallet and dropped it on the table.

"Let's go. This music is killing me." Abby hopped off of her stool too fast, stumbling on her three-inch heels. Chris caught her by the arm, pulling her against his chest. She smelled like spring flowers and warm sunshine. For one wild crazy moment, he thought he was going to black out.

"I told you those shoes were dangerous." He glanced around the jam-packed club, searching for the quickest way out. "Follow me."

Without giving her a chance to answer, Chris wrapped his arm around Abby's waist, guiding her through the crowd of partyers. Twice someone bumped into them, almost knocking Abby over. When they reached the exit, Chris pushed his way through a group of giggling young stars. He recognized one of the starlets from a recent movie he'd seen: *Blondes Have More Dumb.* The title was even dumber than the movie.

Outside, the night air was cool and breezy but a welcome change after the bar. "I'm parked over here," Abby said. "You want to ride together or take separate cars?"

"I'll drive."

Abby hesitated a moment before agreeing. "I can't stay out too late. Chester's home alone. Plus I plan to spend some time with Mom and the three Gs tomorrow."

"I promise not to keep you out all night. Scout's honor." Chris grinned, displaying three fingers in front of him.

"You are no Boy Scout, Christopher

Clay. Remember, I know you and your reputation." Abby swatted his hand playfully as she followed him to his car, carrying her slut shoes in her hands.

Right then, right that very minute, Chris Clay wanted to drop to his knees and tell Abby he'd given up his bad-boy ways and was a stand-up guy just waiting for her to notice. But he couldn't do that. Even if by some miracle he did drop to his knees and profess all, his gut told him Abby would laugh at him and not believe a word of what he said.

Chapter 28

Leaning back on the headrest, Abby sighed. "I can't believe I ate three chili dogs! I just know I am going to regret it later. You should have stopped me after the second one."

Chris reached across the seat and tugged Abby's hair the way he always did. "I couldn't stop you if I wanted to. Damn, I missed those hot dogs. It's been years since I've had one." Chris thought it had been years since he'd enjoyed himself so much, but then he remembered dinner at the Polo Lounge, and that was almost as good. Almost, but not quite, because he had Abby all to himself now.

"Hang out with me, and I'll show you what fine dining is all about." Chris laughed. "Do you ever have popcorn for dinner? You don't look to me like you have any kind of weight problem." Jesus, did he just say that? In the world of women, all men knew not to mention age or weight. *Do you ever have popcorn for dinner?* Shit, talk about shooting yourself in the foot.

"All the time," Abby quipped. "Hey, do you want to know something?"

"From you, everything," Chris said, his tone serious, no longer light and teasing.

He felt Abby staring at him but couldn't take his eyes off the road since the traffic was backing up outside the Buzz Club.

"I was going to say . . . I was . . . I like you . . . that's all," Abby said lamely as she stared out the passenger-side window at the groups clustered outside the bar.

He reached across the console and took her hand in his. "I like you, too, Abby. More than you know."

There, he'd said it. He waited for her to

punch him, yank his hair, anything, but she simply remained in her seat, quietly staring out the window. Maybe he shouldn't have said that, hell he *shouldn't* have said anything. He'd probably just ruined a lifelong friendship.

"I do, too," she said so softly he wasn't sure she had spoken at all.

Chris managed to steer the Toyota Camry into the parking lot without banging into another vehicle. He suddenly had that kid-at-Christmas feeling all over again. Squeezing her hand, he found a parking spot next to her MINI Cooper. He shut off the engine, then turned toward her.

Oh, be still my heart. "Did you just say what I think you said, and if so, does this mean you'll have dinner with me sometime? Like maybe tomorrow?" One of LA's top ten, and he couldn't come up with something more original. But it is what it is, and he was being real, very real. More real than he'd been in all his thirty-three years.

Abby turned to him, an impish twinkle in her eyes. "Depends."

When he saw she was teasing, Chris played along, just like he always had in the past, only this time it was different. Special. Hell, it was downright intoxicating. "On what?"

"Lots of things. First, of course, is where you'll be taking me. I don't want to eat caviar and drink thousand-dollar-bottles of champagne that tastes like old socks. Personally, I like a steak. Rare. Baked potato, loaded. I don't do salads much, but I do like vegetables. They have to be cooked a certain way, not too soft, but crisp, you know, where you can almost hear them snap as you bite into them?"

Chris stared at Abby, unsure if she was serious or if this was just Abby being Abby. That was exactly the way he liked his vegetables, and he liked his meat rare and his potato loaded. Well, damn.

Taking a deep cleansing breath, he brought her hand to his lips. He kissed the tips of her fingers. One at a time. Softly, slowly, knowingly, as though he'd done it before. This was better than his fantasy, better than anything he could've strummed up in his wildest dreams. He took her other hand and repeated the process, slowly, lovingly, one finger at a

time. When he heard her gasp, it was almost his undoing.

"Anyplace you want to go, we'll go," he
promised, continuing to dot light kisses
along her wrist.

Abby pulled her hand away, touching
the delicate area on the inside of her wrist
where his lips had been. Surreal was
what it was. How had an invitation to have
a hot dog turned into something so sensual, so intoxicating? With Chris? Not just
Chris, but the man of her dreams.

"I've imagined this moment since the
first time I saw you. It seems like light-
years ago," Abby said lightly. Uncertain if
he'd heard her, she cleared her throat,
deciding if one of them didn't halt this
slow, sensual seduction, she wouldn't be
responsible for what happened next.

Hating to do it, but knowing she had to,
Abby removed her seat belt and reached
for her purse on the floorboard. She
turned to Chris. "I have to go. Chester . . .
I have to take him out. So, I guess I'll . . ."

"Yeah, yeah. I'll call you first thing in the
morning. I promise. It's okay to call you
early, right? You know, like in a few hours
from now. I probably won't sleep, so I'll be

up early. I know you get up early, but that means different things to different people. Yeah, yeah, I'll call you. Do you want me to follow you home?" *Jesus Christ, I sound like a fourteen-year-old in heat.*

Yes, she wanted him to follow her home, come inside her house, and do things to her she'd only dreamed of, but she couldn't say that. Yet. Instead she said, "Thanks, but I'm fine. I do this all the time, remember? Be sure you call me. Early. You're right, I sleep like you do. Early is good. I'll . . . well, I'll be up, so it's okay to call early. You know, really early." *I have to get out of here right now.*

"You really have to go?"

"Oh, stop it! You know what I'm talking about. Seriously, I have to go."

"Okay, Abby. Tomorrow we'll talk. Early. Real early."

Abby nodded and walked over to her car as she watched Chris watch her. She gave a slight wave before removing her keys from her pocket. She hit the UN-LOCK on the remote pad. In a daze, she dropped onto the seat, tossing her purse on the passenger seat. Never, ever in a zillion years had she envisioned this.

What had she missed all the years? Chris had never come on to her, never really flirted with her. He'd always been a good friend who teased her, called her Shorty, and . . . and he'd kissed her fingers. Each and every one of them. She wondered if she'd ever be able to wash her hands again. Maybe she could protect her hands the way Ida did and wear latex gloves.

Shaking her head to clear her thoughts, she inserted the key in the ignition, started the MINI Cooper's engine, then shifted into reverse. She was so intent on what she was doing, she just missed the Corvette that swerved into the parking spot next to her, barely missing the back of her bumper.

What a jerk, she thought as she backed out of her parking space. Abby thought it almost looked like the guy was trying to deliberately hit her! Someone who probably had too much to drink and shouldn't be on the road to begin with. She watched the shiny blue vehicle for another second or two, waiting to see if the driver got out, maybe to apologize? When she saw that wasn't going to happen, she yanked the gearshift to DRIVE and forgot about the Corvette. She should've flipped him off. For sure, her mother or Sophie would have. No, Sophie would've gotten out of her car, kicked his shiny Corvette, then kicked him in the balls, after which she'd flip him the bird while her mother cheered her on. Or it would be vice versa, with Typhoon Toots doing the kicking and Sophie cheering her on.

Refusing to allow the moron in the Corvette to spoil what she thought of as a perfect evening, Abby pulled onto the main road and glanced in her rearview mirror, looking for Chris's Toyota. When she didn't see him, she felt a tinge of disappointment. Had she really wanted him to follow her all the way to Brentwood even though she'd told him it wasn't necessary? She had to admit that a part of her had. Abby hadn't experienced genuine love and concern from either of her two short-lived relationships. Did she want that from Chris now? Again, she admitted it wouldn't hurt her feelings, but it was too soon, too new to start what-iffing everything Chris said or didn't say.

Chris had been her friend forever.

Seeing him as anything more than that would take some getting used to. Smiling, Abby knew she could and would get used to the idea.

Twenty minutes later, she zipped her MINI Cooper into its spot under the carport. Glancing at the digital clock on the dash, she saw it was only a little after one. Plenty of time to do what she needed to do. Slipping her heels off before getting out of the car in order to avoid another tripping accident, she hooked the leather straps around her index finger, then reached for her purse. She could hear Chester panting on the other side of the door as she inserted her key in the lock. "I'm coming, boy."

Opening the door, she bent over to receive several affectionate wet kisses from Chester before he sprinted out the door into the front yard. Abby waited inside the doorway for him to christen each and every bush before calling him inside.

After she changed into her Wonder Woman nightshirt, she carried her laptop to her bedroom, where she set it down on top of the comforter, propped a couple of pillows behind her head, and went to work. Chester jumped on the foot of the bed, where his blanket and pillow lay on top of the comforter, just waiting for him. "You've got it made, Chester, but you know that, right?" Abby said.

"Woof, woof!"

Abby laughed and returned to her work. Lingering thoughts of Rag and his mysterious disappearance had plagued her all day. She checked her e-mail to see if she'd received a reply from the e-mail she'd sent him that morning. Nothing.

Remembering the desk chair that was out of place in Rag's office, she wondered if it was one of his gambling buddies searching for him. But why skip in and out unnoticed? Why not ask around the office, see if any of his employees knew of his whereabouts? None of it made sense. If the paper hadn't recently been sold, Abby doubted she'd give another thought to Rag's disappearing act. Wouldn't he want to be around to gloat or remind the staff that the new bosses would bring in their own staff? Of course he would. She recalled his words quite clearly. She was positive. One didn't misunderstand when one's job was about to be taken away.

Abby had even called her mother to cry on her shoulder. Two and two definitely weren't adding up to four.

Abby actually considered calling a few of Rag's known Vegas hangouts, see if anyone there had seen or heard from him, but immediately dropped the idea. He'd serve her ass up on a platter in tiny slices if she was to do that and he found out about it. Too risky, for the moment. Maybe there was a woman, a girlfriend? She tried to recall any mention of his latest squeeze, but there were too many to narrow them down to a few. He rarely mentioned a name anyway. If he did, it was usually "babe, "doll," "broad," or some other chauvinistic reference to women.

Maybe she should ask Chris to look into Rag's disappearance. He was an attorney. Surely he had or knew an investigator who could check into Rag's affairs without its becoming public. Yes, Chris would know what to do. She considered the late hour, but he had said he wasn't going to go to sleep and would be calling early. She felt hot all over as she thought about their conversation. What would he think if she called him instead of waiting

for him to call her? It's Chris, she told herself. He wouldn't care what time she called.
She raced to the kitchen, where she'd left
her cell phone in its charger. She punched
in his number as she returned to the bedroom.

"Chris Clay."

Abby smiled. "Remember, you're supposed to say hello?"

She heard what sounded like rustling
covers, then the click of a lamp switch.

"I should have known it was you.
What? You couldn't wait for me to call
you? No one else calls me this late except
your mother. I always say that, don't I?"
He was acting like he was fourteen again.
Fourteen must have been a good year in
his life.

"Were you in bed?" Abby visualized
his broad shoulders splayed across the
bed, his classically handsome features,
jet-black hair mussed from her fingers
raking through it. And then she visualized
herself nestled next to him.

"Yes, but I wasn't sleeping. I might never
sleep again. I was just waiting for . . . you
know, early, to call you. Abby?" Fourteen
and one month.

"Oh, sorry. What?"

"You asked if I was in bed, and I told you I was," Chris repeated.

"You want me to call back tomorrow?" she asked, then remembered it *was* tomorrow.

"No, I'm awake. Actually, I was just thinking about you. So what gives?"

"You'll think I'm crazy, but I'm certain you already do." Abby took a deep breath, releasing it. "I'm sure you heard Mom and me discussing *The Informer* at dinner last night." She paused, allowing him a second to follow her. When he didn't reply, she continued. "Rag, my boss, didn't show up for work today—yesterday, that is. That in itself isn't unusual. He's known to spend his weekends gambling and drinking in Vegas. He rarely shows up on a Monday, but he'll call with some half-baked excuse. It usually takes him a day to ride out his hangover. Here it is the middle of the week, the paper has been sold, and he's nowhere to be found. I thought about calling the casinos where he hangs out, but he'll kill me if he finds out, which leads to my reason for calling. I figured as an attorney you might have an investigator or know of one that I could hire to find Rag. I know what you're going to say, but before you say it, don't waste your breath. Of course I'm a reporter with contacts. I'm simply hesitant to use them. When Rag decides to grace us with his presence, as I said, he'll have my ass for checking up on him. So do you think this is something you can help me with? We can still do that early call. This call is just . . . a ball." *Oh, God, how lame was that?*

Several seconds passed before Chris spoke, and when he did, his words were a complete shock.

"I'm afraid I can't, Abby."

"Can't or won't?" she replied, more than a little miffed at his response.

"Neither. It's simply a conflict of interest. Your mom asked me to do a bit of work for her. I'm sorry. That's all I can tell you."

And here she'd thought after the fingertip kissing, Chris would be putty in her hands. Wrong. That had to mean their entire evening was a conflict of interest. She needed to say something. "I see. Then I guess I won't bother you anymore. Good night." Abby snapped her cell phone shut. She made a mental promise to herself to never ask Christopher Clay for another favor as long as she lived.

Even into perpetuity.

Chapter 29

Toots, Sophie, Mavis, and Ida gathered around the dining room table in Toots's bungalow. For some reason that bungalow had become the unofficial meeting place. She had to admit she liked it that way because she was lazy. If she decided to smoke, she could. Hers was a smoking bungalow. If the others didn't like it, tough titty. Since she was footing the bill for this little vacation, what she wanted should count for something. Which reminded her of the ten-million-dollar hit she'd taken. She was so angry, she knew she was capable of chewing nails and spitting rust. At the moment she had to deal with her friends. She had the rest of her life to plot the death of the person who stole her money. She and the girls were doing Jell-O shots just then. She'd worry about her ten million dollars tomorrow.

"Mavis, all you have to do is pour it down your throat. You don't actually eat it," Toots said when she saw Mavis using a spoon to eat her lime green Jell-O. Toots had requested the Jello-O shots when she observed two young women tossing them back by the pool. One more new experience to add to her growing list.

"I'm savoring it."

"Leave her alone, Toots. If she wants to use a knife and fork, it's her business," Sophie admonished.

"Okay, *okay.* But just one; remember, Mavis is on a diet. The last time I heard, alcohol was fattening."

"Will the two of you stop fussing already," Mavis said.

They went at it like they usually did.

"If Sophie would keep her unwanted opinions to herself, there wouldn't be any *fussing,* as you put it," Toots said.

"Whatever! You're as bad as I am, Toots, admit it. Now give me another one of those shots. I plan on getting good and drunk tonight."

Toots removed another round of shots from the refrigerator. "Any particular reason?"

"I called home today and spoke with Walter's nurse. He isn't doing so well. She said his vital organs were starting to shut down. With his liver gone, what does she expect? She acted like I was supposed to be surprised or sad, whatever. She said it could be just a matter of hours before he's gone. Then she insinuated that most wives would be at their husbands' bedsides. I wanted to ask her how many bedsides she'd been at where the dying husbands had beaten the daylights out of their wives, but I was good. I told her to call if he took a turn for the worse. So does that answer your question?" Sophie slurped another shot and reached for another. "Why don't we make a toast, Toots? Mavis? Ida?"

"I'm ready," Toots said.

Mavis held her empty shot cup in the air. "I'll just use the empty shot glass."

"I'll pass," Ida said from her chair at the head of the table.

"To Walter, may his passing be painful and his insurance settlement speedy!"

They all chimed in, touching the little shot glasses together. "To Walter!"

Toots watched Sophie out of the corner of her eye. Sophie was a tough old bird, but she knew her old friend was indeed hurting. Not so much because of Walter's imminent passing, but the sadness that came with endings. "I can have a private jet ready whenever you need to go, okay?"

"That'll work, Toots. Thanks."

The little group mumbled and muttered and continued to drink. And smoke.

Sophie held up her empty cup. Toots opened the refrigerator and took out the two remaining shots and handed both to Sophie. "You can have these. I don't think I can handle any more. You were right to want to get drunk tonight, Sophie. After Leland's funeral, I drank an entire bottle of wine. I think all widows should get snockered. Dulls the pain of knowing you have to wear black. But that's only when you don't care. I didn't care, and it's pretty obvious Sophie doesn't care, so there you are!"

"I already told you I was not wearing black. I'm going to wear red. I don't want to do the mourning thing, Tots, Tits . . . you know what I mean? I just want to bury Walter, cook his ass up, and be done with it. I'm not even sure I want to stay in the city. It's so nasty, with all those garbage bags tossed on the sidewalk. It stinks, too. Why should I go back? Can either of you give me a good reason?" Sophie was drunk, her words beginning to slur. "Ida?"

"You can come to Maine and live with me. I have a beautiful little cottage. You wouldn't have to pay me anything either," Mavis said.

"Oh, Mavis, you're too damned kind. You'd get sick of me in two days. I could move in with Ida, she'd like that, wouldn't you?"

The look of fear that crossed Ida's face sent Sophie into another fit of laughter. When she caught her breath, she said, "I'm joking, okay? What do you do with your garbage, Ida? I've been meaning to ask."

"Sophie, you're such a smart-ass," Toots said.

"Well, I'm an honest smart-ass. So"—Sophie turned to Ida—"really, what do you do with your garbage when you're afraid to touch it?"

Toots lost it then. She doubled over, grabbing her stomach.

"Sophie," Ida said, "you always were a bitch. I'm going back to my bungalow. Good night, Mavis, Teresa."

"I guess that means she isn't going to answer my question. Good night, Ida, sleep tight, don't let the bedbugs bite." Sophie couldn't contain her laughter, couldn't stop slinging stupid comments at Ida.

Ida left, and Sophie continued as if she'd never been interrupted.

"Maybe I'll find a place out here. The weather's perfect, I haven't smelled anyone's garbage yet." Sophie reached for a cigarette, stuck it in the corner of her mouth, then lit up. She took a deep drag, holding the smoke in as long as she could before releasing it in one big puff. A glorious smoke halo sailed upward to settle over Toots's head.

"You shouldn't be so hard on Ida. We

all know she's a nutcase, but she is our friend," Toots reminded her.

"Oh, screw Ida and the horse she rode in on," Sophie snapped. "I'm sick of her phobia, her disease, or whatever the hell she has. It is my opinion Ida would snap out of her craziness if there was a man in her life. By the way, I decided not to keep Walter's insurance money. I'm going to donate it all to charity. What do you think of that?"

"That *could* be the solution to Ida's problem, but she'd never admit it. You might be right, Sophie, it could be as simple as Ida can't live without a man. She didn't become this germ freak until Thomas died. I wonder if she just needs a good lay, you know, an all-nighter?" Toots said thoughtfully.

"Oh, you two, I swear! I'm going to go before I laugh myself silly. I have a seven A.M. workout scheduled." Mavis hefted her bulk off the chair, grabbed Coco, hooked the tiny leash to the Chihuahua's bejeweled collar, then waddled to the door. "I'll see you girls in the morning. And don't do anything that I wouldn't do. Night."

"Good night, Mavis. Call my room as

soon as you're finished with your workout,"
Toots said, remembering what a struggle it
was for Mavis to walk from the bungalow,
but she swore she was moving a little
faster than she had the day before.

"I will. Night, Sophie."

Sophie waved her hand in the air.
"Night, Mave."

As soon as they were alone, Toots put
on a pot of coffee. "You want to stay
here tonight? You're too drunk to wander
around searching for your bungalow, and
I'm too tired to cart your ass around."

"I'm not *that* drunk. I just like yanking
Ida's and Mavis's chains, shock them a
bit."

"I figured as much. Were you serious
about donating your money to charity?"

"Yeah, I was serious, but on second
thought, how about if I just give it to you to
offset your loss? So, any word on the thief
who got their hands on your ten mil? I
wanted to ask earlier, but never had the
opportunity."

Toots was stunned at Sophie's offer.
That five-million-dollar payoff was what
had kept Sophie sane all these years.
She knew now it was never about the

money, hence the offer. As she waited for the coffee to brew, Toots removed two cups from the cabinet, Half & Half from the refrigerator. The sugar bowl was already on the table.

"You aren't drunk, are you? You have to be the biggest fake in the world. And to answer your question, no, I haven't heard a word. I was hoping Chris would call with some news, but nothing yet. I wonder if I should contact my bank in Charleston? Maybe they could track this money faster than Chris. But within an hour, that news would be all over town."

"No, I'm not drunk. How astute of you to notice, Toots. But to answer your question, I don't see how it could hurt, and I would bet anything Chris doesn't have the connections your banker has. I know about stuff like this. Remember, I was married to a banker. Walter was a lousy husband, but he was damned good at his job until he started hitting the bottle. Unless you care about the town gossiping about you, I'd make the call."

"I'll do it when the bank opens. You know there's something about what Abby said this afternoon that keeps bothering me. Remember how she said she was worried about her boss, the one who gambles and drinks?" Toots poured them each a cup of coffee and brought them to the table.

"Yeah, I do." Sophie poured cream in her cup. "What are you thinking?"

"Well, it makes sense that he's the obvious one to have stolen my money, then took it on the lam. Abby said he was knee-deep in debt, the paper is mortgaged to the hilt, and suddenly my ten million dollars shows up in Chris's escrow account. Her boss knew it was coming. Who else knew? Then some hacker gets into the account, and, poof, the money disappears before Chris can transfer it to *The Informer*'s account as payment for the purchase. Finally, to top if off, the slimeball disappears. I don't know why I didn't think of it before."

"And Chris did say the money was transferred to a bank in the Cayman Islands. I think you're onto something Toots. Maybe we need to make a quick trip to the Caymans."

"That's exactly what I need to do, but haven't you heard? They've been hit by a hurricane. I saw it on the Internet this morning when I was checking my e-mail. The airport is closed, and most of Grand Cayman is without power, according to what I read. It could take days to get that island up and running again."

"So what will you do?"

"That's just it. There isn't anything I *can* do, at least not until Grand Cayman is back together. I'll keep checking the news and the Internet. Really, now that I've laid it all out, I can't believe how obvious it is! I lose ten million dollars, removed from Chris's escrow account before he put it into the account of *The Informer,* and the owner of *The Informer* disappears.

"I'm a strict believer in common sense, too. The only problem is, I can't come out and accuse him because, if I do, then Abby will know I'm the one who was buying the paper, the sucker who was bilked out of ten million dollars. Abby would be humiliated if word got out that her mother was buying the paper, the *failing* paper, mind you, where it just so happens she works, then, boom, she gets ripped off before she even has a chance to make the purchase. That would make terrific headlines for the other tabloids. The ultimate scoop, and it won't be Abby's scoop."

"I can see the headlines now. 'Rag Rakes in Riches!' Isn't that what Abby called him?"

"Yes, actually she told me once it was his initials. They just call him Rag behind his back. You're right, that wouldn't look good. When I find him, I'm going to wrap my hands around his neck and choke him until he can't breathe."

"Then you'd go to prison for the rest of your life," Sophie informed her.

"I didn't mean it literally. It's just a figure of speech. I assume the feds will go after him since this involves bank fraud. They'll send him up the river for so long he'll forget what he did to get there in the first place."

"That's too good for him if you ask me."

"True." Toots reached for the coffeepot and brought it to the table, refilling their cups.

"So when the hurricane damage is clear, are you going down there?"

"Maybe. I'll see what Henry says. I'm sure he has a few contacts there. Like you said, bankers know other bankers, that kind of thing. If he thinks I need to go, I will. I'll have to run all of this by Chris of course. I trust him, he's smart, but I don't think he wanted to get involved in this transaction; he just did it as a favor. He tried to talk me out of buying that damn paper, but I didn't listen."

"Just so you know, I'd do the same thing if I were in your shoes. Shit, I'd do it in my own shoes. You did it for Abby, not yourself. We want what you want for her because we all love her."

"I know that, and Abby does, too. I just know she wouldn't appreciate me sticking my nose in her business. She set up some ground rules a long time ago, and for the most part, mother or not, I try to stick by them. I might not like them, but I do try."

"When we were leaving the paper today, I heard her ask you about owning the paper. What was that all about?"

"That made my blood run cold. I think she suspects something. At first I had the silly thought she might ask me to buy the paper as an investment, but that didn't happen. My gut is telling me she suspects something. It's a mother-daughter thing."

"You are her mother, so that means

you're probably right. I wouldn't bring it up again; let her be the one to come to you. That's my advice, for whatever it's worth."

"I'm not going to say a word. As far as Abby's concerned, we're here for a vacation and to spend time with her and nothing more. Now, I don't know about you, but my old ass is dragging. I say we toss this coffee and call it a night."

"You always have the best ideas, Toots. I'm going to crawl onto the sofa and call it a day. As long as you don't mind."

Toots nodded. Out of habit she rinsed out their cups and turned off the coffeemaker before heading to her room.

"Night, Sophie."

"Night, Tits."

Toots heard Sophie giggle as she closed her door.

Chapter 30

Chris crawled out of bed, making his way to the kitchen. After his conversation with Abby, there was no way he could sleep. He prepared a pot of coffee before going outside to sit on the terrace.

A huge wave crashed against the sand just as a cool breeze whipped across the terrace. He dropped down on one of the iron chairs, minus the cushion.

He went over his last conversation with Abby. No way could he think about the earlier conversation, at least not immediately. There was no way he could ethically snoop into the disappearance of her boss without compromising Toots's trust in him. He was caught in the middle between the two women he cared for very deeply. Hell, he was head over heels in love with Abby, if he wanted to be completely honest with himself.

He heard the coffeemaker's final gurgle. He went inside, poured a cup, and brought it outside to the terrace.

Had he been too anxious tonight when he told Abby he was interested in her and not in a brotherly way? Was it too soon? No, it wasn't, because he'd felt this way for years. Tonight, an opportunity presented itself, and he took it. Abby told him she really liked him, and he'd taken it from there. Had he misunderstood her? Was she just telling him she liked him and nothing more? No, because if that was the case, when he'd kissed her soft fingertips, she would have smacked him silly. He rather thought she'd liked it. He knew he did.

Chris made a mental note to call Toots first thing in the morning. There was no way he could disclose what had happened between Abby and him, but in all fairness to Toots, he felt ethically bound to tell her what Abby had asked him to do.

He looked at the clock, saw it was almost two in the morning. Too late to try to sleep, but it wasn't too late to dream about Abby.

Chris returned to his bedroom, where he crawled under the covers, but he was more restless than ever. He turned on the television, flipped through ESPN, CNN, and FOX News. Nothing worth watching. He clicked on The Weather Channel just for the noise. When he heard the meteorologist mention the Cayman Islands, he turned up the volume.

"All scheduled flights have been canceled. Power on most of the island is out. . . ."

What the hell? Odd, knowing that Toots's money had been wired to a bank in the Caymans. Had someone known of the impending storm, deciding to transfer the money when they learned a hurricane was expected to hit the barrier islands? No, it was too stupid to consider, but whoever the culprit was, Mother Nature had certainly lent him or her a helping hand.

The island was without power, which meant the banks, along with most everything else, were shut down. Which also happened to mean that if the thief was on Grand Cayman, that person wouldn't be able to access the money he or she had blatantly stolen from Toots either. Maybe Chris could find a way to contact the Bank of Bermuda. If he could, there was a good chance that he could catch the worthless creep who had helped himself to Toots's money.

Micky guzzled the last beer from the twelve-pack he'd brought home after wasting his evening chasing down the hot little chick from the paper. She knew where that piece-of-shit boss of hers was, he'd bet money on it.

He'd gone back to the paper, thinking he'd sneak inside again, only this time he planned to take one of the laptops he'd seen on Rag's desk. Not bothering to park in the alley, he'd pulled his Vette in the back lot at the paper. Just as he was about to get out of his car, he'd seen the blonde girl with Rin Tin Tin leaving. On a whim he followed her, thinking she could lead him straight to her boss. He followed her to a fancy neighborhood in Brentwood, parked across the street, and watched her. When he saw her sashaying out the door in that sparkly shirt and those fuck-me shoes, he knew he'd made the right decision when he'd followed her.

The Buzz Club, what a joke. He'd gone inside after the girl. The place was jam-packed with Hollywood types. He'd spent ten minutes trying to inch his way through the crowds. He didn't find her, but knew she'd have to come out eventually, so he'd parked his Vette across the street and waited. How the fuck was he supposed to know he couldn't park there after hours? Some idiot from the city had told him to move his car for the street cleaners. He wanted to tell him to shove it but changed his mind. He was trying to recover fifty thousand dollars. He couldn't afford any more trouble.

He'd watched the parking lot, saw the car parked next to that yellow junk pile she drove back out of the parking spot. He raced over to get the empty spot and al-most hit the bitch's car. She'd left the Buzz Club with some guy, and he'd missed it.

He had a plan, an idea. He wasn't go-ing to wait for the blonde to lead him to her boss.

It was as good a time as any to put his plan into action. He found the shirt he'd tossed earlier on the back of a chair and put it on. Socks, shoes, wallet.

Inside the garage he took his gas can, putting it in the trunk of his car. What better way to gain attention than a fire? Micky laughed.

The Informer was about to go up in flames. He figured it wouldn't take much, given all the paper the place must have in storage.

Damn, he thought as he cranked the Corvette over, *when you're good, you're good.*

Chapter 31

Toots called Henry Whitmore as soon as she woke up. It was six o'clock on the East Coast, three o'clock on the West Coast.

"I hope to God this is a life-or-death emergency, Teresa. It's six o'clock in the morning."

"Shit, I forgot. Listen, Henry, you need to wake up and pay close attention to what I'm about to say. Are you awake?"

"Yes, yes, go on."

Toots explained what happened and her suspicions to her banker. "I know I'm right about this. Before you say I told you so, I'll admit I should have listened, but it's Abby. You know a mother isn't rational when her child's happiness is at stake." Yes, it was a lame excuse, but it was the truth.

"I'll get right on this. Don't you dare make another financial decision without discussing it with me first. Do you understand me, Teresa?"

"Yes, I do. Call me the minute you have any news."

Toots hung up the phone, then dialed Chris on his cell. He answered on the first ring. "Did I wake you?"

"It's only 3 A.M. Toots. Why would you think I wouldn't be awake," he said, his voice laced with sarcasm. "Are you and Abby okay?" he asked.

"Yes, we're fine. Or at least I am. I'm sure Abby's at home. She was preparing to do some research on the Internet when I left her office this afternoon. Listen, I think I might know who took my ten million dollars."

For the second time, Toots explained her theory.

"It makes sense, but Abby's bound to find out. Especially if the FBI gets involved.

I won't tell her, but you better watch yourself since she might put two and two together. She's smart," Chris said. He wondered if Toots knew how smart her daughter really was.

"I know she is, that's why I've got to do every deceitful, underhanded thing in my power to see that she doesn't."

"I'll do what I can, Toots, but remember, if she finds out, it's your ass, not mine."

"You're a good man, Chris. Call me if you learn anything."

Toots hung up the phone. She dialed Abby's cell phone number on the chance she'd be awake.

"Morning, Mom. I won't ask why you're calling this early, and yes, I was up. Chester's bladder doesn't care what time it is."

"I wanted to invite you for lunch. Think you can fit that in your schedule today?" Toots crossed her fingers.

"I have to eat sometime. Where do you want to go?"

"Let's meet in the Polo Lounge at noon. Is that convenient for you?"

"Sure, it works for me. Are you bringing the three Gs? I haven't seen Ida yet. Tell her I miss her and want to see her. And I don't have any germs or whatever it is she thinks everyone has. By the way, how does she justify the rest of us walking around and not succumbing to whatever it is she fears? Do you know?"

"I'm sure Sophie and Mavis will want to see you; where Ida is concerned, I can't make any promises. She's really messed up. Dr. Sameer seems to think he can help her. He gave her some medication, but I don't know for sure if she's taking it. I think a good swift kick in the ass might do her more good than anything, but I'm not a doctor."

"Frankly, Mom, I'm surprised Sophie hasn't taken it upon herself to do just that."

"Well, she's told Ida what she thinks about the situation in no uncertain terms. I think she might be finished with the verbal and go to the physical any hour now."

"I know. Just one more reason why I love her so much. Listen, Mom, I've got to let Chester inside. I'll meet you at noon."

"I'll see you then, Abby."

Toots hung up the phone, made her second pot of coffee of the morning, plotting and planning what she would like to do to the creep who had ripped her off. Ten million dollars wasn't anything to sneeze at. Yes, she had more money than she'd ever live to spend, but it belonged to *her,* not to some third-rate tabloid failure. The more she stewed, the angrier she became. She poured a cup of coffee, then found the remote. She clicked on The Weather Channel and waited impatiently for an update on Hurricane Deborah.

"Thousands are still without power. Again, all flights except for emergency medical and those organizations providing humanitarian aid remain canceled. Stay tuned. . . ."

A banner at the bottom of the screen displayed names of organizations that needed donations and volunteers. Toots scribbled the address down on a pink notepad. She'd send one of them a check, hoping that it might speed up the recovery process. Like her check would make that happen, but she always donated to worthy causes.

She glanced at the time on the television. Almost 5:00 A.M. Damn, she was getting off to a late start. At home she would've already cussed Bernice out at least once and smoked a minimum of three cigarettes. Spying the pack of Marlboros on the table, she lit one up and sucked in the nicotine as though it were pure oxygen. She loved to smoke. Wonder what the surgeon general would make of that thought? Didn't matter. She knew it was bad for her; that was one of the reasons she'd never considered quitting.

Toots almost jumped out of her skin when she heard a light rap on the sliding glass doors. She looked up and saw Sophie. Motioned for her to come inside. "You scared the daylights out of me. When did you leave? The last time I looked, you were on the sofa. I figured you'd sleep in since you stayed up so late. Any news on Walter?"

"I needed a shower, so I left about an hour after you went to bed. What I need right now is some coffee," Sophie said.

Toots filled the cup she'd rinsed out earlier. "Here."

Sophie fired up and drank half a cup of coffee before uttering another word. Toots guessed her friend must really be worn-out because it was a rare moment when Sophie's mouth wasn't running like a rabbit.

"I turned my cell phone off after talking to that bitchy nurse last night. I haven't turned it back on. It's too early to deal with bad news. I figure if he bit the bullet in the past couple of hours, it won't matter one way or the other if I know the minute it happened or not. So"—she took a drink of coffee, another hit off her cigarette—"did you call the banker and Chris?"

"I did. Chris seems to agree that there is a possibility I might just be right. The bad news is that he told me Abby asked him to look into the disappearance of her boss. Chris told her he couldn't. Said it was a conflict of interest."

"Oh, shit, what'd she say to that?"

"He didn't say, and I didn't ask. I invited Abby for lunch. I'm sure the subject will come up. I don't know what I'll tell her. Any suggestions?"

Sophie stretched, turned her head from left to right before answering. "Hmmm, let me think a minute. Could the conflict be that you've hired Chris to do something legal like drawing up a will or something? Or maybe to hire him to scout some property for you to buy. That might get you off the hook."

"I suppose I could tell her that, but it doesn't sound very plausible. But then I *am* an old lady with whims. I'll simply tell Abby that I needed Chris to draw up papers for a legal matter that I can't discuss with her. Actually, that is the truth. I'll just wing it from there if I have to. Poor Abby, what did that girl do to deserve such a sneak for a mother?"

"You're trying to help her, Toots. We all want what's best for her. Like I said, I would be doing the same thing if I was in your shoes." Sophie finished her coffee, got up, and poured another cup. "You want more?" she asked, before returning the pot to its cradle.

"No, this is my second pot. I'm about to drown in all the caffeine I've consumed."

"I need it today. I told Mavis I'd look after Coco while she was with her trainer this morning. I haven't heard from her yet."

"She must be running late. She said they were meeting at seven," Toots said.

"I'd better go check on her. She's usually very punctual. I'll be back as soon as I find her."

"If I don't answer, I'm in the shower."

Sophie nodded, another cigarette dangling between her lips. She left the same way she'd entered.

Toots used her time alone to check her e-mail, hoping for a message from Henry or Chris. Nothing yet. Before the gang piled in, she took a fast shower and dressed in an aqua skirt with a floral blouse. Quickly, she twisted her hair in a topknot, then applied a thin coat of mascara and a touch of lipstick. She checked herself in the mirror. Lavender half-moons under her eyes. She dotted cover-up beneath them, knowing a good night's rest was all she needed to make them vanish.

At times it was hell being a woman, she thought as she went back to the living area. She'd lowered the volume when Sophie came in. Now she raised it, changing the channel to a local news network. If she was going to live there part-time, she figured she needed to start boning up on local affairs. Maybe she would learn something newsworthy she could share with Abby at lunch that afternoon.

Fires from the Santa Ana winds dominated the news; hundreds of people were being evacuated. More than seventy-five homes had been lost in the fire. She made a mental note about not buying a house in a fire zone. She also didn't want to live in an area where there were mudslides. California had great weather, but there were pitfalls as well.

Sophie tapped on the glass again, this time with Coco. "Mavis was waiting for me. She's so enthusiastic about losing weight. It kinda makes me sick, ya know?" Sophie said before putting Coco on her designated pillow.

"You should be ashamed of yourself. Mavis is the best of all of us. If it wasn't for her, we probably wouldn't have made it out of high school, let alone college. She's a good egg, and I don't want to hear you bad-mouthing her, you got it, Sophie?" Toots said in a voice Sophie had never heard.

"What the hell crawled up your butt in the last fifteen minutes? I was simply stating a fact. She's excited about losing weight. I don't know anyone as heavy as Mavis who would get excited at the thought of spending time walking her ass off on a treadmill. Don't be so touchy, or you'll end up like Ida. One nut in the bunch is one too many if you ask me."

"Nothing crawled up my butt. You complain too much, that's all. If you really want to know, I'm proud of Mavis. Ida, too. Yes, Ida's a little whacko right now, but we both know she hasn't always been this way. Give her time, she'll return to being the snooty bitch she's always been."

"I'm sure you're right. I just can't understand someone's being afraid of germs. I spent years working in a germ-infected doctor's office, and it didn't kill me. I never missed a day of work, did I ever tell you that? Even when Walter banged me up, I still went to work. That was the only place I could relax."

"Well, you should've left him after the first time, but it doesn't do any good to look back on bad times. Personally, I would have hired a goon to, you know . . . take care of him."

"Trust me, I thought about it. The repercussions were just too damn risky. If he'd ever found out I even considered something like that, I probably wouldn't be here talking about it. Walter was very dangerous back then."

"Well, you *are* here, and that's what counts. How about I fix us both a big bowl of Froot Loops? I need a massive sugar fix."

"Sounds good to me. What about Coco? Think we ought to give her a bowl, too? She's awfully small."

Toots laughed. "She's supposed to be small. You're not supposed to give dogs sugar."

"I knew that. I just thought she might want a treat."

"Mavis has given the dog too many treats. It's a miracle she isn't overweight."

Toots's cell phone rang. She answered immediately. "Abby. Yes, I saw the fires just a few minutes ago. What? Yes, of course it's not important. Call me the minute you have more news.

"You're not going to believe this, Sophie. Not only did that lowlife jerk rip me off for ten million dollars, Abby said someone tried to set fire to *The Informer*! Think insurance."

"Talk about your investment going up in flames," Sophie said. "Is she okay? I hope no one was hurt."

"She's fine. She wasn't at the office, thank God. As far as she knows, the building was empty when the fire started."

"I seem to recall you sending me an e-mail saying you needed some excitement in your life. It looks like you're getting more than your share." Sophie grinned.

"Yes, I guess I should be careful what I wish for, huh?"

Chapter 32

After he doused the offices with gasoline, Micky Constantine tossed a match in Rag's office, then raced like a madman to leave the building. He'd parallel-parked across the street this time because he knew once the place exploded, he'd only have a minute at most to get the hell out of Dodge.

As he pulled out of his space, he saw three fire trucks pulling into the back parking lot. What the fuck? They couldn't be there already! Tromping on the gas to get the hell away from the place, he wondered if anyone had seen him enter the building. Then he remembered he'd left the gas can behind in Rag's shabby office. Son of a bitch! How stupid was that? He didn't dare go back for it; they'd have his ass locked up in a heartbeat. Maybe it would burn. Yeah, it would. He'd seen something like that in an episode of *CSI*. But that poor bastard on TV got caught. They were always stupid on TV. He was way too smart to get caught.

Leaving the sounds of sirens behind, Micky banged his fist on the steering wheel. This was all Rag's fault. If he had paid him his fifty grand like he was supposed to, none of this would have happened. If he got caught, which he knew wasn't gonna happen, Rag's ass was going down with him. All he had to do was find him.

With the pedal to the metal, Micky was back at his house in record time. He pulled the Vette inside the garage, locked the main door, then went inside to the front room. He clicked on the TV, surfing through several channels until he found what he was looking for.

A woman reporter wearing a dark blue dress that looked like something an old maid would wear stood in the alleyway behind the paper with a microphone in her hand and a notepad in the other. When he hit the volume, her clipped voice filled the room.

"Firefighters managed to control a fire earlier this morning at the offices of The Informer, *a noted tabloid. When I spoke with one of the firefighters, he told me arson is suspected. He went on to say a gas can was found in the offices of* The Informer's *owner, Rodwell Godfrey. When we tried to contact the owner, WLAV learned that he's been reported as a missing person by a concerned staff reporter, Abby Simpson. . . ."*

Abby Simpson. That was the little hot chick that drove the yellow car. She reported her boss missing. *I don't think so.* Micky was sure that was just a lie she'd told the reporter to cover her ass. She knew where Rodwell Godfrey was hiding, and he intended to do whatever he had to get the information out of her. *Missing person, my ass.*

A day ago, Richard Allen Goodwin had thought Hurricane Deborah a blessing from

Mother Nature. Twenty-four hours later, he was sure it was a curse from hell.

He'd attempted a trip outside the hotel, hoping to see what damage there was, maybe find a woman looking to make a few dollars. What he found had not been even close to what he was looking for.

Florida National Guard troops, invited in by the British authorities, were posted everywhere. They were in the hotel lobby, outside on the streets. They were posted outside the casino, which had closed down because the hotel was being powered by generators. The management explained they would only power what was necessary, meaning the casino wasn't necessary to the owners, but it sure as hell was necessary for him. What other reason would he be here? Did those stupid people really believe that visitors to the Cayman Islands came for the view or the beach? Apparently the dumb-asses did, because they had shut down the casino.

Even worse, he had no way to access his new bank account.

Chapter 33

When Abby learned *The Informer* was about to go up in smoke, she called the police to report Rag as a missing person. Yes, he'd been missing for more than twenty-four hours, and no, she didn't suspect he was behind the fire.

Once she'd had time to calm down after learning that the only damage to the building had been in the office area, Abby had a change of heart. It made perfect sense, too. No doubt Rag needed money to pay off whomever he was hiding from. A fire at the paper would be the perfect way to collect on the old building's insurance policy. But was he still the owner? If he wasn't, what good would setting a fire do unless he was planning to scam the insurance company?

Of course she'd just heard her name splashed all over the news for reporting her boss missing. It was only a matter of time before Rag or one of his buddies came looking for her. She wanted to call Chris, ask him what she should do, but then she remembered last night's promise that she wouldn't ask him any favors. What was it Chris had said? Something about his having a conflict of interest where Rag was concerned. As far as Abby knew, Chris and Rag didn't even know each other. How was her mother connected to this?

The only way Abby was going to get an answer was to go straight to the horse's mouth. She placed a call to her mother's cell phone.

"Abby! I thought you were at the paper. Any news on who started the fire?"

"Nothing yet. I wanted to call and reinvite myself for lunch. Are you and the three Gs still up for it? I want to discuss something with you in private."

"Absolutely. I didn't cancel the reservation."

"Then I'll meet you there."

Abby hung up the phone. Chester ran around in circles, his signal that he needed to go out. "You're going to have to hang out here again, Chester." Abby opened the French doors. The huge dog raced off.

Twenty minutes later, Abby was zipping down the freeway. She turned the volume up on the radio when she heard *The Informer*'s name mentioned. The announcer said no one was hurt in the fire, but the building was closed while the blaze was under investigation.

Damn! Damn! Damn!

She was out of a job! She knew something like this was going to happen. That rotten, dirty, scum-eating jerk Rodwell Godfrey better hope the goons who apparently wanted his hide found him before she did. Now what was she supposed to do? She had a mortgage to pay, an animal to care for. Chester's vet bills were not cheap. Was it poetic justice that her very rich mother just happened to be in Los Angeles? Probably, she thought as she lowered the volume on the radio. Didn't matter because she would not ask her for one red cent. Somehow or other she would manage. She still had a bit of money tucked away for an emergency. She would dip into it if she had to. As soon as the offices at the paper were cleared, she would go back to work and earn a paycheck.

But then the voice of reason popped into her head. If Rag was nowhere to be found, and the building was shut down for a damned arson investigation, she might as well cut her losses, look for another job. More than likely the new owners would bring in their own staff just as Rag had said.

Maybe *The Enquirer* or *The Globe* would hire her. But something told her any connection to Rodwell Godfrey wasn't going to earn her brownie points in the job market. She should have stayed with the *Los Angeles Times,* where she could have written boring stories about politicians and their affairs. And it would have been a nine-to-five job.

Oh, the hell with it. All she wanted to

know at the moment was what Chris and her mother had in common with the man who was ruining her life.

Abby pulled off the freeway, and within minutes was dropping off her MINI Cooper for valet parking at the Beverly Hills Hotel.

Knowing that her mother and the three Gs would be waiting in the Polo Lounge, Abby went straight to the restaurant, not bothering to call her mother's cell. She spied Mavis, Sophie, and her mother out on the patio. They waved at her when they saw her heading toward the table.

"Oh, Abby, you look so nice today!" Mavis toddled over to where her god-daughter stood on the opposite side of the table and gave her a big hug.

"And you do, too. I love your new hair color. It's perfect."

"Thank you. It was all your mother's doing," Mavis said.

"Yes. Mother seems to be *doing* a little bit of everything these days." Abby took her seat.

"What is that supposed to mean?" her mother asked. Her stomach immediately started to kick up a fuss.

"You tell me," Abby said, a bit ticked

that her mother and Chris were both keeping her in the dark, sharing secrets. Maybe.

"I would if I knew what you were talking about, Abby, but I don't. Why don't you just ask me whatever it is you want to ask. I know you, Abby. You're miffed." Toots smiled when the waiter came to the table to take their orders. God forbid anyone in California frowned. And everyone seemed to have the whitest teeth.

"I'll wait until we're finished with lunch, if that's okay with you. I'm starved."

"Of course it's okay. Now let's order."

They all ordered salads except Abby, who ordered a steak, rare, with a baked potato fully loaded and a side of green beans. It brought back her conversation with Chris the previous night. She should've kept her stupid thoughts to herself. He probably thought she'd lost her mind. Just then she didn't care.

After they'd finished, they discussed the paper's situation.

"I suspect Rag may have something to do with the fire. He's in debt up to his neck. I'm sure the building is heavily insured. Rag is probably hiding somewhere just waiting to collect his money so he can gamble it away. That's if he's still the owner. By the way, I am officially out of a job. The fire marshals won't allow anyone inside the building until the investigation is complete. Then, of course, there's the missing old owner and possibly the absent new owners. I wonder if they even know the paper is no longer operational, at least until the repairs are made and we're given the go-ahead. All this crap is giving me a terrible headache."

"I have some aspirin in my purse." Mavis fumbled through her bag, finally producing a small container of aspirin.

"Thanks." Abby popped three aspirin, washing them down with her glass of ice tea. How had her life become such a mess? One day it was almost perfect, or as close to perfect as she wanted, then the next day everything went to hell.

"I think I'll take a walk, then a short nap. I stayed up too late and drank too many Jell-O shots last night. What do you say, Mavis, want to come with me?" Sophie's knee nudged Mavis, who immediately understood they were to make themselves scarce so Toots and her daughter could talk.

"Yes, of course, I am supposed to walk as much as possible."

"Abby, spend some time with your mom. We're going to take a hike," Sophie said.

Abby hugged her godmothers good-bye. How did she get so lucky to have so many caring women in her life? Her mother of course.

When Sophie and Mavis left, the waiter brought a dessert menu. "I'll have apple pie and coffee with an extra scoop of vanilla ice cream."

Abby smiled. Her mother and her sugar addiction. It was a miracle she wasn't diabetic. "I'll have the same."

"So, you want to tell dear old mom what's going on?"

Abby nodded. "Did you speak with Chris today?"

"I did. I called him this morning. Why? Is he in trouble?" Toots asked, knowing he wasn't.

"Not that I know of. Last night we had dinner. I told him how worried I was about

Rag. I sort of asked him if he would take a look into his so-called disappearance. He told me he couldn't."

"Really?"

"He said he was doing a bit of work for you." There, it was out.

"Yes, he is. I can't discuss it with you, it's a . . . well, it's a personal issue, Abby. I'm sorry."

Dumbfounded, Abby said, "That's it?"

"I'm afraid that's all I can tell you, Abby. I know we share almost everything, but there are some things a daughter doesn't need to know about her mother. Now, can we leave it at that?"

Abby shrugged. "I suppose I don't have a choice. As long as you're not dying or donating your fortune to a mad scientist, I think I'm okay with allowing my mom to have a few secrets."

"I can honestly say no to both. Now, I know this is none of my business, but you said you were out of a job. I'm sure it's just temporary. Is there anything I can do, give you a loan, pay off your mortgage?"

Abby laughed. How like her mother to think she could solve all problems with money. "You know I don't like taking your money. I'm fine. I've got a little bit of savings. I can get by for a while. If I get in a bind, you'll be the first to know. Thanks, Mom. I know you mean well, but I can't take the easy way out."

"Your father was the same way. Stubborn, mule-headed, and as strong-willed as they come. I'm glad you inherited those traits, Abby. I just don't want you to live from paycheck to paycheck while your dear old mom is alive. You'll come to me at the first sign of trouble, right?"

"You know I will."

"Good."

The waiter returned with their pie and coffee. They made small talk. Abby told her of her plans to work in her courtyard, what she wanted to do with the rest of her house. Both loved decorating, and they got so caught up in discussing the details of what Abby planned to do that they were surprised when they saw they'd lingered over dessert for more than an hour.

"Why don't you come to the bungalow? I'll see if we can't get Ida out of her Clorox condo."

"Mother, you're terrible, but I do want to see her before you leave. Speaking of which, how long do you plan to stay? You probably told me but I don't remember."

"Oh, a few weeks at least. Ida's got to work with Dr. Sameer, Mavis loves her personal trainer. Sophie may have to leave early to take care of Walter's funeral arrangements."

"Good, I'm glad you're staying for a while. Now let's get out of here before our waiter kicks us out. He's been eyeing us for the last ten minutes."

Toots added a generous tip to their bill.

Hand in hand, mother and daughter walked down the path leading to the bungalows.

Chapter 34

Sophie lit another cigarette and puffed furiously. Smoking always seemed to help when her jittery nerves got the best of her, but smoking wasn't working this time around, because her nerves were twanging all over the place. She felt like her head was going to spiral right off her neck and sail away into outer space.

She patted her pockets for her cell phone. No cell phone. Then she remembered that she had left it on the pink marble counter in the bathroom. She took a moment to wonder if she'd deliberately left it behind because she didn't want to hear it ring.

Back in her bungalow, Sophie ran into the bathroom and looked down at the phone. She'd turned it off earlier and hadn't turned it back on. She bit down on her lower lip as she stared at the small gadget.

Sophie wished then that she was tougher, more in control. She hated to admit, even to herself, that she didn't want to be alone when she turned the phone on. She needed Toots for backup. Earlier, Toots had called her room to tell her Abby was visiting with Ida, who had finally agreed to leave her Clorox haven to meet with her goddaughter.

Chalk one up for the Germ Queen.

Sophie jammed the cell phone in her pocket and raced down the pathway that led to Toots's bungalow. Any other time she would have paid attention to the rainbow of flowers and the emerald green lawn, but not today. A skinny minute later, she was tapping on the sliding glass door. She waited a moment before she stepped inside.

"Hi, Sophie. Mom said you might stop over. Did you enjoy your walk?"

"Actually, I did. Walking always makes me aware of how old I'm getting."

"Phooey, you'll be around forever," Abby teased.

Sophie licked at her dry lips. She homed in on Toots. "Can I talk to you a minute, Toots? In private if you don't mind."

Toots glanced at the others. Seeing that they were engrossed in a lighthearted conversation, she motioned for Sophie to follow her into her bedroom.

"You look terrible, Sophie. What's wrong?" Toots whispered as she closed the door for privacy.

"Remember last night when I told you I turned my cell phone off after I talked with Walter's nurse?"

"Yes? So?"

"I never turned it back on."

"What are you waiting for? Turn it on. If it's bad news, we'll deal with it."

Sophie nodded and clicked the POWER button. She saw that she had six messages. Her voice was barely a croak when she said, "There are six messages."

"Just do it, Sophie," Toots encouraged.

Sophie listened to the messages. Four messages were from Walter's nurse, one was from Lila, her neighbor of thirty years, and the last message was from the morgue. Sophie's hands shook as she deleted the last message. Her eyes filled with tears as Toots wrapped her arms around her.

"It's okay to be sad, Sophie. It's okay to cry your eyes out, too." Toots held her close as Sophie cried like a baby.

Toots reached for a wad of tissues from her nightstand.

Toots helped her to a chair, where Sophie wailed and cried, her arms beating at the arms of the chair until she couldn't cry anymore. What seemed like a long time later but was in reality no more than ten minutes, Sophie said, "Okay, I'm finished bawling."

Toots reared back, her eyes full of questions.

"What?"

"Are you sure you're okay? One minute you're bawling your eyes out, then, just like that"—she snapped her fingers—

"you're done? I clocked you. Exactly ten minutes."

Sophie's lips stretched into something that resembled a weak smile. "When something is done, Toots, it's done. Crying isn't going to solve anything. I had to cry for the would-haves, the could-haves, the should-haves. I did it. It's like you wearing black for ten days. You had to do it. Well, I had to cry. End of story."

Toots burst out laughing. It only took Sophie a minute before she joined in. Another minute, and they were both rolling around on the bed like two teenagers. They laughed until their sides hurt.

"Oh, Sophie, you're an old broad just like me. We don't need a man in our lives anymore. I say screw 'em all. Unless, of course, the absolute right one comes along. And then we might have to fall back and regroup." Both women went off once again into peals of laughter.

"Right now, duty calls. I have to go back and do what I have to do. Walter had no family, so it's just going to be me and any of his old friends who care to come for his send-off."

"I have an idea, Sophie. If anyone knows how to plan an event—remember it's always an event, not a funeral—I do. I've done it eight times, so that more or less makes me an expert. After eight husbands, I have the formula down pat. How would you like it if I flew to New York with you? We could have a respectful service, you can take care of your insurance paperwork, then we could shop for a few hours, get you some new Fifth Avenue duds, and jet right back to Los Angeles. Thirty-six hours, tops."

"You'd do that for me, Toots? Now, with all this mess going on at the paper? God, yes."

"Of course I will. There isn't anything I can do about the paper right now. Henry promised me he would do whatever possible to get my money back, though it may take a while, given all the hurricane damage. Chris is working on getting his hacker friend to see exactly what kind of electronic trail he can come up with. All I need to do now is call the airport's general aviation center. I'll hire a jet to fly us there and back, so what say you, Sophie Manchester?"

"I say yes, Teresa Loudenberry, or

whatever the hell your last name is these days. You're one hell of a friend, Toots."

"Stop with the mush before I have to kick your worn-out old ass."

"How do you know my old ass is worn-out? Walter . . . never mind . . . forget Walter. Let's get out of this bedroom and go tell the others before Ida starts a rumor that we're lesbians."

"You sure you're okay?" Toots asked, serious once more.

"If I told you I used to pray for this day, what would you think of me?"

"Truly? I think I might say something like, why didn't you help it along? No, I don't think I'd say that. All good things come to those who wait. That's how you have to look at it, Sophie. You did what a lot of women wouldn't have done. You stayed and made sure the son of a bitch spent his last years in comfort. There should be no regrets on your part. Hey, do you want me to sing at the service?"

Sophie blinked. "Now, that's an offer I can't refuse. Yeah, Toots, warm up those pipes of yours and send him off on a high note."

Toots dabbed at her eyes. "Come on,

let's go tell the others, but we have to be sure we don't get too close to Ida, you know, tears dropping on her or something."

"Screw Ida."

"That might work if there was a man around, but there isn't." Toots started to laugh and couldn't stop until Sophie banged her on the back a few times.

In the living room, the others looked up expectantly when Toots and Sophie entered the room.

"Sophie has something to tell everyone, so listen up." When Toots was sure she had their undivided attention, she looked over at Sophie. "Okay, you have their attention. Spit it out."

"Walter kicked the bucket." She held her hand, palm out, in front of her. "And it's okay, I don't need a bunch of *I'm sorries*. I haven't made it a secret that I've waited for this day longer than I can remember. I'm going back to New York to arrange for his funeral."

"Event, Sophie. It's always an event."

Abby rolled her eyes. "Mother!"

"It is an event, no matter what you say," Toots assured her daughter. "I don't think Sophie is going to hire a seven-piece string band, but she's given me permission to sing at the service. Dying is an event in one's life. Don't even try to dispute it," Toots said firmly.

"I am terribly sorry, Sophie. I know how you've waited for this day, but it still has to be a shock," Mavis said.

"I'm sorry, too, Sophie. When I lost Thomas I didn't want to go on living. But now—"

"You don't have anything to live for. I remember," Sophie said.

"That isn't what I was going to say. What I was going to say is the past few days have been an eye-opener for me. With Dr. Sameer's help, I am going to overcome this disease. I don't suppose any one of you even bothered to notice my hands."

They all stared at Ida's hands. She'd taken off the latex gloves.

"Yes!" Abby said. "That's wonderful, Ida, and you've only been to see the doctor once. I'm very proud of you."

"As we all are. I know this is difficult for you. Now I am going to make an appointment for you to get a manicure as soon as Sophie and I return from New York."

"I don't know if I'll be ready for that, but by all means make the appointment if you don't mind. It will be a goal for me. Mavis and I have been discussing goals and how best to achieve them," Ida said.

"That's the spirit, Ida! Next I'll be stuffing both your hands in that garbage can I mentioned," Sophie teased.

"I would never do that under any circumstances, Sophie. Really, even if I wasn't so . . . off-the-wall!" At first blush it was looking like just maybe Ida was becoming more like the old Ida they loved.

"I know, I wouldn't either, but it sounded good, admit it. So, now that we're all here, why don't we order some more of those Jell-O shots?"

Toots shook her head. "Not today. We'll have a drink with dinner, but Jell-O shots are out of the question until we get back."

"I can't believe what I'm hearing. My mother and my godmothers doing Jell-O shots." Abby pretended to be horrified.

"We enjoyed every one of them, too." Toots laughed.

"Mavis ate hers with a spoon," Sophie said.

"Sounds like my four favorite people in the world had a good time. I don't want to be a party pooper. Sorry, Sophie, you know what I mean. I've got to get back to the house. Chester is waiting on me. Mom, call me and let me know when you'll be going to New York. Looks like I'll be working around the house for the next few days, at least until I find out what's going on at the paper. I plan to keep my end up, so when the new owners decide to show up, they won't call me a slacker."

Abby doled out hugs and kisses before she left. She promised to call that evening.

Sophie waited until the door closed behind Abby before she said, "She's one in a million, Toots. You better hope when she finds out, if she finds out, what her old mom is doing behind her back that she doesn't . . . oh, what am I saying? If she does, you'll deal with it. We'll all deal with it.

"I . . . I have some calls to make, so if you'll all excuse me, I'll get right to it."

Sophie's friends nodded solemnly.

Mavis said, "I'm going to meet with the hotel dietitian tomorrow. Is that okay? I know this isn't free, so if you don't want me to know what all this is costing, Toots, just say the word."

"The word is I want you to do whatever you need to do to get your weight off. I don't know if the rest of you have noticed, but I think you're a bit lighter on your feet, Mavis."

Mavis smiled. "I think I am, too. I've lost eight pounds since coming to Charleston, then here."

"I knew you could do it, Mavis. Just one day at a time."

Ida got up from her perch on the sofa. "I'm going to go back to my bungalow now. Mavis, would you like to join me for dinner tonight?"

"That would be wonderful. I need to go myself. Toots, Sophie, if you need me to do anything for you, just ask, okay?"

"Thanks, Mavis, but no, just stay here and run up Toots's tab. We got it covered."

Together Ida and Mavis left for their own bungalows, their arms linked. Both Toots and Sophie rolled their eyes at one another. Progress with a capital *P*.

It took Toots twenty minutes to arrange

for their flight to New York and to book two rooms at the Four Seasons.

"We can stay at the apartment, Toots."

"I know we can, but we're not going to do that. I don't want you going back there, at least not yet. Do you need me to make any calls?"

"Thanks, but no. This is something I have to do myself. It won't take long."

With nothing else to do to occupy her time, Toots decided to make a pot of coffee. While it dripped, she walked out to the terrace and lit a cigarette. She didn't know why, but suddenly she felt *good.*

As Sophie thought about the calls she needed to make, she debated with herself about who to call first. After deciding that she would begin with returning the call from the morgue, she said to herself, *No, I want to call that nurse. I'm going to give that prissy bitch a piece of my mind. I'm going to do it right now while I'm good and pissed.* Sophie punched in the ten-digit number.

"Everything okay?" Toots asked ten minutes later when Sophie joined her on the terrace.

"It is what it is, Toots. Hey, what are you going to sing at the service?"

"I'll come up with something. I plan to practice on the plane ride. You might want to think about buying some earplugs before we leave."

Chapter 35

The private jet was wheels down at one o'clock in the afternoon. Within minutes, a waiting limousine whisked the two women to the Bank of Manhattan, where Sophie took from her safe deposit box the papers she needed to file a claim on the five-million-dollar life insurance policy she had waited all these years to collect. Their next stop was the Daley Funeral Home on Fifty-seventh Street.

Within an hour, with Toots at the helm, all of Walter's final arrangements were taken care of. Walter Manchester was going to the big bank in the sky in a top-of-the-line spiffy bronze Springfield casket. The one-hour viewing with a closed casket was scheduled for seven o'clock. A five-minute service was set for seven the following morning, with interment at seven-thirty following the short ride to the cemetery. A florist on Fifty-first Street promised bookoo flowers to be delivered to the funeral home.

Sophie had to hand it to Toots, she knew how to pull it all together. "How come we aren't embalming Walter?"

"Takes too long. Casket is closed. You said you wanted it *done.* This is how it gets done. Do you have a problem with any of this?"

"Absolutely not."

"Okay. Then let's hit Fifth Avenue. Our return flight is scheduled for nine tomorrow morning. We're going to be seriously jet-lagged, but the sooner we put this behind us, the quicker you can get on with your life, Sophie. Unless you want to hang around here and have a pity party."

Sophie thought about it. "I'm good with it all. Let's shake it, girlfriend. I hear Saks calling my name."

"Funny you should say that. I heard my name being called, too."

Walter Manchester's event went off without a hitch. Toots sang "Ave Maria," a bit off-key, but Sophie didn't seem to notice or care.

Toots wished she'd had just a little longer to prepare for the event, but considering the time constraints, she was satisfied. She dropped a yellow rose on top of the Springfield casket, said, "So long, Walter," and stood back to watch as Sophie approached.

Sophie laid her rose next to Toots's, tears rolling down her cheeks. "I don't know where you're going, Walter . . . gone, but I don't think you and I will be meeting up . . . ah, later."

Toots reached for Sophie's arm. "Okay, we did it, and now we're outta here. Listen to me, Sophie. Do not look back. This part of your life is over, and it was Walter's loss. You're a wonderful person. God put you on this earth for a reason, so don't ever think you failed. Walter failed you. End of story."

It was wheels up right on time. The two

old friends landed at LAX at noon and were back in their bungalows in time for lunch.

"I like the way you do things, Toots. I could get used to this sort of lifestyle," Sophie said as she looked at the room-service menu.

"You better get used to it, old girl, because you're about to move into a higher tax bracket. What will you do with all that money?"

"I might take a trip in a rocket ship. You can do that now. It's two hundred thousand dollars. Big-ticket stuff. I really don't think I will live any differently than I do now. Though I am going to buy a house. With a huge yard. And I'm going to plant flowers. All those years of living in the concrete jungle, I think a house will be my only extravagance. And lots of flowers. Maybe I could buy a home in South Carolina. I could grow tobacco. I'm going to give a lot of it away, Toots. That's a definite. I'll invest some of it."

"I'll help you plant the garden."

Chapter 36

Micky was awakened by a loud banging on his front door. He rolled over in bed to look at the alarm clock. *Fuck, who in the hell comes for a visit at three o'clock in the morning?* He crammed the pillow over his head, hoping to shut out the noise. When he saw it wasn't about to let up, he called out, "Give me a minute, will ya?" He found the jeans he'd worn the day before lying in a heap on the floor. Reaching for them, he pulled them on as he stomped his way to the door, yelling, "All right already, I'm coming, dammit!"

Micky peered through the peephole, a

frown building between his eyebrows before he opened the door. He didn't recognize the man standing in front of him. Maybe his document pal sent someone to collect his money.

He yanked the door aside, preparing to tell the dressed-up dude to take a hike.

"Are you Michael Constantine?"

Michael Constantine. "Depends on who wants to know. Who are you? What do you want?"

"James Wilson. Orange County arson investigator."

Double shit fuck and hell. Play it cool. Micky seethed. "So? I'm supposed to be impressed?"

Wilson stared at the weasel standing in front of him. "I don't much care if you're impressed or not. I have a few questions I'd like to ask you."

"About what?" Micky stepped away from the door as he tried to put some distance between the investigator and himself in case he had to bolt.

"Do you drive a 1987 royal blue Corvette?"

"Yeah." This wasn't sounding good. He hadn't had an accident. Why the hell was this dude asking him about his car? His gaze went to the coffee table, where he'd tossed his keys.

"I'd like to have a look at it."

"You got a search warrant?"

"Do you really think I would come all the way out here at three o'clock in the morning without one?"

Micky took a step toward the door. He saw two patrol cars parked across the street. "Yeah, you can look at it. Give me a minute. It's in my garage."

"I'll just follow you if you don't mind."

Play it cool, Micky, play it cool. He hadn't left anything in the car to link him to the fire. He'd left the gas can there, but a gas can was a gas can. Half the world owned gas cans.

Micky picked up his keys from the coffee table, motioned for the investigator to follow him through the kitchen to the door leading out to the garage. He flipped the lights on, tossed Mr. Big Shot arson investigator the keys. "Be my guest."

Wilson took a radio from his pocket, spoke into it, then, two minutes later, four police officers joined him in the garage.

"What are they here for? What are

you looking for? I didn't do nothing." Micky hated the fear he was hearing in his voice.

"Just let us do our job, Mr. Constantine. That's another way of saying I don't have to tell you anything." He tapped the warrant in the breast pocket of his jacket. Micky felt like his guts were going to roar up through his throat and out his mouth.

For the next thirty minutes, investigators searched the trunk, they opened the hood to inspect the engine. They went through the glove compartment, looked underneath the seats. They went over the vehicle with a fine-tooth comb. When he saw Wilson go through the trunk a second time, he thought he would black out. Had he spilled gas? He tinkered with engines; gas could be explained away. What the hell were they looking for?

Mr. Arson Investigator dropped something inside a plastic bag. "Micky Constantine?"

"Yeah?"

The arson investigator said something to one of the patrol officers that he couldn't hear. The officer nodded, then walked over to stand in front of him. "Mr. Constantine, you are under arrest. You have the right to remain silent. . . ." The cop clipped a pair of cuffs on his wrist before he finished reading him his Miranda rights.

"What's the charge? Man, you ain't got nothin' on me. I'll sue your ass off for false arrest."

"Tell that to your attorney, Mr. Constantine. We found these," Wilson said as he held up a plastic bag with a pack of matches from Carl's Garage.

"What the hell is that supposed to mean? Since when is it a crime to have a pack of matches? Carl's a friend," Micky blustered.

"No, Mr. Constantine, having a pack of matches isn't a crime. But when you find a pack of matches at the scene of a fire, matches from Carl's Garage with your fingerprints all over them, that's a crime."

Son of a bitch! He thought for sure the matches would burn in the fire! *This is all Rodwell Godfrey's fault. When I find the son of a bitch, I'm going to slit his throat and watch him bleed like a stuck pig.*

Then it hit him like a lightning bolt. He wasn't going to find old Rag because his ass was going to be reclining in jail.

"I ain't dressed, man, you gotta let me get some clothes."

"Where you're going, they will be providing you a very nice one-size-fits-all orange jumpsuit. Now move." The officer who handcuffed him gave him a shove.

"Hey, watch it! That's police brutality!"

"Of course it is." The officer grinned.

An hour later, Micky was booked and fingerprinted in the Los Angeles County Jail.

They brought him to a room the size of a bathroom, where they left him until the sun came up. He had to pee and he wanted to know what they were gonna do with his Vette. A plainclothes officer entered the room.

"Micky Constantine, I'm Special Agent Brett Gaynor. I think you and I need to have a talk."

"You FBI?"

"That's correct. I would like to ask you a few questions."

"Hey, I ain't stupid. I'm supposed to get a phone call. I wanna call my lawyer."

"And you will be able to do that, but not right now. First I have a few questions I want you to answer. You don't want to answer them, fine. Let me say this, it would be to your benefit to tell me everything you know about Rodwell Godfrey."

Son of a bitch, I should've known.

"I ain't saying a word till I see a lawyer."

Special Agent Brett Gaynor stood up and walked over to the door. Before leaving, he turned around. "Rodwell Godfrey has committed bank fraud. If you're involved, you're facing life in San Quentin. Last I heard, it wasn't a day in the park."

Micky Constantine proceeded to piss all over himself.

Chapter 37

"Henry Whitmore, I owe you and Sally dinner and a trip to the Bahamas," Toots said, her face lighting up like a Roman candle.

"We'll do that as soon as you return to Charleston."

"Can I ask how you managed to do this? I was resigned to taking a ten-million-dollar loss. I can't tell you what I've been through, Henry. I don't know how to thank you."

"Actually, it was quite simple. It's almost impossible to wipe out an electronic trail unless you're with the CIA, and it's

my understanding they aren't always successful. You had already told me that the
money was transferred to the Bank of
Bermuda on Grand Cayman. Fortunately,
the banks in the islands are very professional. Given their location and the fact
they are at an extremely high risk for hur-
ricanes, their systems are controlled by
satellite. The loss of power may appear to
have closed the financial centers down,
and I'm confident there are some who are
unable to access their clients' accounts,
but not so with the Bank of Bermuda. Of
course they're running off generators now,
but they are able to access accounts. I
made a few phone calls and learned that
your ten million dollars was transferred to
an account in the name of Richard Allen
Goodwin. Does that name mean anything
to you?"

Toots thought for a moment. Richard
Allen Goodwin. Abby's boss. It had to be
him. New name, same initials.

"No, that name doesn't mean a thing to
me, but the name Rodwell Archibald Godfrey does. He was the owner of *The Informer,* and I'm virtually certain that he's
the one who took my ten million dollars! I

think I can guarantee they are one and the same."

Henry chuckled. "Actually, Teresa, it was just a matter of time before the transaction was discovered. Whoever this man is, he's not very smart. After I spoke to the president of the bank, he called Emmanuel Rodriguez at the Bank of Los Angeles, from which the money was transferred. After confirming the fraudulent origin of the money, the Bank of Bermuda has agreed to transfer it back to your stepson's escrow account. It might even be there already."

"No, he isn't very smart. Listen, Henry, whatever you do, this information can't be made public."

"Teresa, there's nothing I can do to prevent it from happening. Bank fraud is a federal offense. Your thief will be charged in federal court. Where the media go with it is beyond my control."

"They have to find the man first before they can charge him, right? What happens if they can't find him? If he gets wind that he's about to get caught and disappears, then what happens?"

"Teresa, that's the least of your problems. Getting your money back should be all that's important. Let the authorities worry about catching and punishing the man who stole your money. If you plan on going through with the purchase of the paper, be sure you have a good lawyer and do it in person. That's the best advice I can give you."

"I appreciate the advice, Henry. Thank you again."

Toots broke the connection and immediately dialed Sophie. "Can you come over right now. I'll make some more coffee. We need to talk."

"You got me just in time. I was about to hit the Jacuzzi. It better be important, Toots. I don't get to do Jacuzzis very often."

"Oh, shut up and get your ass over here." Toots hung up the phone.

Five minutes later, wearing her red-and-blue-plaid robe, Sophie knocked on the slider before coming inside. "First I want a cup of coffee. You said you had coffee."

Toots poured them each a cup and got the Half & Half from the refrigerator. "You're not going to believe who I was just talking to on the phone."

"George Clooney? Tom Hanks?"

Toots rolled her eyes. "You need to have sex with someone, Sophie. Henry Whitmore called. He found my ten million bucks! It's being wired back to Chris's escrow account as we speak. That's the good news. Do you want to hear the bad news?"

"What could possibly be bad about recouping your ten million dollars?" Sophie asked before lighting up.

"Give me one of those." Toots lit her cigarette. "It was wired to an account in the name of Richard Allen Goodwin. *Rag.* We were right, Sophie! Abby's boss took my money and ran with it. The bad part is, if they find him, he'll be charged with bank fraud, and Abby will find out what a sneak and a liar she has for a mother."

"And if they don't find him?"

"I don't know. I'll call Chris and ask him. He needs to hear the good news, too." Toots called Chris immediately, repeating what she had told Sophie.

"So will they charge him if they can't find him?" Toots asked, her voice irritated.

"Of course, they have to charge him if they can identify him as the person who defrauded the bank. But as of now, there is only circumstantial evidence that Rag is the person who pulled off the fraudulent transfer. What we know is that the initials on the account into which the money was transferred are the same as his initials. We know that Rag disappeared. That's not enough to determine that this Goodwin and Rag are the same person. And if they can't identify him as the hacker, and I seriously doubt that he was, then they may not have enough evidence to charge him or anyone else until they can connect the dots. But once they have enough evidence, he will be charged. It's the law, Toots.

"I'm not sure if they have to name the person who got ripped off, though. It's not an area of the law I know that much about. I suppose it's possible that we might be able to keep your name out of it, at least for a little while. So, do you still plan to buy *The Informer*?"

"Of course I do. I'm doing it as much for Abby as for myself. It's win-win for both of us. You know how I love my tabloids. The first thing I want to do when the sale goes through is to remodel that entire building. I want *The Informer* to become a force to be reckoned with. I want people to beg for a job. I want customers to line up to buy our paper. I want my daughter to be happy."

"I don't know how you can do all that and at the same time remain anonymous."

"I've already thought it through, Christopher. Rag was up to his ears in debt; the bank that held his mortgage is really the owner, right?"

"Yes."

"So, nothing has changed. We pay off the loans, the bank sells us the paper, possibly at a discount, and we set up a corporation whose CEO wishes to remain anonymous. I'll just work behind the scenes. If we all agree to keep our collective mouths shut, it should work. You're the attorney. Make it happen, Christopher."

"I know you want to make this work for Abby. I'll do my best, but I can't make any promises, Toots. As a matter of fact, I wanted to ask you if I could recommend another attorney, a corporate attorney. He's a friend, Toots, and he's very good. Otherwise, I wouldn't recommend him."

"Abby said you told her there was a conflict of interest. I guess I shouldn't have asked you to get involved with this, so yes, set up an appointment with your friend. Are you and Abby at odds over something, Chris? She didn't seem happy when your name was mentioned at lunch. Did something happen I should know about?"

If you only knew, Toots. "Yes. No. Sort of. We're always at odds over something. That's what usually happens when two know-it-alls butt heads. We'll both get over it."

"Of course you will. Do your best to arrange a meeting with your friend as soon as possible. I want to wind this up so I can get down to business."

"I'll get it set up right away. Just be careful, Toots. Now what are you and your quirky pals up to? Do you care to share any details, or is this NTK?"

"We buried Sophie's husband, but you know that. Ida has another appointment with Dr. Sameer tomorrow. She's actually been going without her latex gloves, can you believe it? Mavis is trundling along and determined to lose her weight. I think she will, too. She's certainly motivated right now."

"I don't think I've met Ida yet. I'll wait

until she's comfortable enough to shake my hand," Chris said.

"That's a good idea, I'll tell her. She's starting to set goals for herself. She's even allowed me to schedule a manicure here at the hotel. That's another thing I need to talk to you about, Chris. We can't stay at the Beverly Hills Hotel forever. I was thinking about buying a house. Will your attorney be able to help me with that, too?"

"He's a corporate attorney. But I know dozens of realtors who could show you around. Are you looking for something close to Abby?"

Toots thought about it. No. Abby needed her privacy. "Actually I was thinking about looking into purchasing Aaron Spelling's mansion."

Toots thought she heard Chris laughing. He probably thought she was joking, which she was. "Is that supposed to be funny? If I'm going to live this bicoastal life, Christopher, I plan on doing it in style. You know me, I never go halfway when I can go the whole way."

"Do you realize what that palace is going for?"

"No, that's why I need a realtor, to show me around. I was joking. But I do want something comparable. I'm sure Sophie, Mavis, and Ida will want to stay out here as long as they can. They love being close to Abby."

"I'm sure they do. Let me call a friend of mine. I'll give her your number if you don't mind, and you can take it from there."

"That should work. I really want to do this, Chris. Not a word to Abby. I'll tell her myself at the right time. Christopher, your father would have been very proud of you. You're a good man, just like he was."

"That means a lot, coming from you, Toots. I know you don't say that about just anyone. Gotta run. I've got a hot date with Hollywood's next big star. I'll give my realtor friend your number."

"Thank you, Chris. We'll be talking." Toots was on a roll. "Pour us another cup of coffee, Sophie. I'm calling Abby."

"Yes, Your Highness." Sophie saluted.

Toots held up her middle finger as Sophie burst into laughter.

Toots hit Abby's number on her speed dial.

"Hi, Mom."

"Do you ever not answer your phone on the first ring?"

"Are you kidding? I'm a reporter. Our cell phones are our lifelines to what could be the next front-page story. So, what's up at the Pink Palace?"

"That's why I called. I'm thinking about purchasing a house here, but I wanted to ask you how you would feel about having your mother living in such close proximity. I like the weather here. I'm thinking your godmothers might want to spend their winters here, too. So I wanted to ask, how would you feel if your old mom purchased a winter place here?"

"I would love it! You can help me finish my house, and I can help with yours. What about the house in Charleston? You're not thinking of selling it, are you?"

"Never, Abby. That's my real home. I'll never leave Charleston for good. But I know how much you love it here. It would be wonderful to see each other more often and not just on holidays. I wanted to see how you felt. I don't want you to think I'm invading your privacy."

"Mom, you know me better than that. I'd love to be able to pop in and visit you a couple of times a week. Vice versa. Other than Chester, there are no men in my life."

"I simply do not understand that. You're as beautiful as those stars you write about. Speaking of stars, I just spoke to Chris. He said he had a hot date tonight with Hollywood's next big star. He certainly is a ladies' man." Toots chuckled.

Abby felt like she'd been socked in the gut. *Hot date. Hollywood's next big star.* She thought then about the early-morning call that had never materialized.

"Abby, are you there?"

"Uh . . . Chester just jumped the fence. I'll call you later, Mom."

"Good-bye, Abby."

Chapter 38

Abby felt as though her entire world was falling apart. She was out of a job, her boss was MIA, she knew she had little hope of finding a position at either of the other two tabloids in LA, and that lying sack of crap, Christopher Clay, was letting her down, too.

Christopher Clay had a hot date with another Hollywood bimbo! Just what a girl needed to hear from her mother. And to think she'd toyed with the idea of actually apologizing to him. She absolutely refused to think about how much time she'd spent remembering how he'd kissed her fingers. She was just another notch on his whatever!

Abby stomped her way to the kitchen, where she yanked out a bottle of Clorox from under the sink and poured it over her hands. Godmother Ida had nothing on her. *From here on out, it's war.* She hoped the rat fink would call her so she could hang up on him. She wondered how long it would take him to figure out she was wise to his tricks.

She felt like crying.

Then she started to worry about what would happen if she suddenly found herself in Chris and her mother's company. She wondered if she would have the guts to tell the sweet-talking-oh-I-really-like-you-more-than-you-know player to take a hike.

Chester was the only man in her life, and as far as she was concerned, it was going to remain that way. Chris could kiss any hope of seeing her again right out the window.

She went to the kitchen, where she took a bottle of water from the fridge. Maybe she'd have her mother invite her to the hotel for Jell-O shots. Maybe what she needed was to get snockered. She didn't do too well with liquor, so she tossed that idea down the drain.

Her life had been just great, humming along like a well-oiled wheel until Rag told her he was selling the paper. From that moment on, her life had taken a turn downhill, and there didn't seem to be much she could do about it. Options one, two, and three were dismal at best.

Abby wished she could stop thinking about the paper. Rag skipped out, maybe had one of his hoods start the fire so he could collect the insurance. Where was the sense to that? How could Rag collect insurance on something he no longer owned?

Abby shook her head to clear her thoughts. None of it made sense, and at that precise moment she was too tired to try and put the pieces of a very strange puzzle together.

Abby opened the door and called to the shepherd, who came on the run. She fondled the big dog's ears, and, before she knew it, tears were rolling down her cheeks. Sometimes life just wasn't fair.

She sniveled as she filled Chester's water bowl. "It's just you and me, big guy. We are going to spend a lovely afternoon together weeding the garden."

"Woof!"

For the next two hours, Abby pruned, pulled, and dug through the overgrowth in her backyard, or her courtyard, as she liked to call it. With each vicious yank of a weed, she cussed out Chris Clay.

Two hours later, when she took a second break, she looked around at her work and was surprised to see how much she'd accomplished. The garden was starting to look like a real garden. She thought it looked casual and free-flowing, which was her goal. She swept the brick patio, bagged up the discarded vines, then turned on the sprinkler, hoping to revive the grass without a major replanting. She crossed her fingers that the fertilizer she'd added earlier would kick in and produce a velvet green lawn. She was realist enough to know it might not happen.

"Inside, Chester. You and I have a hot date with a bag of microwave popcorn and whatever Lifetime movie is playing tonight.

Maybe it'll be one of those thrillers where the woman hires a hit man to shoot her boyfriend. What do you think, Chester?"

"Woof! Woof!"

Abby leaned down and wrapped her arms around Chester's neck. He returned the hug by placing both paws on her shoulders.

"You are the man of my dreams, Chester. The love of my life," Abby said in a choked voice.

Chapter 39

Micky had spent the last three hours telling Special Agent Gaynor everything that had gone down, in the hopes of cutting a deal. With nothing to fall back on, he'd turned into a snitch. He hated being a snitch. So what if he'd tossed a match where he shouldn't have tossed it? No one got hurt, the place hadn't gone up in flames. Hells bells, the fire department showed up before anything serious happened. Someone had seen him leave, seen him race away from the scene, and the SOB had written down his license number and called the police. Just his stupid dumb luck.

So he was being interrogated by the fucking FBI all because he'd done a pal, a former pal, a favor by setting him up with a new identity. He conveniently ignored the fact that providing false identities was a federal offense of its own. He had a really bad feeling that he wasn't going to cut any deals.

"And this is it? You have no clue to this Rag's whereabouts?"

"Look, for the hundredth time, no. If I knew where he was, I would've personally gone after him and kicked his ass. I was looking for him myself." Micky told them about the locker at LAX where he'd left the phony documents and how he'd gone back to collect his fifty grand only to find out he'd been ripped off.

"I'm telling you the truth. What? You want me to make up some lies? I don't know what else you want me to say."

"I've sent a detective to view surveillance videos. When we're satisfied you're telling the truth, we'll talk again."

Micky wanted to punch the feeb out, but his hands were handcuffed, and he'd just rack up more charges against himself. He wasn't *that* dumb.

"How long does this shit take? Do we have a deal or not?"

"We'll let you know." Micky felt like crying.

Micky doubled his fists, squeezing them until his knuckles turned white. "I'm gonna sue this place. When I get through with them, they will be sorry they ever laid eyes on me. I got connections!" he blustered.

"Why don't you tell me about these connections while we're waiting on those tapes."

Fuck. "I'm just pissed, okay? I've been cooperative. You said you'd cut me a deal if I opened up. I opened up. That was bullshit about me having connections. If I had connections, I'd be out of here by now, and you'd be sucking your thumb, Mr. Agent."

"You haven't been in front of a judge yet. You've been in jail before, Mr. Constantine. Don't think we haven't checked your record. You should be quite familiar with the system and feel right at home inside a jail cell."

"Whatever."

"Good answer. Speaks of intelligence."

"I ain't saying another word until I talk to a lawyer."

Special Agent Gaynor got up when he heard a tap on the glass. "I'll be right back, buddy. Don't you go anywhere." Gaynor laughed.

When the agent left the room, Micky shouted every dirty word he knew. When he ran out of the tried and true, he made up cusswords, knowing other agents could hear him behind the two-way mirror.

Special Agent Gaynor returned to the interrogation room with a stack of tapes. "You are a lucky man, Mr. Constantine. Seems for once you told the truth. We observed you placing the documents inside the locker and Mr. Godfrey removing them. Now, other than your bout with the arson investigators, I'm done with you."

"What's that mean? You said we'd cut a deal?"

"I lied," Agent Gaynor said.

Grand Cayman had been hit hard by Hurricane Deborah. Power in some areas

had been restored, the airport had re-
opened, but departing flights were mini-
mal. Miami and Fort Lauderdale were the
only destinations.

Richard Allen Goodwin had received a
message via a brown-skinned boy of no
more than twelve on a rickety old bike.
Apparently the phone lines were being restored. Goodwin read the message for
the tenth time.

**"It is urgent that you come to the
Bank of Bermuda at once. We need to
discuss an unauthorized transaction
on your account."**

Rag paced back and forth, debating
whether or not to go. Was it a trick of some
sort? He supposed it was possible though
he thought it unlikely that someone had
tried to access his account. It could be that
someone was just another con trying to rip
him off. His nerves started to twitch. He
must have screwed up somewhere along
the way.

If the feds were on his trail, and his gut
instinct was telling him they were, it was
just a matter of time before the FBI made
a trip to the Cayman Islands on account

of him. Maybe they were already at the bank, just waiting for him to make an appearance.

He still had most of the fifty grand, the money he'd taken from *The Informer*'s payroll account. Nope, folks, you won't be getting paid this week. He wished he was back in his ratty office writing out checks.

So, what to do? Stay, and risk going to jail? Or take what money he had and start over someplace else?

He opted for the latter. Quickly, before the kid from the bank returned with another message or most likely the feds, he crammed what he could into one monogrammed bag.

He waited until he was outside the hotel to hail a cab. It wasn't the first time he'd skipped out on a hotel bill. He smirked when he remembered the bogus credit card Micky had gotten for him. He was sorry now he hadn't ordered lobster and champagne from room service.

"Over here!" Rag waved his arm high in the air. A beat-up yellow taxi that looked like it had seen the last of its better days a long time ago stopped right in the middle of the road. "I need to get to the airport. Family emergency."

"Right away, sir."

The driver wasted no time racing to the airport. Rag wondered if he would survive the ride. *Damn, don't these people know how to drive?*

At the airport, he jumped out, tossed the driver a twenty, then raced inside, hoping against hope he could board a flight to Miami. From there he'd see about going to the Dominican Republic. He vaguely remembered hearing it was cheap to live there.

Rag smiled at the girl behind the counter. "I've a family emergency. I need to get to Miami as soon as possible."

"I believe we have three seats on the next flight. It's scheduled to leave in forty-five minutes."

"I'll take one."

Rag gladly paid the eight hundred dollars in cash for a one-way ticket to Miami. Talk about price gouging.

Lady Luck was courting him again. He heard over the loudspeaker that the two remaining flights had sold out, then the announcement that his flight was leaving early. The passengers were already filing outside to board the twin-engine plane. Rag saw that it only held twelve passengers. Yes. Lady Luck befriended him again. The flight lasted a whole thirty minutes. No drinks were offered, no pretzels or peanuts, but who cared?

When he arrived at Miami International, he promptly booked a flight to the Dominican Republic. Nine hours later, Richard Allen Goodwin was sitting in a bar, drinking shots of tequila and celebrating his freedom.

Chapter 40

Toots, Sophie, Mavis, and Ida waited in the Polo Lounge for Abby and Chris to arrive. Toots wanted to share her wonderful exciting news with those she loved the most.

"Abby is always on time. I wonder what's keeping her," Mavis said. "I can't wait to tell her I've lost another four pounds. I know it's not a lot, but it's a start. Being here with you girls was the best thing that could've happened to me."

"We're all very proud of you," Toots said, aware that, with Mavis, praise went a long way and kept her motivated. Toots didn't have a doubt in her mind that her old friend would prevail, but it would take time.

"I think I've put on a pound or two myself with all those Froot Loops and sugar-laced coffee I've been guzzling. I am not going to give up cigarettes, before you say it, Mavis. I delight in puffing as many as I can." Sophie pulled one out of her pack to make her point, but remembered smoking wasn't allowed in restaurants in California.

"I actually went for that manicure today. I do believe those pills are helping me. I only took two showers today. My hands feel so good. I know it's not where I should be, but I'm not obsessing over germs as much as I was. Dr. Sameer says I'm recuperating faster than most of his patients. Actually, I think he has a bit of a crush on me. He's kind of cute, don't you think?" Ida asked, a sparkle in her eye.

Toots looked at Sophie.

Sophie looked at Toots.

"Dammit to hell, didn't I tell you! I knew it! I damn well knew it! It's a man! See? I told you so. You cannot survive without a man, Ida. That's what your problem is, the fear of being alone, and you just say it's germs and blame it on old Thomas. What a phony you are."

"That's enough, Sophie. But, Ida, I agree with Sophie," Toots said, glancing at her watch again. "I bet Abby got caught in traffic. That's the one thing I don't like about this town. Before Abby arrives, I just want you all to know that *The Informer* will be up and running in six weeks, possibly sooner if the renovations are done. Right now everyone is working out of Abby's garage. Abby learned through the grapevine that the new owners plan to remain silent and anonymous. It doesn't seem to bother her. She's just excited that she has her job back and has free rein. The new EIC seems to like her. She's excited about going back to work. Oh, look, there she is. Now remember, not a word."

Abby saw her mother and the three Gs. She waved as she made her way to the table that was by then known as "their" table since Toots had tipped the waiter so generously at lunch the day before. He'd whispered in Toots's ear that theirs were the best seats to observe the comings and goings of the stars, hence the outrageous tip.

"Mom, you are positively glowing. You only glow when you have a man in your life. Did you meet someone? Tell me you're not thinking of getting married again?"

"Oh, for Pete's sake, Abby, give your old mom some credit. I'm just happy to be with my friends and my daughter. I will not get married again! Now, that doesn't mean I won't consider dating anyone, but marriage is out of the question."

"Good. It's about time you started enjoying your golden years. All of you."

Sophie chimed in. "Abby, you make us sound like we're ready for the old folks' home. I, for one, am going to live life to the fullest from this moment forward. I think we should take a vacation."

"Isn't that what we're doing now, vacationing?" Mavis asked.

"Yes, we are. I have spa days lined up for us tomorrow. The full deal. Facials, massages, manicures, pedicures. Remember I promised to get us all a makeover when we got here? I've arranged for that as well. I've hired Cher's makeup artist, too. You know Cher is sixty-three. So if anyone wants to back out now, forget it. Are you up to this, Ida?" Toots asked. That she and the others were stunned at their friend's sudden, hasty recovery was an understatement.

"Yes, I am."

"What about the waxing we talked about?" Mavis asked.

Abby looked at her mother and shook her head. "Don't tell me you're doing that, too."

"No, I won't tell you that, although Ida has had her you-know-what waxed. More than once, I might add."

"And you know this, how?" Abby asked her mother.

"Ida, tell her it's the truth," Toots insisted.

"It's true, Abby. I was always open to new experiences. I still am, I just . . . what I had was a . . . little setback."

Sophie piped up at any opportunity to aggravate Ida. "As long as there's a man involved. Right? I bet you five dollars we aren't going to have to drag you to the wax room or whatever the hell they call it."

"Kiss my bald ass, Sophie," Ida snapped back, a wicked smile on her face.

They all laughed but kept their gazes on the entrance. Abby watched the old dears, suspicious that there was more to this luncheon than she had first thought.

Their waiter, Manolo, approached their table with a bottle of champagne. "Ma'am?"

Toots hated to start the celebration early, but decided that it really didn't matter. A celebration was a celebration. "Yes, Manolo, please pop the cork."

"Mom, why are we drinking champagne at lunch? Working people, of which I am one, do not drink champagne for lunch. Visitors drink champagne, then take a nap."

"Abby, can't we have champagne just for no reason? Why do people think they have to have a reason for everything they do? It's beyond silly. It's like saving the good dishes and silver for when the Queen might visit you. You need to relax, dear."

"Okay, Mom, I'll relax." Abby was more convinced than ever that her mother was up to something, and the three Gs knew all about whatever it was.

Manolo filled crystal champagne flutes with the pink bubbly.

"Even the champagne is pink," Mavis exclaimed. "I can only have a sip. Alcohol isn't on my diet."

"Don't worry, Mavis, I'll drink yours," Sophie said.

"Oh, look, here he is!"

Abby looked where her mother was looking. Chris Clay in the flesh. Abby raked her gaze across his face, then up and down that hard, sexy body.

Chris leaned over and kissed Toots's cheek. Then one by one he gave the god-mothers a kiss. When he came to Abby, he hesitated for a second, before kissing her on her lips. For more than three seconds. In front of her mother. In front of her godmothers.

"I missed you, Abby."

"Missed me? I don't think so. This is Hollywood. I heard you're dating Hollywood's next big star?"

"Who told you that?" Chris asked.

"I did," Toots offered. "Now, will you two stop quibbling? I invited you both here for a special celebration. Chris, you don't have a glass of champagne." Toots glanced around in search of Manolo. The waiter saw her and quickly made his way to the table, where he poured Chris a glass of bubbly.

"I would like to propose a toast," Toots said, a twinkle in her eye.

"To new beginnings!"

They raised their crystal goblets high in the air, chorusing, "To new beginnings!"

"Mom, I know there's more, I know that look on your face."

"Abby, if you weren't twenty-eight years old, I'd tell you to go to your room."

Manolo made another appearance at their table, this time with luncheon menus.

For the next ten minutes, they perused the selections. When the waiter returned to take their orders, there was an air of suppressed excitement around the table.

Each had reached the tip of a personal milestone, and it could only be better from there on.

"I don't want another hamburger. I'm not sure what I want," Abby said as she scanned the menu.

"Let me order for you, Abby," Chris said.

"I think that's a grand idea. She takes forever to decide sometimes," Toots observed.

Manolo returned to the table to take their orders.

Chris spoke up before anyone else had a chance. "This lovely little lady would like a steak, the filet, cooked rare. A loaded baked potato. And whatever vegetable you have. Make sure it's not overcooked; on the crisp side, you know, how it snaps when you bite into it."

Toots and the three Gs stared at Chris like he'd just fallen from the sky and landed at their table.

"How do you know what Abby likes to order?" Toots asked Chris. "Abby never . . . except . . . never mind. I think you two have a secret. Am I right?" Toots looked at her daughter, saw her blush, then looked at Chris and saw him grinning ear to ear. "Well, I can see something is going on. And I think it's wonderful. I've seen the way you two look at each other."

"Mom! Please, not now. Remember we're here to celebrate something, or did you forget?"

"No, Abby, I did not forget. I might be old, but I'm far from senile."

"Stop keeping us in suspense."

"Toots, dear, I agree with my god-daughter. You delight in keeping us on our toes," Mavis said.

"Spit it out, Toots, or I'll kick your tail right here in the middle of the Polo Lounge." Sophie was laughing, her warm brown eyes glowing like amber whiskey.

"Ida, is there anything you would like to add?" Toots demanded. *Why does everyone have to rush everything?*

"No, I just wish you'd get on with it before our food arrives."

"Oh, all right, I won't keep any of you in suspense any longer. This morning I received a call telling me my offer had been accepted." Toots paused, savoring the moment, watching the faces of those she loved most. At their blank looks, she said, "As I was saying, I received a phone call telling me an offer I placed on a lovely home has been accepted."

Had it not been for the bits of conversation from the other diners, the tinkling of silver against china, and the swish of the soft breeze wafting across the patio, Toots would have sworn you could hear a pin drop.

"I am now the official new owner of the home of the late Aaron Spelling."

Mavis, Ida, and Sophie laughed until their sides hurt.

Chris and Abby walked around the table to give Toots a hug.

"Mom, you're nuts, you know that, right? You are also the best mother in the whole world. I am so glad you're my mother. Sophie, Mavis, and Ida, I couldn't have asked for a more perfect trio of godmothers. Now I can't wait to have a sleepover. Just think, we're all going to hang out. And, Mom, as soon as that mysterious new owner of *The Informer* has it up and running, I'll make sure you get the first issue hot off the press!"

Toots smiled until she saw the wicked gleam in her daughter's eye. She knew that look. "What?"

Abby grinned. "You know how I live for a real scoop, right? Well, ladies, and gentleman, I am working on the biggest scoop to hit this town in a long time! It's going to be the first issue! Don't even think about asking me what it is, because then it wouldn't be *The Scoop* of the year.

You are just going to have to wait like everyone else."

Abby turned to Chris Clay, her eyes narrowed to slits, and said, "Do not ever order a meal for me again. I am more than capable of ordering for myself." She turned to the women and worked up a smile. "I'm sorry, but I have to leave, I have a ton of work to do. I'll see you all later." She waved airily as she left the outdoor patio. All eyes were on her retreating back, but Abby didn't look back.

"What was that all about?" Toots asked fearfully.

"I think she knows," Sophie said, "and she's going to expose you, Toots."

"I saw tears in her eyes. At least I think they were tears," Mavis said.

"No!" Ida said in a know-it-all voice. "That was all directed at you, young man," she said, pointing to Chris. "You're the one she's taking on for her scoop."

Chris looked around the table at the women who were now looking at him like he was some alien from another planet. Even Toots, who only looked at him with love and affection. He didn't know if he should cry or get up and run out to his car.

He opted for the car, apologizing as he bolted from his chair.

"I need a cigarette," Sophie said. "Come on, Toots, let's go out to the parking lot."

Puffing furiously a moment later, the women stared at each other.

"Do you think she knows, Sophie? Is Ida right? Chris . . . no, it has to be us. Oh, God, what are we going to do?"

Sophie blew a glorious smoke ring and watched as it settled over Toots's head.

"She suspects, Toots. Ida could be right. I also think there is something going on between Abby and Chris. By the way, did you know a prayer rug was delivered to Ida's bungalow this morning? My maid told me. I say we just continue with our plans. Let's go back and finish that champagne. We have the rest of the afternoon to plot our next move. I have some great ideas."

"You know what, Sophie, I have a few ideas myself. I think, between the two of us, we can guarantee my daughter a few months' worth of scoops. There might even be an exclusive along the way."

Sophie held up her hand, and Toots smacked it. "Hey, Toots, do you realize between the four of us we have two hundred and sixty years of life experience?"

"And that means what?"

"We draw on all those years of experience. You said you wanted to make Abby a force in the tabloid industry. What, you want me to draw you a map?"

Toots laughed, the sound tinkling across the parking lot. "I like the way you think, Sophie. I think you're almost as devious as I am."

"I'm going to take that as a compliment, Toots."

"One more thing, I'm not ready to quit smoking."

"Me, either."

"I think it's time to finish off that champagne."